"With effortless and beautiful writing, Karma Brown twists heartache and hope together in *The Choices We Make*, taking you on each character's complicated emotional journey and exploring how the worst-case scenario can still bring joy."
—Amy E. Reichert, author of *Luck, Love & Lemon Pie* and *The Coincidence of Coconut Cake*

"Laughing one minute, then fiercely blinking back tears the next, we tore through this novel—so gripping that we were both excited and scared out of our minds to turn the page. Karma Brown has proven herself to be a master at writing about the many facets of love in this stunning page-turner."
—Liz Fenton and Lisa Steinke, authors of *The Status of All Things*

"*The Choices We Make* describes one woman's desperate longing for a baby and her best friend's desire to help.... [A] story about friendship, and love, and sacrifice."
—Julie Lawson Timmer, author of *Five Days Left* and *Untethered*

"I was already emotionally invested in this beautifully written story of love and loss when an unexpected turn of events knocked the wind right out of me. Heart-wrenching yet hopeful, *Come Away with Me* had me smiling through my tears."
—Tracey Garvis Graves, *New York Times* bestselling author of *On the Island*

"*Come Away with Me* tells the heartbreaking yet hopeful tale of a life lost and a life reclaimed. Fans of Elizabeth Gilbert's *Eat Pray Love* will flock to this novel.... Karma Brown is a talented new voice in women's fiction."
—Lori Nelson Spielman, author of *The Life List*

"*Come Away with Me* is full of lush locations, memorable characters, and a turn of events that is nothing short of jaw-dropping. Brown's work is as smart as it is effortless to read."
—Taylor Jenkins Reid, author of *Forever, Interrupted* and *After I Do*

"[A]dventurous, heartbreaking yet ultimately hopeful... This emotional love story will stick with you long after you've turned the final page."
—Colleen Oakley, author of *Before I Go*, on *Come Away with Me*

"Brown's debut knocks it out of the park.... An impressive study of loss, reconciliation, and brave choices with a stunning, three-hanky ending. A strong ensemble of supporting characters fills out this impressive story that carries away the reader's heart and imagination."
—*Publishers Weekly* on *Come Away with Me*

"Brown's novel is cathartic and heartbreaking...will leave you in tears, so definitely have a box of tissues handy."
—*RT Book Reviews*, 4 stars, on *Come Away with Me*

"A warmly compelling love story... Have tissues at hand for Brown's deeply moving debut."
—*Booklist* on *Come Away with Me*

Also by Karma Brown

COME AWAY WITH ME

THE CHOICES WE MAKE

KARMA BROWN

MIRA®

MIRA

ISBN-13: 978-0-7783-1893-4

The Choices We Make

Printed in U.S.A.

First printing: July 2016
10 9 8 7 6 5 4 3 2 1

For my sister, Jenna, because she made me a mother.

THE

CHOICES

WE

MAKE

Author's Note

I am often told my daughter has my eyes and looks exactly like me. I love hearing this because it's a beautiful reminder to be grateful for how she came to be.

The first time my husband and I talked about having kids was the day I sat in my oncologist's office, raw and reeling from my shocking cancer diagnosis at the age of thirty. Along with words like *chemotherapy* and *radiation*, I was also told the lifesaving treatment would bring with it more than debilitating nausea, fatigue and hair loss. It also could cost me my fertility. So the first time my husband and I talked about kids was also the moment I learned I might never become a mother.

Luckily my oncologist was forward thinking and determined I would know motherhood. What followed were exhausting and rushed fertility procedures that left us with twenty-one embryos on ice, all set for when I was cancer-free and ready to start a family.

Despite our plentiful embryos and a boatload of determination, my body was too damaged from treatment, and pregnancy was impossible. However, my sister, Jenna, had promised she'd carry a baby for me if I ever needed her to, and so without hesitation that was exactly what she did. With this promise and one of our perfect embryos, Jenna made us parents in June 2008 through the incredible gift of gestational surrogacy.

It took 1,825 days for us to become parents. It was not an easy road, nor one I would wish on anyone despite our fairy-tale ending. But every injection, procedure, medication, worry, challenge and dollar spent was worth it. Because I am a mom.

The Choices We Make is not our story. But my experiences are scattered throughout the pages, as is my gratitude for my sister and all the women who have helped others know parenthood—it is a gift never to be taken for granted.

The world breaks everyone and afterward many are strong at the broken places.

Ernest Hemingway

1

HANNAH

When the phone rings at seven o'clock on Tuesday night, I think it's odd but I don't worry. You save that for the calls that come in the middle of the night, the ones that wake you in a panic and surely mean someone has died. Normally I don't even answer our landline—a relic from my high school days, so basic it doesn't even have a display screen. Ben thinks we should cancel the service, as no one calls us on it except telemarketers, my mother every so often, and my best friend, Kate, though generally by accident because she has an irrational fear of updating her contacts list.

Deciding it must be a telemarketer as Mom is at her bridge club night and I just spoke with Kate an hour ago, I continue chopping peppers for the fajitas and wait for the answering machine—circa the same year as the phone—to pick up.

"Hannah? Are you there?" The voice is strained, uncertain but familiar.

Tripping over the puppy, asleep in the middle of the kitchen floor, I wipe my hands on the thighs of my jeans and grab the phone.

"Hello? David?" The puppy, awake now, nips at my leg, her high-pitched attempt at a growl more amusing than annoying. "Get off, Clover!" I whisper, trying to sound like the leader the dog obedience instructor told me I need to be. Clover ignores me, continuing her assault on the hem of my jeans. I look over at Ben for help, but he's reading his tablet on the couch, oblivious to it all.

"Hannah—" David says my name again, but this time in a rush. As if he's been holding his breath and is only just allowed to let it out. I gently shake Clover off my leg and throw a treat from my back pocket toward the couch. She promptly chases it before jumping up and snuggling her tiny, fluffy white body against Ben while she crunches the biscuit. He rubs her head, murmuring, "Good girl," and I place my hand over the mouthpiece. "Remember who feeds you," I say to her before speaking into the phone again.

"David, hey. When are you and Kate getting here? My impatient and apparently ravenous husband has already eaten most of the guacamole." I glance at Ben, and he smiles before leaning forward to grab his cell off the ottoman, which was buried under a few magazines and stuffed dog toys. He frowns at the display screen and when he looks back at me his face is creased with concern. A ribbon of anxiety wraps around my chest as I think of my cell phone, forgotten upstairs on the bathroom vanity. I tap my baby finger against the curved plastic of the handset, not liking how my insides feel. "Wait, how did you get this number?"

Ben stands quickly, Clover tumbling off his lap.

It's then I realize David isn't responding because he's crying. Suddenly I hear a lot of other noises, too. Beeping, like an incessant alarm clock. A garbled voice over a loudspeaker. The sounds of busy people, doing important things.

"David, where are you?"

Ben is beside me now, showing me his phone's display. A string of missed calls from David.

"Hannah... I'm at the hospital... I don't know what happened... Everything was fine, and then she just..."

"What's wrong?" My heart pumps furiously. "Is it one of the girls?" Kate must be panicking, which is likely why David was calling instead of her. The ribbon of anxiety winds tighter.

And with his answer, I see the moment my life changes.

14 MONTHS EARLIER

2

KATE

June

I checked my cell again, the fifteenth time in the last five minutes.

"Call me," I told David. "I want to make sure this is working."

"It's working," David said, cutting up strawberries and bananas into small pieces. Even though our girls were eleven and seven, David, a paramedic, still insisted on their food being bite-size to prevent choking.

David licked strawberry juice off his fingers and looked up at me. "Give her time, Katie. It's barely six o'clock."

"I know, but I had such a good feeling this time. And if it were good news, she would have called by now, right? Right?"

David scraped the fruit into the girls' bowls, then placed them on the table beside their dinners—barbecue chicken drumsticks, with carrot and cucumber sticks. "Ava! Josie! Dinner!" he hollered up the stairs before coming back to the kitchen.

"If it's good news, maybe she and Ben are celebrating by themselves first," he said. "And if it's bad news? Maybe she's not ready to talk about it."

The girls came bounding into the kitchen. "What's for dinner?" Ava, our eldest, asked.

"Chicken and veggies," I said, pouring two glasses of milk and handing them to Ava. I topped up my glass of wine and handed David a beer. He wasn't back on shift until the morning, which meant we could have a relaxed dinner after the girls went to bed and binge watch Netflix.

"I don't like chicken," Josie said, scrunching up her nose.

"Yes, you do," David replied, pushing her chair closer to the table after she sat down. She protested by shoving the plate farther away.

"I don't!" Josie crossed her arms over her chest, and I tried to hide my smile behind my wineglass. She looked just like David when she was mad, her dirty-blond eyebrows knitting together in a stern V shape.

"Since when, jelly bean?" I sat across from her at the table and nudged her plate back, taking a sip of my wine. Josie was my sweet and spicy kid—one moment snuggling contentedly, the next slamming doors and declaring life unfair and utterly disappointing. She was named after my grandmother Josephine, who had been a midwife during the war and who, according to family legend, was not a woman to mess with. I had only vague memories of Grandma Josephine, her death coming a day after my sixth birthday. But I do remember she always carried those red-and-white-swirled peppermints in the bottom of her purse, usually stuck to old pieces of tissue, that she drank a shot of whiskey every morning in her tea and that she suffered from frequent migraine headaches— something I had unfortunately inherited.

"Ever since she watched *Chicken Run* at Gram's," Ava said, biting into her drumstick with enthusiasm. While Josie was my loud and emotional child, Ava had always been more even-keeled, like David, and usually had her nose in a book.

But she had a wicked sense of humor—which I liked to take credit for—and was quite skilled at pushing her sister's buttons.

Sensing an opportunity to do just that, Ava ripped her teeth through a large chunk of skin and meat and chewed loudly as she leaned closer to Josie, making smacking noises with her lips. I shot Ava a warning glance, then got up and made Josie a peanut-butter-and-honey sandwich, cutting the crusts off—which I knew I had to stop doing one day soon. Placing it on her plate and taking the drumstick for myself, I avoided David's stare. We had argued just last night about how quick I was to offer options if the girls didn't eat what was put in front of them.

Nibbling the drumstick, I looked back at my phone.

"Kate, she's okay." David swallowed the last dregs in his beer bottle. He got up to grab another and stopped to kiss the top of my head before sitting back at the table with me.

But I knew she wasn't. Hannah had been my best friend for twenty-five years, and I knew her better than anyone else.

3

HANNAH

Ben and I had been married for 2,190 days, and we'd been trying to get pregnant for nearly every one of those.

We met in Jamaica, at the wedding of my college friend Jasmine, who also turned out to be Ben's first cousin. He was tall and funny and had a thing for useless party tricks, like balancing a salt shaker on its edge and folding a dollar bill into a tiny collared T-shirt, which I found irresistibly charming—especially after a few rum punches. With skin the color of steeped tea with a long pour of cream thanks to his Jamaican mother, and deep blue eyes he'd inherited from his American father, Ben regaled me with stories of his childhood in Jamaica, where his mom had been a chef and his dad the lead architect for a string of luxury resorts on the island.

Over too many drinks we laughed, and danced, then stumbled back to my hotel room after a late-night ocean swim. It was one of those perfect nights, the kind that you think back to when life is getting you down. I'd been thinking about that night a lot lately.

Now, six years later, I should have been used to seeing that single line or the words *Not Pregnant*, but every time it caught me by surprise. We'd moved on long ago from the bottle of wine and legs up in the air while we giggled at the prospect of having just made a baby thing. Even though we were actively trying to get pregnant, we rarely had sex anymore. I missed having sex.

I had become an expert at answering the blistering and insensitive, though well-intentioned, "So when are you two going to have a baby?" question. No longer did I answer with the enthusiastic "We're working on it!" response I used to give early on—now I simply offered, "Soon, we hope." The assumption that Ben and I didn't have a baby because we weren't trying to have one really pissed me off.

God, we were trying so hard.

The knock on the bathroom door startled me, and the plastic test stick dropped from my hand.

"Hannah? Everything okay in there?"

I cleared my throat. "I'll be right out." I picked up the white plastic stick with its one dark blue line, and threw it harder than necessary into the trash can beside the toilet, jamming a balled-up handful of tissues on top of it. I had promised Ben I wouldn't do a pregnancy test this time, would wait for the call from the doctor's office with the official blood test results. But I was having a tough time kicking the habit.

A moment later I unlocked the door and stepped out into the hall, disappointed Ben wasn't still standing there waiting for me even though I knew I would have been irritated if he had been. I found him in the kitchen, sitting at the island with a six-pack of Anchor Brewery beer and a bouquet of yellow tulips—two of my favorite things. My cell phone vibrated in my hand, and I glanced at the screen. "West Coast Fertility & Associates." There was no point in answering it.

I started crying. *Damn it.*

"Hey, babe." Ben jumped off his stool and wrapped his arms around me.

"Stupid hormones," I blubbered, my face pressed into his chest. When I pulled back I saw a wet spot on the blue-and-white gingham-patterned cotton of his shirt, which I uselessly tried to blot with the sleeve of my cardigan.

Ben, his arms linked around my waist, leaned back and looked into my eyes. "Everything is going to be fine. You'll see."

I nodded.

"We'll do in vitro next month, and I have a really good feeling about it," he said.

I nodded again. "Thanks for the flowers," I said, craning my head around him to look at the tulips on the counter. I didn't want to talk about next month. Or IVF. "And the beer. I take it at least three of those are for me?"

Ben laughed. "Well, I figured you might need it," he said. "And if not, I was prepared to drink the lot." He winked and I stood on my tiptoes to kiss him.

"I love you, Ben Matthews."

"I love you, too, Hannah Matthews."

I extricated myself from his embrace. "Listen, I just need to go call Kate. You know how she frets."

"I'm sure she can wait for one beer," Ben said, cracking the lids on two bottles. "Here."

"Thanks." I took it from him, then picked up my phone. "I'll be right back, okay?"

Ben nodded and took a sip from his bottle, settling in on the couch. I headed to the bedroom upstairs and shut the door, then put my phone and beer on the nightstand and picked up a pillow from the bed.

Covering my face with it, pressing so hard my knuckles

dug into my cheekbones, I screamed into the four-hundred thread count Egyptian cotton pillowcase until my throat hurt and I had no air left.

4

KATE

"Don't talk about the girls, or babies, or anything to do with eggs or sperm." I grabbed the taco shells out of the pantry and arranged them on the cookie sheet before sliding it into the prewarmed oven. David stirred the simmering beef on the stove top, shaking in some extra chili flakes.

"How would I even bring eggs or sperm up?" he asked before blowing on a spoonful of beef and popping it into his mouth. He swore under his breath, then grabbed his glass beside the stove and took a large gulp of water.

"Is it spicy? Did you put in too many pepper flakes?" I asked, even though I had no business commenting on his cooking. I was—had always been—a horrific cook, something I blamed on my upbringing. My mom could make exactly five dishes—scalloped potatoes with ham, spinach frittata, pasta with red sauce, chicken enchiladas and turkey potpie. I had since learned, thanks to David, how to make from-scratch pancakes, roast chicken with potatoes and beans, and a decent Mediterranean bread salad, but all of us were happy he shouldered most of the cooking. "It's temperature hot," he said. "Spice is perfect."

"I feel so guilty every time," I said, sighing. I whirled the margarita mix in the blender with two cups of ice, yelling over the blender noise. "It was so easy. Like, you barely touched me easy. Why can't it just work for them? One time."

The doorbell rang just as I finished rimming the glasses with rock salt.

"Remember, it's like nothing is different," I said as I headed out of the kitchen.

"Got it. No eggs. No sperm. Nothing is different." David scraped the beef into a large bowl and set it on the island beside the lazy Susan filled with tomato, onion, hot peppers, lettuce, salsa and cheese.

I opened the door, took one look at Hannah and immediately welled up.

"Shit, shit, shit!" I furiously wiped away the tears. While I was definitely the crier of the two of us, I had been determined not to shed a tear tonight. "I'm sorry. I suck."

Hannah gave me a tissue from her pocket. "Thanks a lot. Now I owe Ben twenty bucks."

"What?" I took the tissue. "You made a bet I'd cry?"

"I knew you'd cry," Ben said, leaning in to kiss my cheek.

"I told him you would at least hold it together until after the first pitcher of margaritas." Hannah handed me the bowl of her famous guacamole along with a large Tupperware container. "I've been stress baking," she said, with a shrug. "Chocolate peanut-butter cupcakes."

"Well, now that Katie has completely ruined the evening," David said, wincing slightly when I smacked him in the arm. "Let me just say I'm really sorry, guys." He shook Ben's hand, clasping his other hand against Ben's arm.

"Thanks, man," Ben said. Hannah looked down, her long,

blond ponytail falling to the side, and I could tell she was just holding it together.

"The margaritas are ready, and I'm putting an extra shot in yours tonight," I said, grabbing her hands and pulling her with me to the kitchen. "Come on. It's time to get drunk." David walked behind Hannah and put his hands on her shoulders, squeezing them gently as we all moved into the kitchen. With their blond hair and similar height—David only a couple of inches taller than Hannah—we often joked I had married the male equivalent of my best friend.

"I think I need two extra shots," Hannah said, taking a seat at the island and letting out a shaky breath.

"Done!" I freehand poured the tequila and we laughed.

Three pitchers of margaritas, a bottle of red wine, a mess of tacos and two rounds of Cards Against Humanity later, Hannah was drunk and snoring beside me on the couch. Watching her sleep, I brushed strands of hair out of her face and lay my hand against her cheek. "I'm going to help you, Hannah. I don't know how yet, but I'm going to fix this."

5

HANNAH

Though my hangover was mostly gone by Monday morning, I still felt like crap. My period was coming and, though I was ready for it, the thought of it still gutted me. One more month and a thousand dollars down the drain—quite literally. I sighed as I pulled out the box of tampons I'd hoped to tuck away with the pregnancy tests.

After throwing my hair into a ponytail—being a recipe developer meant I never wore my hair down at work—I quickly brushed my teeth, already feeling dull cramps in my abdomen. Ben was in the kitchen, downing a quick cup of coffee before he had to leave for the office.

"You all right?" he asked, swirling the mug in his hand, then drinking the last mouthful, his eyes still on me.

"All good."

He watched me for a few seconds more, then put his mug into the sink. "I'm going to be late tonight," he said. "Dad and I have to work on the proposal." As a junior partner at his dad's firm, he was currently involved in trying to secure a major project—the redesign of a chain of boutique hotels that stretched along Southern California's coastline—and they were only two weeks away from presenting to the client.

"Dishwasher's clean," he added, seeing me eye his mug—which he had placed unrinsed in the sink—with irritation. "I'll unload it when I get home, okay?" He was using his cautious, soothing tone; the one reserved for days like this. I think he figured if he stayed calm, I would, as well.

I longed to explode with anger, with sorrow, to yell at Ben if for no other reason than to expunge the sadness out of me. But Ben's tone said, let's be gentle and quiet and polite with each other. Like not looking an angry, aggressive dog directly in the eye—if we averted our gazes from our failure to become parents, we might be able to walk away unscathed. I wondered sometimes if Ben believed that being nice enough would smooth the disappointment out, like a hot iron over wrinkled cotton.

So, as always, I took the same tone with him, because this was the dance we danced—the steps well rehearsed, the cadence predictable. "Sure, sounds good." I opened the fridge and grabbed a yogurt, then scowled and put it back. The thought of eating something creamy and cold made my stomach turn. Pouring a large mug of coffee, I popped the lid on the acetaminophen bottle and shook out two—three—pills.

Ben raised his eyebrow, leaning back against the counter. "Headache? Or gearing up for your meeting today?"

"Something like that," I said. There was no point in telling him about the cramps. He'd run out of ways to say, "Sorry about your period" ages ago. I envied his ability to drink his coffee and go to work and to not analyze and obsess over every twinge in his abdomen.

He pushed off the counter's edge and kissed me, tasting like coffee with a hint of mint toothpaste, and was gone a moment later. Sipping my coffee, I replied to my sister Claire's text about Mom's birthday party, then saw the voice-mail icon flash on the screen. With a deep breath I put the phone on speaker and listened to the message from West Coast Fertility I'd been avoiding.

"Hi, Hannah, it's Rosey from Dr. Horwarth's office. We got your blood test results back and I'm sorry I don't have better news for you but—"

I hit the end call button, then placed the three acetaminophen tablets on my tongue and chased them down with coffee.

6

HANNAH

July

Once we got home from the clinic I read through the IVF information sheets while Ben made dinner, writing down the injection schedule on our fertility calendar in the kitchen drawer. Then we ate in silence—Ben had made me his mom's jerk chicken, but even the spicy dish, my favorite, couldn't lift my spirits.

"Hannah," he began, his voice unsure. I was in the middle of scrubbing the marinade dish and stopped briefly when he said my name, clenching my teeth. He had to know I didn't want to talk about it. *The dance, Ben*, I wanted to say. *Stick to the steps we know.*

"What's up?" I asked, keeping my tone light, back to scrubbing. As though I was only thinking about the dish in my hands.

"I know we're going to try IVF, but there are…other options, too. What about adoption? We haven't talked about it in a while."

I slowly counted to five, scrubbing so hard I splashed water onto the countertop. "I can't talk about this tonight. I can't, okay?" Reluctantly I drew my eyes to his face, willing him to see this wasn't the time.

"Okay." Ben nodded, but I saw the shift in his face. The way his jaw tightened as he took a deep breath in through his nose. "So when?"

"When what?" I knew I was being unfairly evasive. After all, this wasn't only my disappointment. Ben wanted to be a father more than anything.

"When will you be able to talk about it?"

"I don't know."

"Hannah, I—"

"I don't know!" I shouted, my rubber-glove-covered hands flying out of the sudsy sink, dripping soapy water all over the mat under my feet. "I have no fucking idea, actually. But if you don't mind, I'd rather just do these dishes in peace and not think about babies or getting pregnant or IVF or any of it, okay?" My voice rose, unsteady and breathless. "Or at the very least, I'd like twenty-four hours to be pissed off about my still-shitty uterus before I even consider taking someone else's castoff." As soon as I said it I wanted to take it back. Stuff the words back into my mouth and swish them around until I could change their meaning. Because it had nothing to do with adopting anyone's "castoff"—a truly horrible way to phrase it, and I had no idea where those words came from— and everything to do with me being terrified of adoption.

I had this sick fear we'd adopt a baby, I'd fall deeply in love with it and then the birth mother would change her mind in the eleventh hour and I'd be left with empty arms and a broken heart. All I needed to do was tell Ben that, to explain myself so he could at least understand my hesitation. But instead I said those ugly words, which pulled us further away from each other.

Ben started pacing, his bare feet leaving damp footprints

on our kitchen floor thanks to the spilled dishwater. Back and forth, back and forth he walked in front of me, his hands pressed deep into his hips. "This is not just about you, Hannah. I know you have to deal with all these injections and hormones, and poking and prodding, but you are not alone in this. I'm right here, going through it, too, feeling shitty and angry about all the same things you are."

I blinked away tears and tried to focus on his footprints so I didn't have to look at his face.

"At some point we, you *and* me, have to decide when it's enough. It's been six years, Hannah, and I..." He paused, head bent to the ground, voice dropping. "I don't know how much longer I can do this."

"Tomorrow," I whispered. "We can talk about it tomorrow night, okay?"

"Okay," he said. "Tomorrow." Then he turned and walked upstairs, and a moment later I heard our bedroom door click shut. I tried not to think about what might be happening behind that closed door. So I stayed where I was, my gloved hands hanging by my sides, only small droplets of water dripping from them now. My abdomen cramped, and I knew that by morning the pain, and my defeat, would be worse. Then I'd sit on the toilet behind a locked bathroom door and cry so hard I'd get the hiccups.

Ben was wrong—in some ways, I really was alone with this.

7

KATE

September

I heard the door creak open and then Hannah's voice. "Kate?"

"Up here," I shouted back, leaning against the window frame, my body tucked up so my toes just touched the other side of the sill. My pedicure was nearly grown out, the half-moon of each toenail peeking out from under the chipping polish. "It's called Chinchilla," the manicurist had announced—almost proudly, as if the name had been her idea—rolling the bottle of boring beige polish between her hands to warm it. "Our most popular neutral for fall." I didn't care about how trendy my toes were, only that they complemented the black skirt and jacket I wore to the funeral and didn't shout wedding or date night, like my go-to coral color would have done.

It had been a month since my mom died, and I still felt strangely abandoned. My father had left when I was a baby, and despite the monthly letters he sent that I rarely opened—typed on impersonal white paper yet awkwardly personal in detail—my relationship with him was similar to my relationship with my dentist. A once-a-year visit for an hour that was about as unpleasant as a root canal. I only did it because my mom asked every year on her birthday for my father to join us for lunch. I think she hoped one day I'd let him off the hook for leaving us, somehow see in him what she still seemed to despite the disintegration of their marriage and his subsequent escape.

Mom had been alone in her beloved garden when she died—because while her cooking was atrocious, her green thumb was remarkable—one Sunday late afternoon while David, the kids and I made pizza and played Trouble. Now that she was gone I had lost my bearings, and though I could get the girls out the door to school dressed and with lunches packed, the rest of my day was typically spent puttering around the house, making lists of things I had no intention of doing and feeling sorry for myself. My mom drove me crazy at times, like all mothers do, but it had been just the two of us for so long and I loved her fiercely. Sometimes, especially at night, the pain got so bad I was sure I was having a heart attack just like she'd had, certain I'd inherited her silent heart problem and would face a similar fate.

David continually assured me I was not having a heart attack when the pain was at its worst, placing his stethoscope against my heaving chest in the middle of the night and taking my symptoms—racing heart, sweating, nausea—seriously, because he was my husband and loved me. He was more patient with me these days, not like when I stressed about Josie's stuffy nose turning to pneumonia or the sliver in my foot from the deck going gangrenous. He was generally unflappable—he said he couldn't get worked up about a sliver when he spent his days and nights trying to keep very sick or injured people alive—but I knew it was just who he was. And it was one of the things I envied most about him.

Hannah appeared in the doorway of our home office, a

room I intended to use one day when I figured out what job title came after "stay at home mom," with a look on her face that told me my days of holing up in my house were almost over.

"What are you doing?" she asked, stepping into the room and putting a plate filled with chocolate chunk cookies on the desk.

I pointed to her bare feet. "Why do you always take your shoes off? You know this is a shoe-on house."

"Well, you don't have shoes on. And why are you answering a question with a question?"

I gestured to the plate of cookies. "Stress baking again?"

"Work baking. Don't get too excited, though. They're gluten-free. Not bad, but gluten really does make everything more delicious." She padded over to where I sat and gave me a kiss on the cheek. "Are you okay, Katie?"

I pushed her away gently. "Go back to the door. I don't want you breathing this in. You have your transfer in a few days."

Hannah pointed at the cigarette in my hand. "That's what I meant about what are you doing. I know the eighties are back in fashion, but think this might be a tad retro?"

I smiled and took a long drag, then turned my head and exhaled out the open window. "Yeah, but I don't care. Tell me, why did I ever stop smoking? I forgot how good it feels." Hannah's grandfather had been an occasional smoker, and until the unfortunate day when her grandmother caught us red-handed, we used to steal cigarettes out of his silver monogrammed cigarette case after school and run down the street to the park, where we'd hide behind the climber and giggle and cough while we smoked, feeling grown-up and wild and a little woozy from the nicotine.

"Feels good for now, until the lung cancer settles in," Hannah said, dragging a chair up to the window. "Give me one."

I pulled the pack out of her hand and tucked it under my arm. "No fucking way," I said. "You're about to make a baby. I'm not letting you put anything in that body of yours except kale and red meat. Speaking of which, the steaks are in the fridge marinating and the kale salad is in the crisper." Back in the early days of trying to conceive, before the fertility medications and doctors, Hannah had scoured every website and piece of advice she could about baby making and had gone on a strict high-iron diet. It only lasted for a month, but it was also the only other time she got pregnant naturally. Unfortunately she miscarried almost immediately, but I still bought her organic red meat before every procedure, feeling superstitious about it all.

"Technically the baby was already made when my sad little eggs joined Ben's very enthusiastic sperm in a plastic dish a few days ago—did I tell you that's actually what they called his sperm? *Enthusiastic*." Hannah sighed, tugging the pack from my hand and pulling a cigarette out. "Are these menthol?"

"Yup. I went old-school." I lit the cigarette she held between her lips. She took a deep drag and coughed a little. "So you need to eat an extra helping of the kale to make up for this, okay? Promise me."

"No need." Hannah took another drag, not coughing this time. "This really is like riding a bike, isn't it?"

I nodded and lit another cigarette right from the one between my lips, which had burned down to the filter. "Why no need?" I asked.

"It isn't going to happen," Hannah said, pushing my feet off the sill and coming to sit beside me. I didn't comment right away. By now I was well used to her negativity when it came to all things infertility, and had learned jumping too quickly to the positive only pissed her off and shut her down. We rested our feet side by side on the chair she'd just vacated, and I commented on how nice her toenails looked, each covered with a fresh and glossy shade of lilac polish.

"Grape Frost," she said, wriggling her toes a little. We smoked in silence for a moment longer.

"Look, I know it's got to be hard to stay positive after everything, but—" I started.

"The embryos arrested."

I swiveled to look at her. "What does that mean? Arrested?"

"It means they didn't grow. Which means we won't be doing a transfer," Hannah said, looking down at her feet again.

"Okay, so next month, then." I nudged her shoulder, hoping she'd look at me. She didn't. "You've waited this long, you can do one more month."

Hannah shook her head and pulled on her cigarette. The office was filling with smoke, but it was still early in the day. I had time to air it out before the girls came home, and David was on a long shift. Though I had only ever been a fair-weather smoker—picking up the habit during particularly stressful times and dropping it when life felt smooth and easy—technically I had quit twelve years ago, when I found out we were pregnant with Ava. But I kept a pack hidden at the back of my underwear drawer, just in case.

"We're done, Katie."

"What? No," I said, placing my hand on her leg. "No, you are not done. Sure, take this month, take two months if you need to, but you can't give up."

She jumped off the windowsill so fast I lost my balance, dropping her cigarette into my glass of water before I could stop her. Then she peeled back the plastic cellophane on the plate, grabbing a cookie and pacing while she ate it, frowning as she chewed. Someone who didn't know her as well might think the frown was about the arrested embryos, but I knew she was contemplating the cookies' texture and flavor, and how to make them better.

"We're not giving up—we're giving in," she said, her mouth half-full of cookie. "There's a difference. Ben said he couldn't do it anymore. And I sort of agree." She stopped pacing, swallowing the mouthful and staring at the half-eaten cookie left in her hand. "More salt, more butter, less vanilla."

I took the cookie out of her hand and had a big bite. "I say just add another cup of chocolate chips and you're good to go."

Hannah started crying.

"Or not. Maybe pecans?" I said.

"I'm a mess. I look terrible. I'm exhausted. I feel like shit. I'm crying all the time. Like, all the time, Katie," Hannah said. "And you know how I hate to cry. Plus, none of my clothes fit. I'm fat."

I shook my head. "You are not fat. You're beautiful."

"Tell that to my jeans and these zits," she said, pacing again, still crying but less so. "All I do is think about babies. And hate everyone who has one. I can't even stand going to Starbucks in the middle of the day anymore, because inevitably there's some new mom sipping a latte and breast-feeding. *Glowing* in all her fucking new-motherness." She looked at me pointedly. "And you know how much I love my London Fogs."

I nodded, watching her carefully. "I know your love runs deep."

"It really does," Hannah said, sniffing and licking her fingers free of melted chocolate. "And in the few moments I have when I'm not thinking about babies or missing London Fogs, I'm injecting myself with needles. I'm a fucking human pincushion. Seriously. Have you seen my stomach lately?" Without waiting for me to answer she lifted her tank top and uncovered dozens of bruises and angry red dots, all blending together in a mesmerizing pattern better suited to an artist's canvas than my best friend's torso. I forced my eyes back to her face, which was blotchy from the strength of her tears.

I put my cigarette out in the glass where Hannah's half-smoked one still floated and walked over to her. Taking the cookie out of her hands, I grabbed a tissue from the holder on the desk and gently wiped the remaining chocolate off her fingers.

"Thanks," she said when I took another tissue and wiped her eyes with it. "I love you, Katie."

"I love you, too, Hannah. We're both sort of a mess, aren't we?"

Hannah nodded, and a laugh bubbled out of her. "You stink, and so does this office," she said. "David is going to lose it."

"He won't be home for hours," I said, handing her another cigarette and taking one for myself. We lit them off the same flame from the lighter that came free with the pack of cigarettes. I inhaled deeply, feeling the cool burn of the menthol-flavored tobacco hitting my airway.

"Cheers to us," Hannah said, tapping her cigarette to mine. "And for what it's worth, there's no one I'd rather be a mess with."

"Me neither."

We smoked that cigarette, and then Hannah went back to work, leaving me to get the smoke out the office with air fresheners and the big fan we kept in the basement. With the fan blowing full blast and a freesia-scented candle burning, I put the cigarette package back in my underwear drawer, headed to our bathroom with the plate of cookies and took the rest of the boring beige polish off my toenails.

8

HANNAH

October

"Are you seriously making popcorn?" Ben opened the fridge, pulling out a beer and an apple. He rubbed the apple on his jeans—his version of giving it a good wash—and, holding the glossy red fruit between his teeth, opened the beer with a quick twist. He held up the beer bottle with a questioning look, and I shook my head.

"No, thanks. I'm in the mood for something stronger tonight. And you love popcorn." I turned the handle on the Whirley Pop popcorn maker, which was heating up on the stove. It had been a gift from my mom two Christmases ago, a "healthy snack" alternative to help me lose some weight. I had been a rower all through college and still wasn't used to my softer body, though I didn't like to admit that. Apparently one of Mom's bridge friends had a daughter who had a terrible time getting pregnant, until she took up running and lost twenty pounds, then poof, twins. My mom was quite certain if I got thin—like my sister Claire was, like Mom had been her whole life—I'd finally get pregnant. While I had wanted to tell her to take the Whirley Pop and shove it, I thanked her for the gift and then promptly hid it at the back of a kitchen cabinet behind a stack of old bakeware.

Tonight was the first time I'd used the Whirley Pop, and only because we had run out of microwave popcorn.

"Wrong. I love melted butter," Ben said. "Popcorn is just a vehicle for the butter."

I rolled my eyes and continued turning the handle, hearing the first kernel pop. "I want to make tonight fun, or at least tolerable, and popcorn is fun. We can pretend it's movie night...just without the movie."

"Hannah, I love you. But popcorn isn't exactly 'fun,' and looking through classifieds is nothing like movie night." Ben took another bite of his apple, swishing it down with a sip of beer. I scowled, both at his attitude about what I had planned for our night and the whole beer and apple thing. While most people enjoyed salted peanuts or chips with a beer, Ben preferred fruit. He could eat whatever he wanted, blessed with his mom's height and his dad's metabolism, and that he chose an apple over nachos felt a little as if he was rubbing it in.

"I didn't say it was *like* movie night. I said I wanted to make it fun...like movie night." Ben just shrugged, and with a sigh I dumped the hot popcorn in a large bowl. "Can you hit Start on the microwave? Butter's ready to go."

"So how does this work?" Ben asked, taking a handful of popcorn and looking at the screen. I had already opened the site, having found it during my research mission earlier in the day.

"I think it's like any ad site, you search and see what pops up." I typed a couple of words in the search box and hit Enter. I was playing naive, because I didn't want Ben to know I'd already done a pretty thorough search. I needed to know what to expect ahead of time, because Ben wasn't exactly on board with the idea of surrogacy.

Two pages of hits came up, and, taking my own handful of popcorn, I scanned the first page.

"Okay, this one looks good. 'In search of a loving couple to take this incredible journey with,'" I read out loud.

Ben snorted. "Nope. That one sounds too high maintenance."

"Stop it. Just humor me, okay?"

He took another handful of popcorn and leaned over to kiss me on the cheek. "Fine," he said, munching on the kernels. "Tell me more about this incredible-journey woman."

"Thank you." I shifted the laptop so Ben could see the screen better. "Thirty years old, mom of three. Good. We know her equipment works. Married—to the same man—for the past eight years, and she's asking...whoa. Holy shit." I pointed to the dollar amount in the ad, leaving a buttery fingerprint on the screen.

Ben leaned in and squinted. He was supposed to be wearing his reading glasses, which he'd finally had to admit he needed, but he was having a hard time accepting that at thirty-five he was aging...or at least his eyes were. "Forty thousand dollars?"

"That seems a bit high. Thought it was around thirty thousand? Maybe because she's already had a successful surrogate pregnancy?"

"Go to the next one," Ben said, taking a swill of his beer.

I sipped my gin and tonic and clicked on the next ad.

"So this one was a gestational surrogate before—that's when she carries the couple's embryo," I explained.

"I know what a gestational surrogate is," Ben said, getting up to grab another beer and a handful of grapes. "Need anything?"

I shook my head, reading on. "She didn't like the medications when she did the gestational gig—can't say I blame her," I said, looking over at Ben. He nodded, settling back on the couch. We had briefly discussed trying to find an egg donor and maybe giving that a try using my own uterus. But the thought of paying for someone else's eggs, then turning them into embryos, then trusting my uterus to let them grow... It left me weak with anxiety and despair.

I couldn't explain how, but I knew—*I knew*, deep inside—that my body would never carry a baby to term. And I couldn't handle one more negative pregnancy test or chemical pregnancy. Sure, we could also get donor eggs, fertilize them with Ben's sperm to make embryos and then find a gestational surrogate, but the cost to do that would be astronomical. And we'd already spent thousands of dollars to get to this point—surfing for surrogates on date night.

"So she's only willing to be a traditional surrogate, which is perfect for us." Ben nodded again, and I smiled at him before looking back at the screen. I was nervous, so much more invested in this than I cared to admit.

"Married, healthy, two kids, good BMI, no family disease, had a recent psychiatric evaluation..." At that Ben raised his eyebrows but didn't comment. "Huh. Okay. Says she would prefer a Christian, traditional couple, and wants a relationship after the birth." I chewed a stray cuticle, trying to decide how I felt about that. The Christian thing didn't worry me, even though Ben and I were not religious, but a relationship after the baby was born?

"I guess that's not so different from adoption," Ben said, shrugging. "What do you think about that?" I knew he wasn't keen on doing a surrogacy, but I loved him for appeasing my need to look at all the options.

"Let's go to the next one," I said, swallowing the lump in my throat. I was weeks off the fertility medications now, so I couldn't blame the tears that sprang to my eyes on that anymore. What I wished I could say was that I loathed every second of this, no matter what I had said about the popcorn and fun. I wanted to have my own baby, not pay someone else to have one for us.

I hated that I'd dragged Ben into this sad mess, where we were spending our Saturday night reading surrogate classified ads and pretending it was something we wanted to do. I was worried that I couldn't make myself talk to Ben about how much adoption scared me. How I preferred the idea of surrogacy because the baby would at least be genetically linked to one of us. But most of all, and the thing I hadn't said aloud to anyone, ever?

I was deeply ashamed to be an infertile woman. I despised my body for failing me, failing Ben and our marriage, on the most basic of things.

Pushing that shame and sadness down, I read the next few ads out loud. They all sounded similar enough that by the end of the two pages it was hard to remember one from another. The popcorn sat heavily in my stomach, and I regretted putting so much butter on it. I shut the laptop forcefully and turned on the television.

Ben shifted so he faced me. "What are you doing?"

"I think you're right. I don't think this is a good idea." I flicked through the channels. "What do you want to watch?"

He took the remote from my hand and turned the television off. "Maybe we should talk about option C."

"What's option C?" I asked.

Ben swallowed hard but kept his eyes on mine. "Not having kids."

I stared at him, unsure what to say. We had talked briefly about the possibility of not having a family, but for me it was never a real option. But looking at his face I saw the concern, and worry, and realized all of this had taken as much out of him as it had me. So because I loved him more than I hated the idea of never having a child, I said, "Okay, let's talk about option C."

And the truth was option C had some decent stuff going for it. Travel. Financial freedom. Flexibility. The ability to be selfish. Saturday morning sleep-ins and late Sunday brunches. Glass coffee tables with supersharp corners, white couches and expensive throw pillows.

So while I brainstormed and wrote down the top ten places I'd like to travel with Ben, and he sketched out and calculated how much it might cost to design us a dream home overlooking the ocean, my heart wasn't in it.

Option C meant there would never be a baby.

I hated option C.

Around three o'clock in the morning, unable to sleep, I crept out of our bedroom and went downstairs to the kitchen. Bowl of Cherry Garcia ice cream in one hand and my laptop in another, I sat at the kitchen table and fired up the computer. I left the lights off, eating the cherry-and-chocolate ice cream by the laptop's glow, and went back through the ads Ben and I had browsed earlier.

I stopped at the one of the woman who preferred a Christian couple and wanted a relationship after the baby was born. Something about her had stuck with me, perhaps because she was one of the only ones to not romanticize the experience. There were no adjectives like *wonderful* or *incredible* peppered throughout, and I liked how up front she was about what she wanted out of the contract, money aside.

Tapping my spoon gently against the sides of my now-empty bowl, I tried to imagine what it would be like to have another woman carry a baby for me—a baby I had no genetic link to. My mind filled with a million questions and concerns, like how we would pay for it, and how our friends and family would react, and how I could be certain the surrogate wouldn't change her mind in the end and fight us to keep the baby. And if I would love a baby that wasn't mine as much as one I gave birth to.

Ben and I had agreed to put the surrogacy idea on the back burner. He preferred the idea of adoption, worried about the astronomical costs and complications—both emotional and logistical—that came with surrogacy, and as a last resort, option C. With a sigh I shut the laptop and took my bowl over to the sink. While I rinsed it I imagined rinsing out baby bottles after midnight feedings, and the pain in my belly was so intense I doubled over the sink, dropping the ice-cream bowl—the loud clang as it hit the stainless-steel tub echoing through the kitchen.

"Fuck it," I said, drying my hands and opening the laptop again.

Scanning the ad I found the contact information, and before I could even think about what I was doing, I typed her an email. With my finger over the enter key, poised to hit Send, I realized I was shaking. I told myself I wasn't committing to anything. It was just an email, and Ben didn't even need to know about it because nothing would likely come of it.

I hit Return, saw the confirmation my email had been sent and then went back to bed.

9

KATE

My cell phone rang, the familiar bars of Michael Jackson's "Pretty Young Thing" filling the silence of the kitchen. *Hannah*. I jumped, a hand to my chest, only then realizing I was still holding the butter knife I'd been spreading the peanut butter with.

"Shit," I said, glancing down at my previously white shirt. There was a large peanut-butter stain right in the middle of my chest. Why did I even bother trying to wear clean shirts, and a white one at that? I ran my finger over the excess peanut butter and licked it off, answering my phone.

"Hey, you," I said. "How goes it?" I tucked the phone in the crook of my neck and, glancing at the large clock on the wall, swore under my breath and quickly cut the crusts off the bread. My head was still pounding, despite the migraine medication I'd taken at four in the morning, but at least the tingling in my neck and arms was gone and my stomach had settled.

"Hey, are you going to be around for a bit after the girls go to school?" Hannah sounded weird. Out of breath. Like she had a secret she couldn't wait to let burst out of her mouth.

"It's a migraine morning, so David's taking them. You okay?"

"Yeah, yeah, good. Okay, I'll be by in about forty minutes. Want a latte or maybe a tea for your head?"

"Coffee, definitely," I replied. "I haven't had a chance to make any yet. That's probably why my head is still pounding."

"For the last time, set your coffee timer. It will change your life, promise."

"So you say." I leaned into the knife as I pressed it against the sandwich, the soft bread squishing and some peanut butter and jam squeezing out the edges.

"I'll get you a double shot. See you soon."

"See you soon," I said, hitting End with a peanut-butter-covered fingertip. "Shit!"

"Mom, you need to put a dollar in the jar." Ava came into the kitchen and grabbed a triangle of the sandwich before I could stop her. "Is this peanut butter?" Ava asked, holding the sandwich up in the very tips of her fingers as though it were poisoned.

"Yes, it's peanut butter. You love PB&J sammies. What's the deal?"

Ava rolled her eyes. "First of all, stop calling them 'sammies.' You sound really lame."

"Well, excuse me," I replied, tucking the other triangles into Josie's reusable sandwich bag, which was covered with bumblebees and tulips. "And I'm not lame. I'm your very cool, very hip mother."

"Secondly," Ava said, ignoring me, "you know you can't send peanut butter to school. We need that soy nut butter crap."

"Shit," I said, quickly followed by, "Don't say it. I know." I pointed a finger at the jar on the windowsill, which was half-full of dollar bills. "I'll put my money in today and after

school you need to put a dollar in for using the word *crap*."
It had been my idea to do the swear jar, after watching some
parenting show while I was at the dentist's office trying to
ignore the drilling in my mouth. But it had backfired, as I
was responsible for at least 70 percent of the money in there.
I reached into the pantry and grabbed two protein bars and
two fruit cups. "There's no time to make more sandwiches,
so protein bars it is."

"Fine," Ava said, taking her lunch bag from me and putting
it in her backpack. "I'm tired of sandwiches anyway."

"Where's your sister?"

"She's changing again. Something about not feeling the
color pink today."

"Josie!" I shouted up the stairs, just as David started coming
down. "Sorry, can you grab Josie? They're going to be late."

David turned and went back up the two stairs he had come
down, shouting Josie's name as he did.

I finished packing Josie's lunch and tucked it into her backpack, mentally running over all the things I needed to do before they left for the day. My mind felt foggy, an irritating
side effect of the medication I took to thwart the debilitating
migraines that struck every month or so.

David and Josie came into the kitchen, looking as if they'd
coordinated their outfits. Josie was dressed in black leggings
and a tunic, and David wore his all-black paramedic uniform.
"You look lovely." I kissed Josie on top of her head. "Black is
a great color on you."

"Thank you, Momma," she said, her chin tilting up and
a smile coming across her freckled face at the compliment.

"Okay, get going or you'll miss the morning bell." I kissed
the two of them on their cheeks, foreheads, noses and lips, just
like I did every morning. Ava wiped her lips afterward, but
Josie came back for a second kiss. I was grateful I had a few

more years of kisses and snuggles and Josie thinking I walked on water before the hormones kicked in and I became her "lame," forgetful, cussing mom instead of her hero.

David pecked me on the lips when I handed him his lunch, and I pulled him in for another kiss. "Have a great day," I said.

"You, too." He smiled at me, his gaze settling on me in a way that made me feel warm inside. "How's the head?"

"Better," I said. "Hannah's bringing me a coffee, so I'll be right as rain in no time." David kissed me again, and then in a rush they were out the door, and suddenly all was quiet in the house again. With a sigh, I sat at the kitchen table and rubbed the back of my neck while I checked my inbox filled with spam offers and PTA to-dos, impatiently waiting for Hannah, her news and my double-shot latte.

10

HANNAH

We had an off-site photo shoot and I didn't have to be at the restaurant we were featuring until ten. At nine o'clock I rang Kate's doorbell, nervously tapping the toes on one foot as I mentally rehearsed how I was going to justify what I was planning to do.

I could tell she wasn't feeling well when she opened the door, even though she was smiling. Her eyes were dull and her face pale.

"Thank God," she said, kissing my cheek and taking the tray of coffees from my hands. "I really do need to set that timer. David usually makes the coffee, but he didn't get a chance this morning." She smelled like peanut butter and tea tree oil, which I knew she used on the girls' hair every morning before school, claiming it had kept them lice-free even during the school's inevitable outbreaks.

"How's the migraine?" I asked, following her into the living room. I sat on the couch beside her and tucked my legs under me. She took a sip of the latte and closed her eyes. "So much better now. Thank you for this." Then she opened her eyes and looked at me in a way that made me even more nervous, her deep brown eyes holding steady on my face. "Out with it, Hannah. What's up?"

I cleared my throat, shifting to grab my own coffee. "So I've done something... Something I probably shouldn't have. No, definitely shouldn't have."

"What have you done?" Kate asked slowly, as though she was giving both of us time to prepare for whatever it was.

It all came out in a rush. "I emailed a surrogate even though I told Ben I wouldn't, and now she wants to meet, like tomorrow, and I said I'd meet her and I didn't tell Ben and I'm not sure I want to because I know he's going to lose it and she's asking for forty grand to do this and she's really religious and we're not and she wants to have a relationship with the baby after it's born but I really want to meet her. I think. I'm pretty sure—"

"Stop talking," Kate said, and so I did. She casually took a long sip of her coffee and then got up. "This calls for chocolate." A moment later she was back, a huge dark chocolate bar on the coffee table in front of us. Kate popped a piece of the chocolate in her mouth and sucked on it, melting it on her tongue. I didn't bother reminding her chocolate was one of her headache triggers.

"First of all, I have to say I'm sort of impressed. I mean, going on a secret surrogate-hunting mission? That is a very un-Hannah-like move."

I squirmed, knowing she was trying to make me laugh but feeling worse by the second. "I didn't mean for it to be a secret, I just... I don't know. I just did it before I could think too hard about what I was doing."

Kate nodded, looking at me thoughtfully. "Who is this person?" she asked, snapping off another square of chocolate.

"Her name is Lyla. She's a mom, married and healthy, and she wants to be a surrogate. My—our—surrogate."

Kate narrowed her eyes. "How did you find her?"

"A classified ad." I tried not to cringe, hearing how it sounded. I mean, you went to the classifieds to find a dining room table or tickets to a sold-out concert, not for a woman to carry a baby for you.

Kate paused, the chocolate square partway to her lips. "You're kidding me."

"Nope, not kidding."

"And you're sharing this with me instead of Ben because…?"

"Because I needed to tell someone who was going to be on my side," I said, my voice dropping. The sweetness of the chocolate locked up my throat and I coughed hard a few times.

Kate rubbed my back. "Oh, honey. Ben is always on your side."

I shook my head. "Not this time, Katie. Sure, he humored me and went through the ads with me, but I know he doesn't want to do this. He thinks it's… He wants to try adoption."

Kate took my hands in hers and gently tugged on them until I looked at her. "And you don't?"

"I'm not sure what I want anymore," I replied. "No, that's not true. I know exactly what I want."

Kate squeezed my fingers. "You want a baby."

I nodded. "A baby. And when I read through Lyla's ad, something just… I don't know, something just told me to email her. I didn't even consider what I'd do if she responded back."

"When are you going to tell Ben?"

"After I meet with her? I mean, maybe once I see her, talk to her, I'll be sure it's not the right thing to do." I looked at Kate, then looked away quickly when I saw her face—she was right, of course. I had to tell Ben.

"Besides, you can't go alone. What if she's nuts? Has some

kind of weird secret agenda, like pretending to be pregnant so she can get your money and then take off?" I didn't want to admit that very thought had crossed my mind more than once.

"You're right. This is a bad idea. Sorry, I just—"

"You just want to be a mom," Kate said, holding my hands tighter. "Listen, I still think you should talk to Ben before you go meet any sort of potential baby mama, but if you really want to go through with this first, I'll come with you. I don't want you going by yourself."

"Thank you. But… I should never have sent that email. I can't shut Ben out of this, no matter how much easier it might be." Kate gave me a small, sad smile. "I'm going to cancel." My phone's alarm went off. "Gotta run. I need to be at the restaurant by ten."

I stood and hugged Kate tightly. "Thanks for talking me off the ledge."

"Thanks for the latte. I needed it. You gonna be okay?"

I nodded. "Fine. You know me—I'm not a quitter."

"No," Kate said, shaking her head. "You are not."

"Let me know if you need a hand with the girls after school, okay? You can put your feet up and I can make dinner."

"Deal," Kate said. A minute later I was waving at Kate as she stood in her doorway, heading toward the BART station. Fifteen minutes later while I waited for my train, I pulled out my phone and checked my messages. One from Ben, wanting to take me out for dinner tomorrow night; one from my mom, making sure I wouldn't forget to call my uncle George after his gallbladder surgery; and another one from Lyla, confirming our meeting the next afternoon. Ignoring the messages from Ben and my mom for the moment, I hit Reply and told Lyla I'd see her there and was looking forward to it, then got on the train trying not to feel guilty about lying to everyone.

11

HANNAH

As I stood in the coffee line, secretly observing Lyla—who was engrossed in something on her phone—all I could think about was how tiny she was, her hips narrow and legs so short her feet only just grazed the floor when she was sitting down. I had good hips for pregnancy—wide and sturdy. I was also, at five-eight, on the tall side for a woman and so assumed that when Ben and I had a child he or she would probably end up tall—perhaps a volleyball player like Ben had been, or a rower like me.

I still hadn't allowed myself to really consider what I was doing here—that this woman, waiting for her green tea latte and cinnamon coffee cake, was prepared to use her own eggs and body to carry a child for me, a complete stranger. Lyla looked up and smiled, and I smiled back, face flushing at being caught staring.

The guilt that swept through me was deep and swift, and I had the sudden urge to run back out through the coffee shop's front door and pretend like I hadn't agreed to this. Or better yet, I wished I could go back and erase that first email I'd sent Lyla, finish my ice cream and go back to bed instead of hitting Send. I should have told Ben—I had lied to him about something important exactly once in our relationship, back when we were still figuring out who we were to each other, and had promised him at the time I wouldn't do it again. That was not who we were. My stomach knotted, and I felt sick.

"Fourteen seventy-five," the young guy at the cash register said, and I had the feeling based on the tone of his voice that it wasn't the first time he'd told me what I owed.

I mumbled an apology and fished a twenty out of my wallet, handing it to him with a smile. He gave me my change and the place card holder with my number, and I went back to our table.

Lyla looked up as I sat down and I noticed her eyes were brown, flecked with amber highlights that almost looked like there were tiny lights behind her irises. They were pretty. I had accepted that if we were to go the surrogate route, the baby would not look like me. Lyla was quite fair skinned, so at least Ben's coloring would shine through. For some reason that mattered to me—that the baby looked like one of us—though I knew I should have let go of that ages ago.

"They'll bring it out to us." I placed the numbered card on the edge of our table.

"Thank you," Lyla said, her voice exuberant and her smile wide. "So, Hannah, why don't you tell me a bit about yourself?"

Her forwardness caught me off guard, until I remembered this wasn't the first time she'd sat across from a woman she was considering carrying a baby for. I hated that I was the inexperienced one—the desperate one. The one who needed something and who had so much to lose.

"Well, let's see," I said, chewing one of my cuticles—a nervous habit I had been trying to break since I was a girl. You could always tell the state of my anxiety or stress based on the shape of my cuticles. "I'm thirty-five, grew up in Marin—Mill Valley, specifically. I'm a recipe developer at *Femme* magazine, which means I spend a lot of time in the kitchen, cooking and eating, so as you can imagine it's a great job."

"Oh, I love the recipes in *Femme*," Lyla said. "I don't know how you stay so thin, having to eat everything."

I smiled at the compliment and wished I could record it for my mother. "Well, we have a little industry trick. We don't swallow most of what we taste—we spit it out. It sounds gross I know, but it's the only way to avoid buying a new wardrobe every year. I gained about ten pounds the first six months I was at the magazine until I learned the taste-and-spit trick."

"Huh, I never even thought about that, but it makes sense. What about your family? Are they here in San Francisco?"

"My dad died when I was ten," I said, then thanked her when she told me she was sorry to hear that. "My mom lives over in Pacific Heights with my sister and her husband." I cleared my throat and looked over to the coffee bar, hoping our drinks were on their way. The nervousness in my belly was increasing with every word.

"Are ya'll close?" Lyla asked. "You and your sister?"

I looked back at her. "Claire's five years younger than me, but yeah, I guess we're close? Or as close as you can be when you have that many years between you." Claire was an associate partner at her husband Peter Todd's law firm and expected to make full partner within the next year—which would make her the youngest partner at the firm. And it had nothing to do with nepotism. She worked hard; she got what she wanted. As for me, I liked my job—a lot most days. I got to work with food—my first love—and it was the sort of work that allowed room for motherhood, too. But careers and age difference aside, the truth was that Claire and I were different in every way we could be—she was ambitious and confident, petite and pretty, while I was less so in all areas.

Lyla nodded. "I get that. My two boys are quite close in age, but have very different personalities. Luke is the oldest, and a risk taker—he's going to turn my hair gray soon. Jason, my husband, says we're going to spend a lot of time in the ER with Luke." She smiled. "And Johnny is only fifteen months younger, but he's an old soul. He's a very quiet and responsible boy."

"Do you have a picture?" I asked.

"I do!" Lyla shifted her chair to come beside me. She smelled like lavender and mint, and I took a deep breath in, the scent pleasant and relaxing. "Here's Luke last year in the school play." I looked at the screen on her phone, seeing a boy—around six or seven I guessed—dressed in a brown sheet cinched at the waist with a belt and sandals, a huge smile on his face—Lyla's smile. "He played Joseph." I nodded and murmured how sweet he looked, glancing at the next picture she pulled up. "And this is Johnny, also last Christmas." Johnny sat in front of a fully decorated Christmas tree. He wore glasses and smiled, though he showed no teeth.

"They're very handsome," I said. "And really look like you."

Lyla looked at the photos, still smiling. "I get that a lot."

My stomach dropped, thinking again that no one would ever say that about my child—if I could even find a way to have a child. I pushed the sadness away and focused on my coffee and brioche, which had just arrived.

Lyla went on to say she and Jason had just celebrated their ten-year anniversary, and had moved from Texas to San Francisco a year ago to move in with his mother, who was ill. Jason was working as a security guard but wanted to become a police officer, and while Lyla had worked as a medical receptionist in Texas, she was taking care of Jason's mom and the boys now. I commented how tough it must have been to make the move, and she shrugged, saying that she wasn't close to her own family and Jason's mom was like a mother to her.

"So why are you looking into surrogacy?" Lyla asked.

I was suddenly uncomfortable—as much as I knew this was the conversation we needed to be having, I didn't want to be having it.

"Oh, well, wow. Where do I start?" I laughed, but it came out sounding forced, and Lyla gave me a sympathetic smile. "We've been trying for six years, which when you say it out loud seems like way too long, doesn't it?" I shook my head and took a deep breath, hoping it might relieve the tension sitting in a band across my chest. It didn't. "I've been pregnant three times but miscarried very early on. And other than that, no luck. We've been working with a fertility specialist for about four years now."

"I'm sorry, Hannah. That must be real difficult for you and Ben."

"Thanks, yeah, it hasn't been…easy. But I'm lucky. He's amazingly supportive." *Except he has no idea I'm here talking with you, and I'm not sure what that says about me. About us.*

"Are ya'll married?" Lyla's tone was casual, but the way she looked at me suggested otherwise.

"Yes! Didn't I mention that? Seven years."

"Oh, good," she said, stirring her latte and sucking some of the green-tinged foam off the spoon. "Sorry if that sounds strange, but that's real important to me and Jason."

"Of course, I understand completely."

"Do you and Ben belong to a church?"

I had been dreading this, knowing it was important to Lyla, and wasn't sure how to answer. I went with the truth.

"No, we don't." I took a bite of my brioche and left it up to her to decide what to do with that.

"That's okay," Lyla said, forking her cinnamon cake and popping the piece into her mouth. I waited while she chewed and swallowed. "I just need to let you know I won't do any genetic testing with the baby or anything like that and I'm pro-life." She said this casually, as if we were discussing a new restaurant opening or the weekend weather forecast.

I sat there with my mouth open for a moment, surprised at how quickly we were at this stage of the conversation. "Of course," I said again, swallowing hard. I hadn't thought any of this through, and it was becoming clear I had not been ready to hit Send on that email.

"Do you have any questions for me?" she asked, pressing the back of her fork into the sugary crumbs that dotted her plate. She licked her fork and looked at me expectantly, her face open and friendly.

Yes, Lyla, I have no fewer than a million questions for you. Like, why are you doing this? How does this whole thing work? Do we pay you in one lump sum or monthly? Will we get to come to all the ultrasounds and be at the delivery? Will you agree to take a multivitamin every day and never drink a sip of alcohol? Will you talk to the baby while it grows, tell it about us?

"A few," I said, trying to decide the best way to ask her the questions that overtook my mind, certain I couldn't find a diplomatic way to ask the most important question: *How will you place this baby into my arms, knowing it is part of you?* "But how about another piece of cake first?"

12

KATE

David and I were sitting in the gym's parents' lounge—really a well-used room with plastic orange chairs and fluorescent lights that made the purple walls practically glow—watching the girls at their weekly gymnastics class and drinking bad coffee from the café next door. Every time I sat watching one of their classes I felt grateful for my mom, who had endured years of thrice-weekly dance classes and competition weekends throughout my childhood and teenage years, never complaining about uncomfortable plastic chairs or bad coffee or the time it took away from her having her own hobbies.

I took a sip from my white plastic take-out cup and grimaced. "Next time, why don't we make coffee at home and bring it?" I silently thanked my mom again. "Oh, almost forgot. I'm meeting Hannah for a drink tomorrow night. That okay?"

"Sure. How is she doing?"

I paused. Long enough for David to swivel in his chair and look at me.

"She's okay."

"And?" he asked.

"And nothing." I gave Josie a thumbs-up after her unassisted cartwheel and smiled big.

"Kate, what's up? I know that look."

"What look?" I asked, but then sighed and took a deep breath. "Fine. She was planning to meet with a surrogate."

"A surrogate? Where?"

"Here. In town."

David let out a low whistle. "I didn't realize they were at that stage of things."

"Well, *they* aren't exactly at that stage of things." I shrugged, then looked back at the girls. "It's been six years and they've basically tried everything. I don't blame her, but I'm worried for her."

"What do you mean by *they* aren't at that stage of things?"

I kept my eyes trained on the girls, even though they were doing nothing but waiting for their turns on the balance beam. "She didn't tell Ben about the surrogate meeting."

"What? Really? So, she was just going to go by herself? Without Ben?" David's eyebrows rose along with his voice.

"I told her I'd go with her, but she said she was going to cancel anyway."

"Katie…"

"What? I couldn't very well let her go alone. She's…she's definitely off-kilter right now."

David sighed and leaned back in his chair. "Do not get in the middle of this, Kate. She needs to talk with Ben, period. You can't go meet a surrogate with her. This isn't like getting dragged to boot camp for moral support or something. This is no small thing, and it's between them."

"Don't you think I know that?"

"Do you?"

I looked back at the girls, trying to mellow the irritation

threatening to take over. "It doesn't matter, because I talked her out of it."

"I hope so. I would lose it if you did something like that without telling me."

We sat in silence for a moment. "How would it even work?" David asked. "They don't have embryos, right?"

"This surrogate would use her own eggs."

"So the baby would be Ben's and this other woman's?" David gave his head a couple of quick shakes. "No way. I could never do that."

"Why? It's not really different from adoption when you think about it. Except at least Ben's genes would get in there."

"But what if this woman decided to keep the baby in the end? I mean, it would be her *baby*, right?"

"It would," I said, frowning at the thought. "I don't think Hannah really thought it all through."

"Shit, Ben would flip if he knew she had propositioned this woman without telling him."

"She didn't exactly 'proposition' her," I said, his choice of words grating on me; my need to defend Hannah boiling up. "It was more curiosity, or a reconnaissance mission, I guess."

"Still...don't you think he'd be open to it? He wants a kid as much as she does. But not telling him?" David shook his head again. "That's a sure way to guarantee he won't go along with it."

"Well, she implied he wasn't on board with the idea anyway."

"That makes it worse," David said. "I love Hannah, but she's playing a dangerous game here."

I pressed my lips together, pausing for a moment. "She's desperate, David."

"Desperate enough to risk her marriage?"

I shrugged. I'd be lying if I said I wasn't worried about Hannah and Ben sticking it out if there was no baby—a relationship could only bend so much under stress before it snapped. And Hannah keeping this from Ben felt like a big crack in their happy marital veneer.

David nudged my shoulder, and I lifted my coffee cup to avoid spilling it on my legs. "For the record, if you ever kept anything big like that from me I'd be beyond pissed."

"Noted, and ditto."

"Are they asleep?" David looked at me from our bed, lying on top of the duvet in his boxers and an old hole-filled T-shirt from his days as a first aid instructor. He had plenty of shirts, including others from his instructor days, but for whatever reason this was the one I couldn't get him to let go of. I filed it under things-to-ignore-even-though-they-drive-me-crazy-because-I-love-my-husband-more-than-I-hate-what-he's-wearing.

"They are." I got into bed beside him. Running my hands over his chest, feeling the softness of the fabric, I remembered back when we were as new as the T-shirt. Pushing it up, the black color now faded to a velvety gray, I planted a row of kisses around his exposed belly button. His abs flexed, and I looked up to see him smiling. "I'm going to lock the door," I whispered into his stomach, kissing it again. I jumped to my knees and scrambled off the bed, my feet padding softly on the hardwood floor of our bedroom. With a quick twist of my hand, our bedroom door was locked—one of the best tips my hippie mother-in-law, a sex educator, had ever given me, even though I had been horrified at the time—and I was back in bed stretched out beside David.

"Do you think they'll be okay?" I asked.

"Who?" His voice was low, his lips caressing my ear and whispering that I had too much clothing on. I obliged by lifting my arms over my head so he could do something about that.

"Hannah and Ben," I replied, only half paying attention to what his hands were doing. "If they can't have a baby, do you think they'll stay together?" My heart beat faster, in part from David's touch and in part from imagining the end of Hannah and Ben, which was unacceptable as far as I was concerned.

David propped himself up on an elbow and rubbed his thumb over my jawline. "They'll work it out. They love each other. And, yes, they've been through hell with all of this. But they are stronger than that. You'll see. It'll be okay."

I smiled, then wriggled out of my underwear with some help from David's persuasive hands. Our bodies knew each other so well—having done this enough times there was never any doubt of a home run for all. My breathing sped up and a moan formed in the back of my throat as David gently spread my thighs, moving between them. When I wasn't sure I could hold out much longer, I lay a hand on his head and pulled his hair gently, forcing him to look at me. I gestured under the bed and he smiled, nodding.

"Which one do you want tonight?" he asked, and I heard him rustling through the box under our bed, which held a variety of adult-only toys and, like the door, also had a lock on it.

"You choose," I replied.

A minute later I was enjoying David's choice for the evening, no longer caring about hole-filled T-shirts I'd dreamed of tossing out weekly with the trash or the state of Hannah and Ben's marriage.

13

HANNAH

Ben was working late, so I said I'd meet him at the restaurant. My mind was still spinning from my coffee date with Lyla, but I had such a good feeling about things. It had been a long time since I'd felt anything but unhappiness and disappointment in the baby-making department, and Lyla had given me something to hope for again.

After we'd polished off another piece of cake and latte each, Lyla basically told me she was in. That she had to chat with her husband, of course, but she couldn't see a reason for us not to take the next steps, which involved lawyers and contracts and doctors and probably a hundred other things I hadn't yet considered. I wasn't expecting her to decide that quickly, picturing many emails, phone calls and meetings between the four of us, and it threw me off. Tears in my eyes, I'd jumped up and hugged her while she was still in her seat. She'd laughed and said I could thank her when she was pregnant.

Though she answered my questions about why she wanted to be a surrogate—with refreshing honesty she said it was a financial decision for her family but also an altruistic one because it meant helping another couple become a family—and gave me some insight into the process, which was about as complicated as I expected, I never got around to asking the most difficult question.

I could lie and say I decided it wasn't all that important—after all, this wasn't her first time. She had walked away from a baby before, so there was no reason to think she wouldn't—couldn't—do it again. But the truth was I had been too afraid in the moment to do anything to ruin things before they even got started. It was a lot like a first date, where you leave out the baggage and unsavory details, because you really want to go out with this person again.

Thinking about how to tell Ben what I'd done—and that Lyla had chosen me, chosen us—left me light-headed with anxiety on the cab ride over to the restaurant. With every passing minute I became more convinced I should have talked with him first, like Kate said. Of course he would have been fine with it. Ben wanted a baby as badly as I did…

Or at least he used to.

These days I wasn't sure if he really *was* willing to do whatever it took, like I was. Would he be okay joining his sperm with another woman's egg, a stranger for whom this was more a job than anything else? Would he feel awkward about bringing home a baby that wasn't actually ours? Was he willing to invite another woman into our lives—us using her for her genetic material, her using us for our willingness to hand over tens of thousands of dollars?

Was I prepared for all that, as well?

Suddenly the idea felt all wrong. Too many variables crowded my thoughts. There were so many ways this could go wrong, and only one way it could work out.

But if it worked, I would have a baby.

My phone buzzed, and I looked down to see a new text had arrived. My stomach lurched when I saw it was from Lyla.

So nice meeting you today. Forgot to ask, do you have a picture of you and Ben? I'd love to show Jason. Can't wait to get started! Chat soon—Lyla

For a moment I did nothing. I read the text a half dozen times, then, fingers shaking, found a great photo of Ben and me, from our last vacation a year earlier in Jamaica for his annual family reunion. When that picture was taken we had been waiting to hear if our latest procedure had worked, distracting ourselves with family dinners on the beach, massages at the spa and long afternoon naps in lounge chairs shaded by palm trees. We weren't pregnant as it turned out, but at the time—sun shining and ocean warm—it felt as if anything was possible.

With a quick note saying it was lovely to meet Lyla, as well, and a promise to be in touch soon to sort out details, I attached the photo and hit Send.

It started to rain just as the cab approached the restaurant, and I grumbled about forgetting to bring an umbrella. The cabdriver kindly offered to walk me to the restaurant door, pulling out a large umbrella from the trunk and giving me his arm. I took it as a sign that my luck was changing. That Ben would be thrilled at my news, once he got over his surprise. I could spin this. He would forgive me for not telling him first.

Inside the restaurant it was dim and heady with scents of roasting meat and the hostess's sharp perfume. I quickly scanned the tables, looking for Ben, and saw him in a booth in the corner. With a smile and a point, I told the hostess I saw my husband, and she walked me over to the table. Ben was facing me and looked up as I walked past the few tables to get to where he sat. He smiled, eyes lighting up as they took me in. I thanked the hostess, then stood in front of Ben.

"What do you think?" I asked, turning one foot out and placing a hand on my hip. I winked and smiled, and he nodded slowly.

"That dress was made for you."

I flushed, suddenly wishing we were home and wearing a lot less. After I sat down—still imagining Ben unzipping my dress and running his hands all over my body—he leaned toward me and kissed me firmly on the mouth. "Those shoes are going to get you in trouble later," he whispered. I smiled, taking my foot out of my red patent leather heel and running it up the inside of his leg under the table.

"Well, look at you." Ben leaned back and grabbed my foot under the table. He rubbed my arch and my calf, and shivers ran up and down my body. I was transported back to the early days of our relationship, when the feel of his fingertips on my bare skin made my stomach wiggly and my cheeks hot, much like now.

"I need a drink," I said, slightly breathless. Ben pouted as my foot slipped from his hand, and I laughed. The waiter was there a moment later and I ordered a gin and tonic with extra lime. Ben caught me up on his day and the project he was working on with his dad, and I told him about my latest recipe—spicy chocolate torte for our February issue—not mentioning anything about Lyla. I had no clue how to bring it up. *So, Ben, today I had coffee with a surrogate who said she'd like to carry a baby for us. You should really try this olive tapenade, it's amazing.*

Ben was ordering our appetizers and main courses and I was trying to figure out how to open up the Lyla conversation when my phone buzzed again. I nibbled the crostini our server placed in front of me, topped with grilled octopus and spiced mango marmalade, and glanced at my phone under the table. *Lyla*. But an email this time. I quickly opened it and tried to read it discreetly.

"Medium rare?"

"Sorry?" I asked, looking up to find Ben and the server watching me.

"Your steak. Medium rare?" Ben asked.

"Sure. Yes, that's perfect." I hadn't had a steak rare in a while, always eating everything fully cooked just in case I was pregnant.

While Ben and our server debated if he should have the flatiron steak or the paella, I scanned the email.

Sorry to tell you this... Jason and I agree that we're better suited to a Christian, more traditional couple... I'm sorry to get your hopes up... I'll be praying you find your perfect match...

I felt dizzy and hot, my face surely going fiery red in the candlelight. The half-eaten crostini dropped from my hand, hitting the table and leaving an oily splotch on the tablecloth.

"Hannah? You okay?"

My mouth open, I looked at Ben and tried to get the words out. *No, I am not okay.*

"What's up? Is something wrong?" He gestured to my phone resting limply in my hand.

I looked back at the screen, which had since faded to black and tried to reconcile what I'd just read. Only half an hour ago Lyla had written she was looking forward to getting started. *What changed?* I racked my brain, thinking of our conversations. Everything was fine until I sent the photo. What happened?

I couldn't hear Ben but could see his lips moving. The whooshing in my head grew louder; then everything focused on Ben's face. On the errant eyebrow hair that grew longer than the others, the one he made me pluck out monthly. On his crystal-blue eyes, which were perhaps the slightest bit too far apart and were now filled with worry. On his beautiful brown skin—much darker from a week in the sun in the picture I'd sent to Lyla. *Jason and I agree that we're better suited to a Christian, more traditional couple...*

More traditional couple. In a flash I knew what had happened, why Lyla changed her mind, and that I could never, ever explain any of it to Ben.

"I'll be right back," I sputtered, getting up so fast my napkin and purse fell to the floor. Ben stood quickly, too, looking unsure about what to do. I asked a passing server where the washroom was and practically ran there, grateful for the individual stalls. Once inside a stall, I locked the door, then sat down when I thought my legs wouldn't hold me up anymore.

I read the email again and then once more, tears coming fast. I heard the bathroom door open and a woman's voice calling my name, identifying herself as the hostess.

"In here," I said, mentally willing the young woman to leave. "I'm okay. I'll be right out."

The door squeaked shut and I heard her exchanging words with Ben, who was obviously right outside the women's restroom.

Shit. I couldn't tell him now. I had fucked up big-time, not to mention the promise I made all those years ago to always tell him the truth—especially about the big stuff. Why had I even sent that first email to Lyla? I was being punished—for lying to Ben, for being so desperate to have a child I didn't see the warning signs right in front of me, for that time, long ago, when I'd wished motherhood away.

Pulling myself together, I flushed the toilet even though I hadn't used it and splashed water on my face. Taking a deep, shaky breath I walked on unstable legs to the door and paused one more moment before opening it.

Ben stood right outside, frowning, the lines on his forehead thick with concern. He took a quick step forward and wrapped an arm around me. "What happened?"

I shook my head, staying in his protective embrace a moment longer. "I think it might have been the octopus?"

"Are you sick?"

"I'm not sure. Maybe I'm allergic?"

"All of a sudden?" Ben led me back to our table, where I sat down and sipped the glass of water he handed me. Then he crouched in front of me, hands on my thighs. "You've had octopus so many times before."

"I don't know. I had a bite and suddenly felt awful. Sorry. I'm mortified." I drew a shaky hand over my forehead and attempted a smile. "You can't take me anywhere."

He let out a long breath and gave me a gentle smile. "Don't worry about that. I'm just glad you're all right." He stood, and I took his outstretched hand. "Let's get out of here."

A few minutes later—after multiple apologies to the waitstaff for leaving before our meals came out—we were in a cab on the way home, my head resting on Ben's shoulder, his arm around me. It was still raining, and I felt empty inside. Gutted by the most recent defeat, which lay overtop of so many other setbacks like a thick woolen blanket.

I would never tell him what I'd done, or why Lyla had gone back on her decision. And I hoped I could forgive myself for it.

14

HANNAH

We'd been living together for three months, dating for six, when I realized I was late. The first few days I ignored it; then a few days later I double-checked the calendar to be sure I had counted properly. Then I looked through my pills, and in horror discovered I'd missed a day. I was so panicked I didn't even tell Kate.

Ben knew something was up and kept asking if anything was wrong—clearly I wasn't hiding my anxiety well. I said things were fine, just stress at work because I was up for a promotion, which I didn't end up getting.

At the two-week mark I told Ben I had an off-site meeting so we couldn't commute in together, kissed him goodbye, then called in sick the moment he left the apartment. After buying as many pregnancy tests I could fit in my hands at the pharmacy—five—I went back home, where I hoped to prove I wasn't about to become a mother.

It was too soon. We hadn't seriously talked about marriage, let alone kids. I hated my job at the newspaper, creating and testing recipes the guy with the byline took credit for, but knew it was a necessary stepping-stone. I was taking night classes to become a pastry chef and wasn't ready to trade any of that for diapers or late-night feedings. And I'd started rowing again a few mornings a week, liking how taut my stomach had become as a result. I didn't want a baby, didn't see how a baby would fit into our lives—not yet.

Ben came home early—around three in the afternoon—and about one minute into the wait for test number five. A nearly empty two-liter bottle of soda was on the bathroom counter beside four used test sticks, all with two blue lines.

I was pregnant.

I heard the front door unlock. I froze, clenching test number five—which also turned out to have two blue lines—in my hand. "Hannah? Where are you?" Ben called down the hall.

"Bathroom!" I shouted. Our first apartment was so small you could literally get from one end to the other in mere seconds.

"You weren't answering your phone, so I tried you at work. Rebecca said you called in sick?" His voice got louder as he came closer to the bathroom. "Why didn't you call me?" We were still in that sweet spot of our relationship, when the sniffles that sent me back to bed warranted a call to my boyfriend, who would worry and fawn over me and make me his mom's pepperpot soup and leave work early to pick up aspirin and cough drops. Not that Ben wasn't caring now, because he was still concerned if I wasn't feeling well, but we had moved past the soup and care package delivery and into the more realistic scenario of a "feel better" text and finishing out the workday.

Ben knocked on the bathroom door.

"Just getting out of the shower," I said, eyeing the mess of test-stick packaging all over the floor. "Give me a second."

I heard him retreat and quickly shoved the test sticks back into the boxes, then crumpled them all up into the plastic pharmacy bag, which I shoved to the bottom of the trash can. I dumped out the rest of the soda and stuck the empty bottle under the counter, reminding myself to throw it down the garbage chute later.

When I came out of the bathroom five minutes later, Ben jumped up from the couch and walked toward me. He had loosened his tie and held a paper bag in one hand. He looked me over, trying to figure out what was going on, and placed his palm against my forehead. His hand smelled like soap and felt cool against my skin.

"I'm fine." My voice wavered, and I cleared my throat. "Just a touch of the flu I think."

Ben looked at me strangely. "I thought you were in the shower?"

"I was. Why?"

He ran his fingers down my hair. "Your hair isn't wet."

I opened my mouth to explain—*just say you wore a shower cap*—and then closed it again, thinking maybe now was the time to tell him about the five positive pregnancy tests in the trash. "Right. The shower."

"What's going on, Hannah?"

"Nothing," I said, too fast and too high-strung. He noticed and swallowed nervously. It occurred to me he thought maybe I really was fine, but that something was wrong between us. "I promise. Everything is okay. Aside from whatever virus has taken over my body. Speaking of which, what's in the bag?" I asked, reaching for it and opening it up.

"Some throat lozenges, aspirin and those fizzy tablets for your stomach. Oh, and a Snickers bar," he said with a smile. "I was trying to cover all the sickness bases. And the chocolate bar is for me because I missed lunch."

"Thank you." I kissed him, then apologized for probably

getting him sick—he didn't need to know that would be quite impossible. "You are the best boyfriend ever."

"I know," he said, winking. "Now get on the couch and let me take care of you." I raised my eyebrows, and he laughed. "I was thinking some tea and aspirin, but I'm open to whatever might make you feel better."

I dutifully drank my tea and took the two aspirin he gave me, then let him snuggle me on the couch under hot blankets while we watched too many hours of television. But while I lay there in his arms, laughing at the television as if I was actually paying attention, all I kept thinking was how badly I had messed everything up.

For a week I panicked about the pregnancy. I told no one, including Kate, because I wasn't yet sure what I wanted to do. I'm embarrassed to admit I even flipped a coin—three to one for keeping the baby, though I was never any good at sticking to coin tosses. In truth I was terrified by both prospects: becoming a mother or choosing not to.

But luckily—or unfortunately, as I'd say now—it wasn't my choice to make. My body chose for me, and two weeks after those five positive pregnancy tests, I miscarried. There was a disturbing amount of blood, and cramping intense enough to send me to bed early in the afternoon with a hot water bottle, which is where Ben found me after work.

"Are you not feeling well again?"

"Not really," I said, sitting up and plopping the hot water bottle to the side.

"Maybe you should go to the doctor?" He looked worried. "It's been over a week."

My guilt kicked into overdrive. "I'm not sick. But I need to tell you something."

"Okay." Ben sat on the edge of the bed and ran a hand up

THE CHOICES WE MAKE

and down my bare shin, his forehead crinkled in anticipation of whatever I was about to say.

I took a deep breath. "I was pregnant."

He stared at me for a moment, his mouth open in surprise, before asking, "Was?"

"I miscarried this morning." I picked at some lint on my shirt, left there from the hot water bottle's fleecy cover. I expected him to ask if I was okay, what happened, how I was feeling about it all, if I needed anything. Those were the questions I was ready for.

"You didn't tell me." It was a statement, wrapped in frustration.

"No, I'm... I'm sorry. I didn't think—"

"How long?"

"What?"

"How far along were you?" Ben's jaw was tight, his hands now on his lap instead of touching my leg. I knew the question he was really asking.

My voice quieted; my heart beat hard in my chest. "I found out two weeks ago."

He looked up at the ceiling and exhaled loudly. "How could you not tell me, Hannah?"

I started to cry, the first tears I'd shed since finding out about the pregnancy. "Honestly? I didn't know how I felt about it. And I wanted to figure that out first. But I guess none of that matters now."

"Does Kate know?"

I shook my head. "No. I didn't tell anyone."

Ben nodded, and I wasn't sure what he was thinking. At least he didn't look as mad as before. He didn't say anything for so long I started to get antsy, needing us to get to the part where he forgave me and we could move on.

"Are you okay?" he finally asked.

I lay back against the duvet and closed my eyes. "Yes," I said. He shifted to lie beside me on the bed, then handed me my hot water bottle, which I pressed onto my painful abdomen.

I swallowed hard, my next words coming out in a whisper. "What if I'm a crap mother, Ben?" My own mother had done what I considered to be a satisfactory job, but she probably wouldn't win any parenting awards. In fairness, she had raised my sister and me mostly alone, and we hadn't made it easy on her. I had also spent enough time with Kate and young Ava— who had just yesterday flushed an entire roll of toilet paper down the powder room toilet, resulting in a very expensive plumber visit—to question if I was cut out for motherhood.

Ben laughed a little when I told him about Ava and the toilet paper, which for whatever reason made me cry harder. Probably because I knew then he wasn't going to storm out of the bedroom and leave me to my cramps and tears and regret. "Everyone thinks they'd be a shitty parent, Hannah. That's what helps keep you on guard to try and do the best job you can." The tears came faster, hot and fresh. "If you think you'll be stellar, you get cocky and miss things. People have been doing it forever. You'll figure it out." I almost believed him. "You'll be a great mom, and I can't wait to watch you in action one day."

I blew my nose, honking into the tissues he handed me.

"I want you to promise me something."

"What?" I blew my nose again.

"If you're not okay, or freaked out about something, you have to tell me. I know you have Kate, and Claire in an emergency." I snorted. Claire was pretty low on my who-to-call-in-an-emergency list. "But I'm not going anywhere. I love you. And for what it's worth? I know having a baby right now wouldn't have been ideal, but we would have made it work.

So, promise me. Nothing but the messy truth from here on out, okay?"

"Okay." I nodded. "Nothing but the messy truth."

Except I didn't hold up my end of the bargain.

What I never told Ben, or even Kate when she hugged me later that day after I confessed to her as well, was that when I realized I was losing the baby I didn't feel sadness, or despair, or even loss... I felt *relief.*

I was relieved I wasn't going to be a mother.

And that's the sort of messy truth you keep to yourself, because perhaps that one time when you whispered, "Please, I don't want to be a mother..." to the universe, it thought you meant forever.

A few days after the Lyla and restaurant incidents, Ben and I were sitting in Dr. Horwarth's office getting the news I knew was coming but was still not ready to hear. How do you prepare for the brutal reality of being told you will never carry your own child? You can't, I realized, as his words washed over me along with the sensation of drowning—I was circling the same stupid drain I'd been circling since that first negative pregnancy test, all those years ago. Except this time there was no rescue mission planned, no life vest, nothing to keep me from sinking straight down to the bottom.

"Remember at the beginning of all this how I suggested you draw a line in the sand, deciding how far you're willing to go and what you're willing to put your body through to make it happen?" Dr. Horwarth clasped his hands on his desk, his face gentle with understanding.

But while he might have understood what we were feeling on an intellectual level, the pictures of his smiling family displayed on the corner of his desk suggested he really didn't get it, couldn't get it.

"I remember," I said, my voice breaking. Ben held my hand, like I expected him to, like he knew he should and had so many times before. But it brought me no comfort today.

"I'm wondering how close we are to that line now. I'm willing to keep trying. We can do another round of IVF... but I'll be honest," Dr. Horwarth said, pausing for a moment. "I'm sorry to say I don't expect to have different results than what we've had."

I was so filled with anger—at my body, at Dr. Horwarth, at Ben for sticking through this with me when he should have left to find a wife who wasn't barren, at the woman in the waiting room who was having a hushed but excited conversation on her phone while she stared at her ultrasound photo, a smile stretched wide across her face. And tickling the edges of that anger was such a deep pain I was afraid of what would happen to me if I let it take over.

15

KATE

November

The waiting room was packed. Checking my watch I saw she was already twenty minutes behind. Settling in, I opened another magazine—this one with a young celebrity wearing a marshmallow-size diamond on her finger and declaring her three-month-long courtship "the time of my life"—and sipped my latte. While most might dread a trip to the gynecologist, I was always happy to be here. Not because of the exams—that would be going too far—but because Dr. Lisa Kadari's practice had a self-serve latte machine, individually wrapped dark chocolate squares in a huge glass bowl and the best magazines. It practically felt like a holiday at her office.

I flipped through the pages—past silly articles on celebrities who did things just like us regular folk, like pick up their own dry cleaning and wash their cars—and put the magazine down a couple of minutes later. Scanning the other titles, I picked up the latest copy of *Femme* and turned to the food and recipes section. It was nearly Thanksgiving, and Hannah had done a two-page spread on putting a holiday-worthy feast on the table in under an hour. Seeing her smiling face in the corner thumbnail photo made me think about how she'd looked nothing like that happy woman at our drink date the other night—her eyes red rimmed, her ponytail disheveled and her spirit broken.

She'd tried to cancel on me; she wasn't feeling well and didn't want to infect me, and could we do it another night? When I showed up at her place thirty minutes later, saying that unless she was vomiting or running a 104-degree fever, she was coming with me, she'd gotten dressed without another word. Ben had watched her carefully as she left the room to get changed, after which we chatted about the nonimportant stuff like work and the girls' recent soccer game until she came back out. But I knew he was worried, like I was. The past few months had taken a lot out of her, and it was as if whatever was chewing her up inside had just showed up on the outside for all of us to see.

Another twenty minutes and two magazines later I sat on the exam room table, waiting for the doctor. There was a knock, and a woman's voice from the other side of the door. "Kate? You all set?"

Lisa Kadari was a petite woman with a big presence. She had thirteen-year-old twin boys—whom she had somehow managed to birth naturally at six and half pounds apiece— golden skin and hair that hung straight down her back in a glossy black sheet. When I asked her once how she got her hair so shiny, she'd said genetics and coconut oil. So I'd gone out and bought a giant tub of the stuff, slathering it all over my hair that night. I'd woken up with an oil-stained pillow-case despite the plastic shower cap and a new pimple on my forehead. That was the end of my beauty experiment with coconut oil.

She came in and took both my hands in hers in greeting, and I could see the remnants of a henna tattoo on her skin.

"My cousin got married this past weekend," she said, holding her hands out—her fingers splayed to show off the temporary tattoo.

"It's beautiful," I said, noting how intricate the designs were as they wrapped around her fingers and snaked up her arm in deep brown vines and leaves and starbursts, disappearing under the sleeve of her pastel-pink blouse, which poked out from her white coat.

"Thank you, I agree. Now, tell me, how are things?"

I dutifully filled her in for a minute or so on the girls and David and life before she asked, "And what can I do for you today?"

At this question I shifted slightly, clearing my throat and looking at my toenails, which I had fairly hastily polished that morning when I realized how ugly they looked bare. My feet were never going to win me any compliments, my toes slightly wonky and nails ridged thanks to years of dance class in too-tight shoes.

I wasn't due for my annual physical for another seven months, and had been vague with the receptionist when I'd called to see if she could squeeze me in.

"I had a few questions..." My voice trailed, and then I laughed. "I have no idea why I'm so nervous all of a sudden."

Dr. Kadari smiled. "Questions about what?"

"About another pregnancy," I replied, the words tumbling out of me quickly.

"You want to have another baby?"

"No...that's not what I want..." Dr. Kadari's eyebrows rose slightly as she waited for me to explain. "David's vasectomy might make that a tad tricky."

"Yes, that's the whole point of a vasectomy," she said, laughing with me.

I took a deep breath and looked down at my toes again.

"So, here's the thing. I'm wondering if I'm in okay shape to get pregnant again. If my eggs are, you know, still young enough and all that good stuff."

She rested her hands on her crossed knees and leaned back in her chair. "Well, you're only thirty-five and have two healthy, beautiful children," she said. "Of course we never can tell about egg quality based on age alone, but I'd say you probably have at least a few healthy ones left." She winked and smiled, and I smiled back, feeling infinitely more relaxed.

"I'm considering doing something and I wanted to get your medical opinion before I say anything to anyone else. Is that okay?"

"That's what I'm here for," Dr. Kadari said. "So tell me, what is it you want to do?"

16

KATE

"I saw Dr. Kadari today," I said, holding hands with David while we walked a few paces behind the girls. We had promised them after-dinner ice cream if they did their homework first, and we were on our way to make good on that promise.

"Oh, yeah? How is she?" David's middle finger traced small circles on my palm, which tickled but not enough to pull my hand away.

"Good. Same. Tiny. Still with that perfect hair." I sighed, running my other hand across my own hair, which was due for a wash.

David laughed watching me. "I hope you're not thinking of pulling that coconut oil out again."

"I gave that to Hannah ages ago. Apparently it's great for baking."

"I thought you just saw Dr. Kadari a few months ago?"

"I did," I began, pausing to yell at the girls to stop at the edge of the sidewalk.

"They always stop, you know." David pulled my hand up to kiss it. "I think soon you might be able to let that one go."

"As soon as you stop cutting their grapes and hot dogs, I'll stop this." I nodded and gestured forward with my other hand when the girls yelled there were no cars. "But, yeah, I saw her a few months ago for my annual. Today was for something different."

"Everything okay?" David's tone was unconcerned, confident that if something was wrong, I'd have told him about it before now.

"Yup."

"Good."

There was a lull, and I ran over in my head how to say what I wanted to say. It all felt so complicated, what had happened with Hannah and Lyla, and after spending three painful hours watching Hannah sit and nurse one glass of wine at the bar, I had made a decision.

Before I could go any further with it, I needed to talk to David. But I couldn't think of how to appropriately express Hannah's devastation so he would see this was a good option—the best option, if you asked me.

We were minutes away from the ice-cream shop, and I needed to get it out before we sat down and ordered.

"I could help her, you know."

David glanced over at me as we walked, but I kept my eyes straight ahead on the girls—who were jumping over the sidewalk cracks and singing some song I was too far away to hear.

"Help who? Dr. Kadari?"

"No, not Dr. Kadari. Hannah. I could help Hannah."

"What do you mean? Help her how?" David asked, now thoroughly confused.

"I could carry a baby for her."

David stopped walking so fast I didn't have time to adjust my stride, and my hand ripped out of his. I glanced between him and the girls, who had reached the ice-cream shop and were sitting at one of the tables on the patio—swinging their legs the way young girls filled with an abundance of energy do when forced to sit still.

He watched me, saying nothing, but I knew he was trying to figure out how to respond. A second later he took the two steps forward to reach my side, then grabbed my hand and pulled me forward a little too hard, toward the girls.

"No," he said, walking a step ahead of me even though he was still holding my hand.

"No?" I responded, this time being the one to stop and pulling my hand purposefully out of his. I'm sure the girls were wondering what the hell we were doing, all the stopping and starting in the middle of the sidewalk.

"No," he said again, hands going deep into his jeans front pockets, his shoulders rolling forward the way they did when he was angry.

I tried not to react the way I wanted to—which was to shout at him to use another word other than *no.*

"You don't get to veto just like that, you know."

He bit his bottom lip, rolling it under his teeth and taking a deep breath as he stared at me, staring at him. "And you don't get to toss out an idea like that without talking to me about it first."

"Isn't that what we're doing here?" I asked, sighing with frustration.

"Look, this is not the time or place, Kate. We're going to go over there, order some ice cream and hang out with our kids, and we'll talk about this later."

"Fine," I said, turning and walking toward the ice-cream shop.

I'm not sure how I'd expected him to react, and I knew how unfair it was to bring it up like that—at a time when we really couldn't discuss it—but it still pissed me off. As retorts of "my body, my decision" tickled my lips, I forced them back knowing what a bullshit response that would be. Of course it wasn't my decision alone—David had to be on board if this was going to happen.

So I needed to figure out how to get David on board.

Much later, after ice cream, showers for the girls, and barely two words exchanged between David and me, we sat in bleached wooden chairs—from my mom's garden patio set—on the rooftop balcony off our bedroom, tumblers of red wine sitting on the table between us untouched.

Sounds of car horns and passersby and a baby crying out an open window a few houses down surrounded us, offering a reprieve from the uncomfortable silence that comes when the angry things you want to say are still mercifully inside— where they can't do damage to anyone but you.

"I'm sorry I didn't bring it up before I went to see Dr. Kadari." In retrospect, sharing this giant decision with my gynecologist—who I saw once a year—before my husband was probably not the best idea.

"It's not about that," he said, swirling the wine in his glass but still not taking a sip. He put the glass back on the table and stretched out his legs, crossing them at his ankles. One flip-flop was slightly askew, but he didn't seem to care. "It's that you even thought it was a real option."

I swallowed hard, willing myself to discuss this calmly. "Okay, so why couldn't it be a real option?"

"Oh, I don't know. Maybe because we have our own daughters to think about. Or the fact that we have busy lives, and you have said more than once you don't want to have more kids?"

"But this baby wouldn't be my baby, our baby."

"You're delusional if you think that's true," David said, his words clipped with frustration.

I tried not to cry, in part at the nastiness of his tone, in part because I wanted him so desperately to see it from my perspective—something that was looking less and less likely with every passing minute. I drained my glass and then took David's.

"Well, cheers to you at least being willing to listen to my side of things," I said, lifting his tumbler up and taking a huge gulp of wine.

"Kate, I don't want to fight with you—"

"Then don't!" The last sip of wine—its tannins bitter in the back of my throat—choked me, and I coughed violently. David turned sharply to look at me but didn't say anything or ask if I was okay.

Once I'd stopped coughing, with another sip of wine—my buzz growing but not dulling the flurry of emotions I was experiencing—I said, "I don't want to fight, either."

David nodded and took his tumbler from my hands, having a sip of the nearly empty glass. "Are you even sure this is something Hannah and Ben would want?"

"Yes."

"How? Have you talked with her about it?" His voice was tight, the look on his face more so.

"No, of course not." I almost had, when we were out for a drink and she looked as if nothing would ever be okay again. I didn't mention that to David, however. I had enough of a fight on my hands at the moment. "But I know she wants a baby more than anything. I could give her that, David."

David muttered something under his breath.

"What was that?" I asked.

He took a deep breath, scrubbing a hand roughly down his face. "Katie, I love that you love Hannah this much. Your heart is as big as they get. And you know I want them to have a baby. But let's look at this from a logistics standpoint. They haven't even been able to make embryos that survived long enough to put them back into Hannah's uterus. How would you carry a baby for them without embryos?"

I closed my eyes, not wanting to see his reaction when I said what had to come next.

"I would use my own eggs."

He slammed his glass down on the armrest of the chair hard enough that I startled and looked over quickly, certain the glass had broken.

"You can't be serious."

"I am."

David stood, leaning on the railing, his profile in my view. His shoulders were hunched, his forearms flexing as he steepled his fingers together repeatedly.

"No fucking way." Cold. Emotionless. Nonnegotiable.

Fine, then. I would give it right back to him.

"Again, you do not get to veto this," I said, tossing in a short mirthless laugh before finishing his wine.

He whipped around to face me, eyes blazing. "Do you really understand what you're suggesting?" he asked. "You're talking about giving Hannah and Ben one of Ava and Josie's half siblings. You're talking about giving away *your own* child. A part of you. Just fucking handing it over!" And in that moment I realized he wasn't mad about the decision or my lack of communication around it. He was upset at the idea of such a precious part of me belonging to someone else.

"But—but that's exactly it, David. This baby would not be my child. Or your child. Or Ava and Josie's brother or sister. It would only be an egg. *One egg.* An egg is not a baby. Or a sibling." I was standing up now, too, facing him, my hands on his chest. Pleading. Shaking with too much wine too fast and the fear that he would never understand how badly I wanted to do this thing. "David, we are so lucky to have our girls. Can you imagine life without them? That is what Hannah and Ben are facing. A future without a child. They will never know what it's like to celebrate that first birthday. Or take pictures on the first day of school. Or write a note for the Tooth Fairy or from Santa, or to hear their child call them Mommy and Daddy. Can you even imagine?"

David watched me, his mouth still drawn tight with anger.

"I can do this. Dr. Kadari gave me the green light, physically. I'm young and healthy, and I know how to carry babies. Besides, Hannah is my best friend. There isn't anything I wouldn't do for her."

"Isn't that sort of the problem here, Kate?" David's voice had softened, but his eyes were still furious.

I cocked my head, unsure which part of it he was referring to.

"You've already decided to do this for Hannah. This crazy thing, that would mean going through a lot of stuff I bet you don't even know the half of, spending nine months being pregnant with a kid I had no part in making, then giving it away. Just like that. Giving your child away. And you didn't even *consider* talking with me about it first? I mean, really, Kate. You're talking about having a baby with another man. What the hell did you expect me to say?"

"Jealousy does not look good on you." As soon as the words left my mouth I regretted them. I knew it wasn't jealousy. I hadn't looked much past Hannah's need and my ability to fill it—and all David was doing was calling me out on my gross oversight.

"Jealous! You think I'm fucking jealous?" He took a quick step toward me, and I instinctively backed away, his tone suggesting a little distance was probably the best option. "Why does it have to be you? Why can't they find someone else?"

My words came out tangled, urgent and without the confidence I'd hoped for. "Because no one else loves Hannah as much as I do. It isn't just about an egg, or making a baby with someone other than you, or being a uterus for hire. It's about doing something for my best friend that will change her life *because I can*. I want to do this, David. Please help me do this. I can't—I won't—do it without your support."

I was crying now, handfuls of his shirt held tight in my fists, our faces only inches apart. He took his hands and wrapped them around the sides of my face and I leaned deeper into him. After a few moments, I felt his lips on the top of my head, then on my forehead and cheeks. He smiled, and I smiled back, knowing I had broken through—he was on my side, like I knew he would be eventually.

"I hear what you're saying."

Relief flooded me. "Thank you, I know it's going to be—"

"Kate, stop. The answer is still no. I'm not okay with you doing this, and that isn't going to change."

And with that he kissed my forehead again, stepped around me and headed inside our bedroom, leaving me to face the night sky, speechless, my cheeks wet with tears and my stomach sour with wine and disappointment.

17

HANNAH

Claire shoved a plate of goat-cheese-stuffed dates and another of miniature bocconcini, tomato and basil appetizers on skewers at me. "Put these on the table out there, would you?" I took the plates, then tucked the bottle of balsamic glaze she passed to me under my arm. "I want swirls, okay? Not zigzags."

Even though she was younger than me, and I was the one with the culinary expertise, my sister never failed to make me feel like I was her assistant in situations like this. But because today was Mom's sixtieth, I had promised myself I wouldn't do my usual when Claire got like this—which was to roll my eyes like a teenager and do the zigzags rather than the swirls, giving her an "Oops, I must have not heard you" when she called me on it later.

Peter and Claire lived in Pacific Heights in a Victorian Queen Anne–style house that was butter yellow—all too yellow, if you asked me—and had colorful stained glass windows at the front. Ben, enamored with the architectural details like the turrets, wraparound porch and patterned shingles, loved the house. But it felt too big and, somehow, despite its warm-colored paint and intimate nooks and crannies, also felt cold and hollow to me. However, Claire would have said I was just jealous and she might have been half-right about that. It was more house than I could ever dream of owning, especially since the years of fertility medications and procedures had drained our savings.

Mom's suite was off the back, complete with a small kitchen, bathroom, sitting area and bedroom, and it suited her perfectly. She never missed an opportunity to tell people how gorgeous the house was or how grateful she was that Claire and Peter made space for her in it. I always felt compelled to add they were never home, between Todd & Associates and social events and weekend getaways, so it wasn't much of a hardship to share the space. But I kept my mouth shut because at least Claire had offered. I couldn't say the same.

We'd organized this surprise party for Mom, which would be mostly attended by her bridge and book club friends, a few neighbors, and Claire, Peter, Ben and me. I had been dreading it for weeks, edgy with all the recent infertility issues and knowing Claire and my mom would want an update. Ben made me drink a shot of bourbon before we left the house, knowing that spending an evening with my mom and sister called for a stiff drink, and thankfully I was still warm and relaxed from the alcohol.

"What else do you need me to do?" I stood in the kitchen doorway, watching as Claire dashed from stove to fridge to island, hands busy but outfit perfectly intact and stain-free under her similarly pristine apron. I almost laughed thinking about my own apron—covered in so many stains you almost couldn't make out the picture on the front, which was a dill pickle with the words *I'm kind of a big dill* written underneath it. David and Kate had bought me that apron when I got the job at *Femme*, and it never got washed—I was superstitious about wiping away the splashes and splotches, because they were the result of a lot of hard work and creativity.

But though Claire looked entirely put together today, she seemed off, distracted, opening the fridge door and standing in front of it with one hand on her hip, staring into the shelves but taking nothing out.

"Did you bring the cupcakes?" she asked, still standing before the open fridge.

I paused. "Of course I brought the cupcakes. You saw me walk in with the cupcakes twenty minutes ago, remember?" As was customary for any family birthday, I'd baked and decorated two-dozen red velvet cupcakes with cream cheese frosting—using my grandmother's recipe.

She didn't respond, now busy lining up wineglasses and champagne glasses on the kitchen island. As she turned she caught the edge of one of the glasses and it fell over, breaking on the granite surface.

"Shit!" she said, jumping back to avoid the glass. She grabbed a dustpan and broom from under the kitchen sink and swept the glass off the counter so quickly I barely had time to tell her to be careful not to cut herself.

My eyes narrowed as I watched her sweep the final shards into the dustpan. "What's the matter with you?"

"Nothing. What do you mean?" She dumped the broken glass into the garbage and tucked the broom back under the sink.

"Something's weird. You're all distracted and clumsy."

"I am not," she said, her voice going up an octave. I gave her a look, and she tilted her head back and sighed as she stared at the ceiling.

"Fine. I'm pregnant."

Of all the things I could have imagined her saying in that moment, this was not one of them. The bourbon started rising back up from my otherwise empty stomach. Claire had never once talked about even wanting a child. The jealousy that lit up inside me was almost too much, and I sat down hard on one of the island's steel stools.

"It's early. Only six weeks. And it was *not* planned," she said, looking back at me, as if that was supposed to explain everything. There were tears in her eyes, and in that moment the jealousy abated just enough for me to see she was struggling with her news as much as I was. At least I didn't have to shout "Congratulations!" and hug her as if it were the best news I'd ever heard.

I nodded and looked down at the counter, where a few tiny shards of crystal clear glass remained. "What does Peter think?"

"He's thrilled, as you'd expect," she said, her voice betraying her irritation. "But he isn't the one who will have to put his career on hold, or wear ugly maternity clothes, or breastfeed." She ran a paring knife through a lemon, her quick strokes slicing it into wheels, and I wanted to shout at her that being a mother was so much more than that. But I was rendered speechless at her next statement. "I considered not having it," she said, quietly to ensure only the two of us would hear her, cruelly clueless that I was the only one who really needed protection from her confession—it was as though she sliced right through my middle with her paring knife. She looked at me then, and my face must have said it all.

"Shit, Hannah. I'm sorry. I didn't mean to say that... With everything you and Ben have been going through, that was majorly insensitive of me. It was just such a surprise, and I'm a mess. My brain has been taken over by this baby." She put down her knife and lay a lemon-juice-wet hand over mine. I tried to smile, then told her I was glad she was keeping the baby, and could tell it made her feel better.

I watched her cut another lemon, noting her smooth, blond ponytail, pink-hued cheeks and diamond stud earrings, all of it pretty and purposeful. Life was so fucking unfair at times. She had the thing I wanted more than anything—even worse, she got it by accident when I had been trying for years. And I had what she wanted: infertility, the perfect excuse to justify a child-free life.

18

KATE

Things had been tense with David ever since the other night, and I was getting antsy with the cold civility in our house. I wasn't angry anymore—that had faded after a day or so along with my self-righteousness. It was a lot to ask of him, to accept my proposal outright. I knew that going in, but I had really believed he would see it from my perspective.

I wished I could talk to my mom about it, and I'd tried to at her grave site. But no matter how comforting people say it is to have a place to visit the people you've lost, the reality is you're talking to a slab of granite that can't talk back.

Tonight was board game night, this time at Ben and Hannah's, and we had just left the girls with a sitter. At fifteen dollars an hour. Just one more reason to miss my mom—not only did we not have to pay her, we always came home to folded laundry, a clean kitchen, and girls who had learned something new from their doting and creative grandmother. Like how to plant an indoor mini–herb garden, or how to crack eggs using only one hand and a butter knife, or how to turn baking soda, vinegar, red food coloring and a plastic soda bottle covered in papier-mâché into an erupting volcano.

The cab dropped us off in front of Hannah and Ben's place, a row house that was typical in Noe Valley. It had been restored inside and out to both keep the architectural details—like the gingerbread lining the roof and the spindles on the porch—and to add some luxuries, like heated floors in the bathroom and kitchen, and a glassed-in sunporch off the back. The house belonged to Ben's parents, and Hannah and Ben rented from them, which was why they were actually able to afford the pretty Victorian in a neighborhood where homes ran well over a million and a half dollars.

We stood on the front step and I rang the doorbell, the chime echoing through the house. David shifted beside me, and I tried to ignore the dull headache behind my eyes and the tingling in my fingertips, forcing a smile as Ben opened the door, scents of spice and something dark and sweet welcoming us in. The sounds of a mixer filled the front hallway, nearly masking the music—Buena Vista Social Club—that Hannah loved and always played when she cooked.

Hannah was in the kitchen, as per usual, her apron covered in dark splotches and the electric beater in her hand. She held a spatula in the other hand and was diving it into the bowl, scraping the sides. I kissed her cheek and peered into the deep red mixing bowl.

"Whatcha making?"

"Mexican chocolate bread pudding," she said. "Left out the raisins though, just for you."

"You really do love me," I said. I despised raisins—their wrinkly flesh sticking in your teeth for hours. I dipped my finger in the bowl, then popped it in my mouth. "So good," I murmured.

"You know there are raw eggs in there," Hannah said,

smirking when I grimaced and slapped a hand to my mouth. "You'll be fine, princess. Ben, can you get Katie a drink?"

Hannah laughed when I snatched the fresh margarita from Ben; the green, slushy drink was filled to the very top of the glass and nearly splashed out. I took a quick sip, getting a hit of the rock salt that mingled on my tongue with the sweet and sour of the drink. "Thank you," I said, taking another sip. I hoped drinking wasn't a bad idea tonight, with a migraine threatening—then I decided I didn't care and took an even bigger sip.

"Maybe I should just give you the pitcher?" Ben asked, laughing. David cast me a quick glance, and I knew what he was thinking—that I should slow down if I didn't want to end up in a dark room with a bucket beside me all day tomorrow—but he wisely said nothing.

"Ha-ha," I said. "This will be fine, thank you."

Ben and David started chatting about work and baseball, which was my cue to tune out and focus on Hannah. Sitting on a bar chair in the kitchen, I sipped my ice-cold margarita and observed her. She looked better than the last time I saw her, though perhaps a bit thin—her cheeks hollow and her apron knotted tightly around her waist.

"You look skinny," I said. "What's up with that?"

"Is that supposed to be a compliment?" She laughed, pouring the chocolate egg mixture onto the cubes of bread, which were piled in a baking dish that looked well loved, a caramel-colored film lining the edges of the white ceramic dish.

"Depends I guess if you want to be called skinny."

"Please, I am not *skinny*." Hannah turned on the oven timer and topped up her margarita. "But I'm for sure going to tell my mom you said that. She'll be thrilled." She smiled wryly at me and pushed the bowl of guacamole toward me. "Eat."

I nibbled a tortilla chip heavy with guacamole. Hannah's

guacamole was amazing thanks to a secret ingredient she refused to ever give up. "How is Ellen doing?"

"Oh, you know. Busy playing bridge, and cruising, but not too busy to mail me articles about how reducing stress can up your chances of getting pregnant."

"She means well, sweetie."

Hannah sighed. "I know. And I shouldn't even complain because at least I have her around to drive me crazy." She looked at me sadly and reached out to rub my hand. "Sorry."

"It's okay. You complain away. I love your Ellen stories."

"You'll love this one, then."

"What? Tell me." I scooped up more guacamole with a chip and leaned on the countertop.

"Yesterday she sent Claire and Peter a giant 'Congratulations, you're expecting!' bouquet to their office and Claire hasn't told anyone at work yet. Peter was relieved because he wanted to tell everyone right away, but Claire lost her shit."

My mouth hung open, the chip not having made its way in yet.

"Oh, right. Didn't I mention Claire was pregnant? Surprise!" Hannah rolled her eyes and dipped a nacho chip into the guacamole.

"Oh. Fuck," I said.

"Exactly my reaction. Not even planned. A big 'oops,' and she's not thrilled about it, either. You know Claire. Motherhood is at the bottom of the list, right under scrub the—" Hannah looked up and stopped talking abruptly.

I turned to see Ben and David coming into the kitchen. "I'm going to show David the office," Ben said.

David cleared his throat and put his beer on the island counter without looking my way, and I hoped Ben and Hannah hadn't noticed the uncomfortable tension between us.

"Office?" I asked after they'd gone upstairs.

"Well, looks like we don't need a nursery, so..." Hannah pressed her lips tightly together.

"Oh, Hann, no tears, okay?" I put a napkin into her hand, which she crumpled into her fist rather than wiped at her eyes.

"I don't want to cry," Hannah said. "All I do is cry. And it isn't just that. I also obsessively Google baby-making tips. And stare at strangers' belly bumps at the grocery store, hating them for it. And fill my stupid online shopping cart with Pottery Barn Kids shit I'm never going to need. I'm one giant infertile cliché."

"No, you are not. You're beautiful and brilliant and everything you cook tastes like perfection and you have great legs. No, seriously, I wish I had your legs. Mine are short and full of varicose veins." Hannah laughed through her tears, and I handed her another napkin that this time she used to dry her face.

"You know what I did the other day?" she asked. "I went into Pea in the Pod and told them I was three months pregnant but wanted to get a head start on clothes, and could I try on one of those belly pillows, you know the ones that make you look really pregnant?"

I nodded, remembering trying one on when I was first pregnant with Ava.

"So I strapped it on and tried on maternity clothes for about half an hour, crying the whole time, which I blamed on the hormones when the salesgirl asked if I was okay. How lame is that?"

"That is not lame," I said, rubbing her forearms.

"Maybe not that part, but then you know what I did?" Hannah leaned in close and lowered her voice. "I bought three outfits. Four hundred dollars!" At first I thought she was crying again, but then I realized she was laughing. She looked up at me, her eyes still damp with tears but with a huge grin on her face. "They're in the back of the guest room closet, under the sheets and towels."

"Keep them," I said, draining my margarita. I thanked Hannah as she filled my glass up again from the nearly empty pitcher. "That way if you decide to eat all the food you make at work instead of spitting it out, you'll have clothes that fit."

Hannah smacked my arm, and my drink sloshed over the glass. "Hannah!" I laughed and jumped back to avoid getting soaked by the errant margarita.

"Okay, enough of this." I slid off my bar stool and walked over to the fridge, opening it to peer inside. "Where are your eggs?"

"Eggs? Why?"

"Ah, here we go," I said, pulling out a carton from the back of the fridge. "Let's go." I shut the fridge door and grabbed her hand.

She laughed. "Where are we going?"

I didn't answer, instead tugging her along until we stood in her backyard, facing the fence that separated her yard from that of her neighbors. I placed the opened carton carefully at our feet and handed her an egg.

"Throw it."

Hannah took the egg from me but continued to stare at me, her mouth open with confusion.

Gesturing toward the fence, I then picked up my own egg. "Throw it at the fence. Like this." I pulled back my arm and then released the egg in a nice, high arc. It hit the wooden fence with a satisfying smack, the yolk dripping down the fence and the shells dropping to the ground below.

"What the hell are you doing?" Hannah asked, now staring at the fence and the mess of egg on it.

"Nothing that a little water won't wash off, and my mom always made me keep our eggshells for her garden, so really you're helping your flowers, right?" I picked up another egg, feeling its cold, smooth surface in my hand. "Look, you said you're tired of crying, right? Well, maybe it's time to get mad.

Just get mad. Throw an egg as hard as you can. Be destructive with something. We have eleven..." I held up the egg in my hand. "Sorry, ten ways for you to do some damage that won't really hurt anything. Trust me—you will feel better."

I pulled my arm back again. "This one is for Claire, for getting pregnant first. That little bitch." I winked at Hannah, and she smirked; then I launched the egg at the fence, where it splattered in a mess of bright yellow. "Oh, that feels so good. I'm telling you. Give it a try."

Hannah squared her shoulders toward the fence and pulled her arm back, like I had, her mouth pursed in concentration as she aimed. "This one is for my crappy eggs." She released the egg and it hit very close to mine. She shouted and laughed, and I raised my eyebrows.

"Damn, that was almost poetic. But see? Better, right?"

"Better," she said, grinning at me before bending down to get another egg.

After we'd finished throwing the dozen eggs at the fence and hosed the mess away, we lay on the grass and stared up at the dark sky, which was overcast and starless. Hannah turned her head toward me. "So when are you going to tell me what's going on with you and David?"

"Is it that obvious?" I sighed and kept my eyes on the black sky. I knew I should keep my mouth shut, knew better than to talk about this when the tequila and migraine were muddling my thoughts, but between Hannah's tears, my fix-it tendencies... "I have this idea and it's going to sound crazy. But hear me out."

"Is it crazy like 'I'm going to jump out of an airplane,' or crazy like 'let's run away for a week to Maui'?" Hannah asked, turning on her side to watch me. "And is it this crazy idea that has David all sullen?"

"No, no and yes."

"So, no airplane, no Maui, which is disappointing, I'll have you know, and yes to David's bad mood. Which makes me both curious and worried. Tell me."

I kept my voice as even as I could, and turned toward Hannah. "I want to have a baby for you and Ben."

"What?"

"I want to carry a baby for you."

"That's what I thought you said, but—"

I sat up. "I can have babies. I've had two of them. My eggs are good. I love you. You *need* to be a mother. I can give that to you, Hannah. I can."

Hannah sat up slowly, keeping her hands firmly planted on the ground as if she needed to hold herself up. "I guess that explains the David thing." Her voice was quiet, tense.

I shrugged and bit the inside of my cheek, pausing for a moment. "I'm working on David," I finally said, to which Hannah sighed deeply.

"Katie, I—" She shook her head and wrapped her arms around her now-bent knees. I waited, impatient for her to finish her thought. "We can't do this."

"Why not?"

"For one thing, because David is not okay with it. Which I totally understand. And for another? I love that you've even considered this, but do you really get what you're offering?"

I was irritated. First David and now Hannah. Why couldn't they see that this was a legitimate option, and a great one at that? "Of course I know what I'm offering. My egg, my uterus, Ben's sperm, nine months, your baby. Got it."

Hannah took my hand in hers and squeezed. "I love you. But you and David are too important to us to muddy the waters like this. You are my best friend. And I need you to stay my best friend, okay?"

"But why can't I be your best friend and your baby mama?" She laughed at that. "I can do it. I promise nothing has to change."

"*Everything* will change," Hannah said, shaking her head slowly. "How can you not see that?"

"You deserve to be a mother, Hannah."

"Maybe so, but it's not your problem to fix."

Hannah's phone beeped, and she looked at me as though she wasn't sure what to say next. "The pudding... I've got to take it out of the oven."

I stood up and brushed some stray pieces of grass from my pants, wanting to escape this moment as quickly as possible. "It was just an idea. Let's pretend like I never brought it up."

Later that night, after David and I were home and in bed— our backs to each other—I finally gave in and turned him toward me, apologizing for everything and telling him the option was off the table. Even Hannah, the one who wanted a child more than anything else, agreed it was an unrealistic idea fraught with too much risk. He was right; I may have been well-intentioned, but I was wrong.

After that, we had spectacular makeup sex and fell asleep in each other's arms. But my sleep was restless as I dreamed of Hannah pulling a tray of tiny babies nestled in polka-dotted cupcake holders out of her oven, declaring it was okay, she didn't need my help, she had found the right ingredients after all—it was all in the eggs. I woke in the morning, headache thankfully gone but stomach unsettled from the rich bread pudding and boozy margaritas and strange dream, wondering if I really could just let the idea go like I'd promised both Hannah and David I would.

19

HANNAH

My blades sliced through the water, the single rowing shell cutting a smooth trail across the surface of the Aquatic Cove, which was still relatively tranquil this early on a Sunday morning. Only a couple of boats dotted the water, and seagulls occasionally pierced the quiet as they dived for breakfast. With each drive my lungs burned and my toes cramped—it had been a while since I'd been out on the water; I was out of shape. I'd barely slept the night before, and it was cold, my fingers numb. But the familiar sense of calm I always felt when I rowed settled into my bones within three sweeps, and I was glad I'd paid my membership fee to the rowing club for another year.

Catch. Drive. Finish. Feather. As I worked my body through the strokes, breath coming faster and arms quivering with the effort, I thought about Kate and the night before.

I want to carry a baby for you.

At first I'd been shocked. Then filled with gratitude. Then certain—no matter how kind and selfless—the gesture had no merit and that Kate would see that as soon as the margaritas stopped flowing.

So when she said she'd drop it, I, too, tried to put it out of my mind. But then while we cleaned up dinner and got ready to play cards, I suddenly became light-headed and nauseous. After excusing myself for a bathroom break, I sat on my bed and tried to catch my breath. Maybe it was some kind of strange delayed reaction, but in that moment—and for only a moment—I indulged the idea. What if Kate *did* carry a baby for me? Yes, it would technically be her baby, but it would be my child to bring home. To a crib we'd set up where the new steel desk now sat—in the office, which I'd been reserving for the nursery up until last week when Ben, in a display of uncharacteristic superstition, suggested half-jokingly that if we turned it into an office, maybe then we'd get pregnant. Like somehow we could trick fate. I'd smiled at his optimism and agreed it was probably time to pick out a desk—knowing full well if we were telling the universe anything, it was that we were giving up.

But a baby, with Kate. It would be different than it would have been with Lyla. Kate was my best friend, and no matter how we got a baby, she would always be in its life. Unlike my fear about Lyla wanting to keep the baby, I wouldn't worry about Kate—she would not break my heart like that. If someone asked me how I knew I could trust her so completely, I would simply answer, "Two decades, that's how." Plus, if we did this, we would have an amazing story to tell for years to come.

But it was a fantasy, and while intoxicating to imagine even briefly, not a reality I could afford to focus on. The complications could be astounding—even if David and Ben, who most certainly would have serious reservations, agreed to consider it.

And so with a few splashes of water on my face and a deep breath, I'd let the fantasy go and had headed back downstairs for cards and another drink.

But as I sweated out the previous night's alcohol and highly caloric bread pudding on the fog-draped water, I thought it again: *What if?*

"How's the bread?" Ben called out from the back patio, where he was grilling jerk chicken over the pimento wood chips he had shipped from Jamaica a few times a year. The smoke curled through our screen door, and I inhaled deeply, mouth watering at the smell.

"Almost ready to go in," I replied, kneading the ball of sweet dough a few times before using my pastry cutter to turn it into eight equal pieces. Rubbing my flour-covered hands on my apron, I lifted the lid on the rice that was simmering away in a combination of coconut milk, garlic, onions, thyme and allspice and almost ready for the rinsed kidney beans. Beside the pot of rice was another filled partway with vegetable oil, boiling gently. Back to the bread, I rolled each piece into a cigar-shaped loaf and then set the loaves into the hot oil, where they bubbled and fried with the heady scent of vanilla and sugar.

We had Ben's parents over every month for an authentic Jamaican dinner—and even though his mom was the expert, Ben and I liked to prepare the food. I loved the challenge of sourcing the ingredients for the recipes—like pig's tail and callaloo, a green leafy plant similar to spinach, for pepperpot soup, or Scotch bonnet peppers for jerk marinade, or breadfruit that could be roasted, fried or boiled with coconut milk—and how my kitchen smelled when the spices and scents all mingled together. Ben loved the food, having grown up with traditional dishes like ackee and salt fish for breakfast, dinners of curried goat with bammy bread and jerk everything.

By comparison, when my mom had to take over all the cooking from my grandmother—who had lost her sight when

I was a teenager—our diet consisted mostly of grilled cheese sandwiches on white Wonder bread with a side of sweet gherkins. Anything that was easy to prepare ended up on our plates. Until the afternoon my grandmother sat me down and begged me to do the cooking, saying if my mother served her another sweet gherkin she might have to jump off the Golden Gate Bridge. My grandmother had nurtured my love of food, of experimenting in the kitchen, and was the main reason I ended up in the career I did. She had been a beautiful cook, though more traditional in her style—with dishes like roast rosemary lamb with mint jelly, lobster rolls on homemade buns thick with fresh creamed butter, spiced butternut squash soup and peach cobbler with cinnamon whipped cream generally on the menu.

I had many times imagined us in our kitchen with our children, Ben teaching them the importance of grilling jerk over pimento wood and how you should never use canned kidney beans for rice and peas, and me showing them how to fold in stiff-peaked meringue when making soufflé or the magic of homemade buttercream icing.

Swallowing the lump in my throat, I used a wooden spoon to push the Festival bread around in the oil and turned the loaves over so they would be fried and crispy on both sides. I was draining the deep golden bread on paper-towel-lined plates when Ben came through the door with the meat.

"Smells amazing," I said, dumping the glass measuring cup of rinsed kidney beans—which had soaked overnight in water and were now plump and deep burgundy red—into the rice and giving it all a stir. "We're all set. Just need your mom and dad. And...there they are," I said, when the doorbell chimed.

Almost an hour later, full of rice and peas, chicken and the crispy-on-the-outside-doughy-on-the-inside Festival bread, we all sat in the backyard under a patio heater that made early

December's chill disappear, eating mango ice cream and chatting about how it looked like rain tonight. Ben's mother, Evie, who was tall but soft around her edges, put her scraped-out glass dish down and sat forward in the teak garden chair, fixing her deep brown eyes on me. "So tell us. What's happening?"

Ben glanced at me, and I focused on my ice cream, which was half-eaten and starting to melt.

"Mom, not now."

"Evie, let's just leave it alone tonight, okay?" Nathan, Ben's dad, looked over at the two of us and smiled. Though a massively successful, creative man, he didn't look the part. He was quite tall, standing an inch or so above Ben, and thin, with salt-and-pepper hair he unfortunately combed over and glasses that were perhaps a decade or so past being fashionable. But he had a face that appeared younger than his sixty-two years, and brilliant blue eyes that Ben had inherited.

"What?" Evie exclaimed, waving a hand to dismiss Nathan's request. "We haven't had an update in a few weeks, and I, for one, would like to know where we're at with the whole grandbaby project."

When we first started trying for a baby, I welcomed Evie's questions and interest. My mom often asked, sure, but in ways that grated on my nerves—like did I realize my chances of conceiving dropped significantly after the age of thirty, or when was I going to stop drinking coffee and eating nitrites and take my fertility seriously? Evie, on the other hand, talked about having a grandchild as if it was the only reason she had been placed on this earth—to spoil it with love and her Jamaican cooking. When her constant questions started to wear thin, Ben patiently reminded me of Sarah—his older sister who had died of leukemia when she was only two and before Ben was born. He had never known his sister, but she was a constant presence in the Matthews house, in the pictures on the walls and in Evie's stories. Ben thought, rightly so I suspected, that Evie saw our child as a way to recapture some of that time she'd missed out on with Sarah.

And so as the years went on I thought a lot about Sarah, which only added more stress to the pressure-cooker situation we were in. Now when Evie brought the baby thing up, which she did in exactly this way every time we saw them, I had to fight the urge to ask her to please shut up. I wanted to shout that we had tried everything, and that unfortunately it didn't look as though there was going to be a baby after all.

"Mom, please stop." Ben stood up quickly, a frown crowding his face.

"Ben, sweetheart, I was only trying to—"

"Stop!" Ben barked loud enough that I jumped. Evie looked as if she was going to cry, and I sat openmouthed and in shock. I'd never heard Ben speak to his mom like that—she walked on water as far as he was concerned. "You want an update? Here you go." Tears filled his eyes, and I knew he was seconds away from losing it completely. It scared me, seeing him like this, but I sat where I was and watched him unravel. "We tried in vitro and not a single embryo lived. Not one." He held up his index finger and shoved it up toward the sky violently. "So we are out of options. And don't even think about bringing up adoption. Apparently it's not an option, either." I started at this—watching him as he stood there in front of us quivering with anger—and wondered what that meant. Last I knew we had agreed to put adoption on the back burner, not eliminate it completely as an option. But perhaps we had both been lying to each other. Me about Lyla, and Ben about being ready to close the adoption discussion for the time being.

Before I could get a word out Ben took off, storming through the house and slamming the front door. I knew he was probably on our front steps, where we often liked to sit with midafternoon coffees or glasses of wine, depending on the day and our moods, watching the neighborhood go by.

"I'll go," Nathan said, rising from his chair and following Ben. I kept my eyes on the back porch screened door, willing them to come back so I didn't have to sit with Evie in awkward silence. My mind raced, trying to figure out what to say to her, and what to say to Ben later after everyone had left and it was just the two of us.

"I had a miscarriage once," she said. I glanced over at her, but she kept her eyes trained on a loose thread hanging from her sleeve. "Sarah was about a year old, and when I found out I was pregnant, well, let's just say I didn't handle things well. There was a lot of screaming, crying and carrying on." She looked at me wryly, a small smile on her lips. "But as my momma told me—that woman loved her Jamaican proverbs— 'If yu cyaa get turkey, satisfy wid John Crow,'" she said, her patois smooth and lyrical. "Which basically means you need to make the best of it and be content with what you have."

"Good advice," I said, my voice cracking. I cleared my throat and took a sip of water.

Evie nodded. "It was. When I lost the baby I sunk in a deep pit of guilt, thinking it was my fault or that I'd somehow caused it by wishing it hadn't happened in the first place."

"I can understand that."

"I'm sure you can," Evie said, watching me closely. "So let me say it to you, because I love you like a daughter and would never want you to feel even for a moment the way I did. If yu cyan get turkey, satisfy wid John Crow."

I smiled and stood up when Evie did, allowing her to wrap her arms around me. "Don't give up faith," she whispered, her mouth close to my ear and her breath carrying the sweet smell of mangoes and cream. "You just never know what's around the corner."

20

HANNAH

I was on my fourth cup of coffee and second cinnamon bun when Ben walked into the kitchen, bleary-eyed in his boxers and T-shirt.

"What's up?" he asked, scratching the stubble forming on his chin. He never shaved on the weekends and by Sunday it looked as though he had dipped his chin in coffee grounds. "It's five o'clock in the morning. On a Sunday."

"Hi! Morning!" I went on my tiptoes to kiss him on the mouth. He smelled like mouthwash, which meant he was up for good. "Want a cinnamon bun? Fresh out of the oven."

"Think I'll stick with coffee until the sun comes up."

I grabbed him a mug from the cupboard, then sat back down and took a gulp of my coffee. "Too hot, too hot. Careful, it's hot."

Ben laughed. "Thanks. I'm guessing this isn't your first cup?"

I held up four fingers and took another, smaller sip.

"That explains a few things," Ben said, sitting down beside me. "What are you working on?"

I tapped my keyboard to wake my laptop's screen up. "I've been thinking that you're right."

"Oh?" Ben sipped his coffee and settled into the stool, splaying his knees to the side and resting his elbows on the island. "I'm looking forward to hearing this."

"We should look into adoption."

"Hannah, I don't think—"

"Hear me out." I turned the computer screen toward him. "I've bookmarked a bunch of sites. Some for domestic adoption. Some for international. And I found a couple of blogs from adoptive parents here in San Francisco. One of them got a baby six months after they finished their home study. Can you believe it? Six months. Here I was thinking it could be years, but that isn't always the case. So I started a profile page for us. It's not live yet—don't worry. And I sent an email to an agency, but seeing as it's—" I glanced at the time in the right-hand corner of the screen. "Five after five on a Sunday morning, I'm guessing we won't hear anything back today."

"How long have you been up?" Ben asked, squinting at the screen while I flipped between pages.

"Since three."

"Seriously?"

"Couldn't sleep. Also, you're not going to believe this, but did you know I could actually breast-feed if we adopted? I'd have to take some medication and pump for a while, but I could breast-feed, Ben."

I glanced over at him then, and in his face I saw so many different emotions I wasn't sure which one I needed to pay attention to first. He looked equal parts curious, concerned and dismayed.

"What? What are you thinking?" I asked, worried he didn't seem as excited about all this as I was.

He closed the laptop. "I'm thinking that things got a bit

dramatic last night and that's my fault, and that you don't need to do this. I'm okay, promise. It's okay."

Shortly after Evie told me not to lose faith and hugged me for a full minute without breaking her grip, Ben and his dad had come back. I could tell Ben had been crying, but he seemed better when he hugged his mom and apologized. We didn't talk about any of it after his parents left, because I knew the best thing I could do for him was to not turn the incident into a discussion point.

"I know you're okay," I said, placing my hand against his cheek. "Honestly, it isn't about that. I had an epiphany last night, oh, around two in the morning when I got up to counting five hundred sheep and realized I wasn't going to fall back asleep."

"You actually counted to five hundred sheep?" Ben smirked and took my hand, kissing my palm.

"I really did. But after I gave up on that, I decided I was tired of being a victim in this whole thing. I'm sick of thinking about how unfair it is, because that isn't getting me anywhere."

"So was that your great epiphany?"

"That, and realizing when I leap forward fifty years and look back over my life, I see two things clearly. One, you and I have had a long happy marriage, and I'm still baking you cinnamon buns on Sunday mornings."

Ben smiled at that and grabbed the half bun still on my plate, taking a giant bite. "I like that vision," he said, after he'd swallowed. "And two?"

"Two, I am a mother and you are a father. I have no idea how it happens, but it doesn't matter. So I want to adopt. Or at least try. Basically I'm going to fake it 'til I make it, or something like that."

Ben leaned forward to kiss me. "I'm in. I'm one hundred percent in." His lips moved from mine to my neck, where they lingered softly. I sighed, a familiar pleasurable sensation starting in my toes and spreading upward.

"I like where you're going with this," I said, shifting away from him despite his murmurs to stay where I was, that he wasn't quite done. "But I need to tell you one more thing."

He grumbled somewhat impatiently.

"Give me a sec. I'll be right back." A few minutes later I was back, a shopping bag in one hand and a large box in the other.

"What's all that?"

I took a deep breath. "After the last negative test I went and bought maternity clothes. Three outfits. I tried on one of those fake bellies and told the salesgirl I was three months pregnant." I held up the shopping bag.

Ben raised an eyebrow, a smile playing on his lips, but he didn't say anything. "Also, I told you I got rid of all the pregnancy tests but that was a lie. Three weeks ago I ordered two dozen more." I shook the box, the tests shifting around inside.

"That's a lot of pee sticks."

"Yes, yes it is." I laughed and put the box on the kitchen table. "I'm going to donate them to the women's clinic in town, and I'm going to give the outfits to Claire. Even though I'm sure she'll say they aren't her style or something equally annoying."

I turned the bar stool around so Ben was facing me, then straddled him and wrapped my arms around his neck, pressing my body tightly against his.

"Where were we," I whispered, kissing him deeply, the mint of his mouthwash now dulled by coffee and sticky cinnamon icing.

"Right about here." He lifted my arms over my head and pulled off my shirt. I shivered as his hands ran over my shoulders, my back, my breasts, and was soon breathless and pulling him off the stool to the floor. In my haste to get our naked bodies aligned and horizontal, I lost my balance and slipped off the stool. He tried to break my fall and I landed on top of him before rolling to the side. We both started laughing, then stopped just as suddenly when my mouth found his.

Ten minutes later and still naked on the floor, his boxers and my bottoms lying beside us, and a couch cushion under our heads, I looked over at him and grinned.

"I forgot how fun that could be." I snuggled into his chest and he threw an arm over me, his fingers rubbing around and around on my still-flushed skin.

"I know," Ben said, sighing. "When did it stop being fun?"

"I can't remember exactly. Somewhere between cycle ten and 'you're never going to carry a baby'?"

"Hannah, don't do that."

"Why not? Might as well joke about it—otherwise it's just sad. I'm tired of being sad all the time."

"You're right. Screw it. Literally." I laughed as he kissed the spot between my breasts, and I held his head there for a moment, feeling his stubbled chin tickle me gently. "It's time to start having fun again."

"I agree. But...one more thing first."

Ben started kissing a trail down toward my belly button. "What?" he asked, between kisses.

I bit my lip. "I think you might freak out, but don't freak out. It's going to be fine."

"Hannah..." Ben stopped midway down my body and gave me a look.

"I put a deposit down on a puppy somewhere between the international adoption search and making the cinnamon buns. A Coton du Tulear, which is basically a small white dog that doesn't shed. My grandparents had one. I've probably mentioned him? George? They're very calm. You won't even notice it's here."

"A dog. We're getting a dog?"

"Yes! You will love it—I'm telling you. They are so cute. And small. Tiny, really. Wait, I'll show you the pictures—"

Ben held up a hand. "Later. I think this is more important than a... What's it called again?"

"Who cares," I said, lying back with a sigh. Ben smiled, then ducked his head and started up where he left off.

21

KATE

January

The letter sat in the middle of the kitchen table where it had already been for eleven days, taunting me to open it. Even though all the other mail that had arrived during that time had been opened and dealt with, this letter remained untouched.

"Is today the day?" David asked, nodding his head toward the envelope after noticing me staring at it, again, while the girls did their homework after dinner.

I sighed. "Maybe."

"Girls, close your books and let's go get some ice cream," David said.

"But it's a school night," Ava said. "We never get ice cream on school nights. And I haven't finished my homework yet."

"How are you my child?" David planted a kiss on the top of her head. Josie, who would do anything for ice cream, had already shoved her book back into her school bag and was getting her shoes on by the front door. "Let's go!" she called out, and David gave Ava a gentle shove toward the front hall, laughing as she continued to protest.

"Thank you," I said, resting my chin in my hands.

He paused by the kitchen doorway. "You know, you don't have to open it. Or the one that comes next month. You already know what's in there."

"I know. But ever since Mom died I can't help but feel like he's all I have left so I should at least hear what he has to say, right?"

"He is not all you have left, Katie," David replied, sounding slightly exasperated.

"The only *parent*," I clarified.

I always found a reason to open each letter in the end— maybe it was something about the business, which I, as my father's only heir, would inherit one day, or that he was sick or dying, or that this was *the* letter where he apologized for taking off on me and Mom all those years ago.

"You don't need him. You never have," David said, and I murmured that was true. David never made me feel as though my anger toward my father was unsubstantiated, even if I probably should have let it go years ago. He did, after all, provide for Mom and me after he left. His greatest crime was leaving what he considered to be an unhappy or unsatisfying marriage—something that was hardly unique or particularly inexcusable. But loyalty ran deep in my bones, had since I was a young girl, and I simply couldn't forgive him for deciding we weren't enough.

"You have me. The girls. Hannah, Ben. A whole bunch of school moms who seem to require your advice on everything. I swear those women couldn't make a puffed-rice-and-marshmallow treat without your approval." I smiled. I often joked about spiking the iced tea I brought to the PTA meetings just to get through them, though in truth I liked feeling needed most of the time. Especially now that my girls were getting older—every day it seemed they needed me less and less, which made me feel a little lost.

"As always, babe, you are right."

He raised an eyebrow. "Can I get that in writing?"

"Ha, ha," I replied, shooing him away when Josie shouted it was time to get a move on from the front porch.

Once the house was quiet again, I picked up the envelope and ran my fingers over the sharp edges, tapping it against my palm with my other hand. Then I ripped it open down one edge, quickly before I could change my mind. A check fell out, but I didn't even bother to look at the amount. I had long ago refused to take money from him.

The letter was typed on letterhead, as always. I wondered which secretary had typed it for him. Probably Susan, whose signature was on the courier forms when he sent me flowers on my birthday and when the Christmas packages arrived for the girls, and whom was mentioned often enough in each letter to make me suspect she wasn't only his secretary.

I started reading, irritated by the shake in my fingers.

Dear Katherine—

Katherine. *How little you know me, Dad.* The only time I'd been called Katherine was probably the day I was born—when my mom filled out the birth certificate details for the hospital administration. *I hope this letter finds you, David and the girls well. I'm sure the holidays were difficult, it being the first Christmas since Mom passed away.* I hated how he referred to Mom as "Mom"—as if he had a right to be so familiar with how he talked about her with me. *I heard from your accountant about the girls' funds, and I'm glad we were able to get it all set up and squared away.*

Without your involvement, I imagined he wanted to write at the end of that sentence. I had left my accountant to handle all the details, biting my tongue in the meeting because I knew it wasn't about me this time. *There's something I've been wanting to talk to you about, but with your mom now gone I suspect we won't be seeing each other anymore, so I'm forced to write it in this letter. Though I want you to know I will be at the restaurant on her birthday, at noon just like always, in case you wanted to join me.*

The words on the page went fuzzy. I blinked rapidly a few times to get rid of the tears that threatened to fall onto the crisp white paper.

I've proposed to Susan, and she has said yes! We're both thrilled, and the wedding is set for the summer. August 10th, and though I have no expectations you'll come, I wanted you to know you're all welcome. Nothing would make me happier than having you and your family there. Susan and I hope you'll at least consider it.

"Damn you, Susan. You're a fool—you should have stuck to typing his letters and picking up his dry cleaning," I muttered.

And then he ended the letter, exactly the way he always did.

With love, Edward McTavish.

Never "Dad," or even the more formal "Your father"—Edward McTavish, like the stranger he was.

I folded the letter up, tucked it back into the envelope along with the check, then grabbed the kitchen shears from the knife block. I poured a glass of wine and sat at the kitchen table, slowly cutting the envelope in half, then in half again, then cutting each of the four rectangles again and again and again, until there were dozens of paper squares neatly piled in front of me and my glass was empty.

22

HANNAH

The office was dingy—threadbare carpet, walls that could use a fresh coat of paint and store-bought artwork hanging in cheap wooden frames—but it smelled good, reminding me of the morning glory muffins my grandmother baked every Sunday morning. Dense and dark and spiced, made with orange juice and zest, carrots, pineapple, raisins, walnuts, coconut and cloves, she called them her "everything but the kitchen sink" muffins. Sometimes I make a batch when I'm missing her, or when I'm stuck on a particular recipe, even though I'm the only one who likes them—Ben said they taste like an experiment gone wrong.

The reason behind the sweet-smelling office became obvious once we announced ourselves at the reception desk—a plate of oatmeal raisin cookies sat under a glass dome, with a sign reading *Please help yourself!* taped to the front of it, and a lit candle labeled Orange Sherbet burning on the other side of the desk.

"Those were fresh baked this morning," the receptionist, a young woman with curly strawberry-blond hair whose blouse was probably open one button too many, said. "Please, have one!"

Ben, never one to turn away a cookie, lifted the glass lid. "Want one?" he asked me, and I shook my head. He slid a cookie onto a napkin, replacing the glass dome noisily.

"Hannah?"

I blinked, still standing at the desk. Ben was halfway to a chair, cookie in hand with a questioning look on his face, and the receptionist's big, welcoming smile was still intact.

"Go ahead—have one. They're delicious." Because I was embarrassed for going catatonic in front of her desk and it seemed she might take offense if I didn't have a cookie, I smiled and took one.

"You all right?" Ben mumbled, his mouth full.

I nodded and nibbled my own cookie. "These are really good," I said to the receptionist, who was watching us, gauging our reactions, as if she was the cookie baker. Who knows, maybe she was.

"Want the rest of mine?" I whispered to Ben when the receptionist turned away to answer the phone.

He stopped chewing. "Okay, what is wrong with you? You never share your cookies with me."

I laughed and placed my half-eaten cookie on his empty but crumb-laden napkin. He popped my half cookie into his mouth, then crumpled the napkin up and tossed it into a wastebasket about five feet away. It went right in. "Yesssss!" Ben said. "Did you see that? Right in. Like a boss."

"I suspect the Warriors are ready to offer you a spot on the team. Any day now."

Ben grinned, then shook his head and laughed quietly.

"What?" When he didn't answer, I asked again, "Why are you laughing?"

"Sorry, I don't mean to laugh. It's just... I sort of can't be-lieve we're here."

"And that's funny because?"

"It's not funny," Ben said. "I'm just happy. That's all."

He said it so plainly, so easily, that I didn't know what to say for a moment. "Well, I'm glad. I'm happy that you're happy."

"Are you happy, Hannah?"

I crossed my arms over my chest and took a deep breath. "I'm at least halfway there."

"That's good enough for now," he said. "I'll take it."

A few minutes and another cookie later for Ben, we were led down a hall so narrow we had to walk single file. The of-fice she ushered us into was cramped; the desk, three chairs and a large putty-colored metal filing cabinet in the corner on which rested a sick-looking fern filled every inch of the space. Just as we took our seats—steel-and-cheap-fabric chairs that looked like garage-sale fare—a man in his midforties, with a head of thick brown hair and a tie that hung a bit too short, walked in.

"Good morning," he said, and shook our outstretched hands. His grip was firm, and he did that thing where he en-veloped the handshake with his other hand—a gesture that made me instantly like him. "I'm Dan Cosgrove. So great to meet you, Mr. and Mrs. Matthews."

"Please, Hannah and Ben." I sat down as he made his way around the other side of the desk.

"So Cheryl Huttner sent you my way," Dan said, open-ing a folder on his desk. I noticed a wedding band, and then almost right away the picture on his desk showing him with a pretty brunette woman and five children of varying ages all wearing big smiles and Mickey Mouse ears, standing out-side the gates of Disneyland. "Cheryl and Fred's son is almost four now. She still sends me pictures regularly, which I love to get." Cheryl was a coworker of mine from the magazine, in the sales department, and had used Dan and his agency to adopt a little boy a few years back. She had gushed about Dan and their experience, and even sent an introduction email on our behalf, which was partially how we came to be sitting there this morning with Dan—Cheryl was so enthusiastic about him, and adoption, I felt as if I had to at least go through with one meeting.

"You have five kids?" I asked, still staring at the photo.

Dan smiled and picked up the frame. "We do," he said. "You should see our house in the morning. One bathroom. Absolute chaos." He then went on to point and name each of his kids—Riley, Jackson, Owen, Mary, Kaileigh—and his wife, Heather Ann, who was a physician at the hospital. "You have a lovely family," I said.

"Thanks, I agree," he said, placing the frame carefully back on his desk. "Now, let's talk about the two of you. I know Cheryl has probably filled you in on what we do here and how we do it, but let me tell you a bit about the process." He sipped from the stainless-steel travel mug on his desk, then leaned back in his chair. "I'm what's called an adoption 'facilitator,' though I prefer 'family matchmaker.' Heather Ann has more than once told me how cheesy that is, and she's generally right about things like that, but that's my unofficial title." He smiled, and Ben and I laughed. "Basically I help connect you to a birth mother and in some cases a birth father as well, to see if we can make a match."

"How are we 'connected'?" Ben asked.

"Great question," Dan replied. "Basically you make a 'brag book'—which is like a sort of family résumé, with pictures and details about you two and the sort of life and experiences you would provide a child with. Then I meet with the birth mother or birth parents to go over the brag book and help facilitate them choosing prospective parents for their child."

"Do you have one of these brag books we could look at?" I asked.

"You bet." Dan opened a drawer in his desk and pulled out a hardback book, about the size of a rectangular photo album, and placed it in front of us. "We're different from a private adoption agency in that we help the birth parents choose, but it is ultimately their choice. At a typical agency, the birth parents relinquish the right to choose to their caseworker, and then that caseworker makes the match on their behalf." Dan sipped from his travel mug again. "Obviously I prefer the way we do things here, because in my experience the best matches are made when the birth parents are involved in the process."

I glanced up at him and nodded, only half listening. My eyes dropped back to the book in front of me, the front of which showed a smiling couple—probably late twenties or early thirties—wearing leis and standing on a white sand beach. Opening the book I found pages of photos—vacations to beaches and ski hills, Christmas trees and stockings, bicycles leaning against park benches, and poses on hiking trails with a dopey-looking yellow Labrador retriever—with captions on each page telling the story of this couple, Hillary and Derek.

With every picture, every anecdote, my stomach dropped a little more, the reality of this couple hitting so close to home. This was Ben and me, with different pictures but the same story.

I had a feeling Dan's desk drawer was stacked high with books just like this one.

Closing the book, I rested a hand on the cover, Hillary's face, her smile, still visible. And suddenly I didn't want to take a baby away from Hillary. I didn't want to be in competition with any of these couples, because they were as hopeful as we were that parenthood was not out of reach, reserved for the luckier ones.

Dan went on to explain the process. Home study, brag book, birth-parent meetings, fees and attorney requirements, and the thirty-day clause—which basically meant the birth mother, or parents, could reverse their decision within the first month. Ben looked surprised at this, though I was sure I had mentioned it—likely in passing, and without admitting my own fear—when we set up this meeting.

"They can change their minds, even after we've taken the baby home?" Ben asked, shifting in his chair as if his jeans had shrunk a size.

"They can," Dan said, a frown pulling down the corners of his mouth. "Now, I've only seen it happen once in all the years I've been doing this. But it is something you need to know can happen. I've found in many cases having an open adoption helps alleviate this."

"Open adoption means there would be an ongoing relationship with the birth mother, or parents, right?" I asked.

"Exactly." Dan nodded. "More and more that's how adoptions are going these days, and studies tell us it's likely in the best interest of the child to maintain some type of relationship."

"That would be fine with us, I imagine... Ben?" I said, turning to look at Ben for confirmation. But he was staring at Dan, not acknowledging my question.

"I don't know if I could handle that," Ben said, turning to me. I was about to ask what specifically he couldn't handle, because I was not sure what part of the conversation had caused the panicked look on his face. "If we took a baby home...how could we give it back?"

"I know," I said. "But remember, Dan said it doesn't happen. Not often, anyway."

Ben nodded, but his face remained grim and I knew exactly how he felt. Every attempt we'd made at becoming parents had been frustrating and constricting, like trying to run for your life while wearing a straightjacket—it was never going to be easy. Even choosing *not* to have a child wouldn't be easy, though it would be simple by comparison. But once again, we were faced with the unfairness of having to choose an option from a list of only difficult, potentially heartbreaking paths.

So you chose the option you hated the least, or the one you thought you could live with once the dust settled.

23

KATE

Our bedroom was dark except for my e-reader's ghostly glow creating a bubble of soft light around me. Though I had tried to shut it down a few times and go to sleep, my mind kept going back to the letter and the fact that my father was getting remarried. For reasons I couldn't articulate to David when I'd tried earlier, I was furious. So angry I'd started crying when I told David about the letter—which made me angrier, that my father had gotten under my skin.

As quietly as I could I pushed down our quilt and swung my legs over the side of the bed, my feet landing softly on the hardwood floor. I held my breath and started toward the bathroom, cringing when the old floorboards squeaked under my weight. "Katie?" David's voice was scratchy. "Are you okay?"

I could lie and say yes, totally fine, go back to sleep, but suddenly I wanted nothing more than to be wrapped in David's arms. To unzip my chest, which felt tight with anxiety and guilt I didn't fully understand, and let it all spill out into the darkness so I didn't have to carry it around with me anymore.

"Not really," I said, still standing where I was, shaking a little in the cool night air of our room.

"Come here." David sat up and turned on his bedside lamp, the soft glow blanketing the room. I squinted with the light, then made my way back to bed and under the covers David held out. Snuggling deep into the warmth of our bed, I leaned back against his chest and linked my fingers through his, holding them tightly. "What's going on?" he asked, kissing the top of my head.

"It's Mom's birthday next week," I said. "Edward said he'll be at the restaurant."

"Do you want to meet him?" David asked.

"Of course not," I replied, my voice loud in the quiet of the night. "What would I even say to him?"

David nuzzled his lips into the crook of my neck and planted a warm kiss there. "Whatever you want. Or nothing at all. I can't imagine Edward expects you'll show up. But you can if you want, Katie. It's okay if you do."

The tears started, rolling down my cheeks. "I only went to those lunches for Mom. If it had been up to me—"

"I know—you wouldn't have gone. But I also know you, and I suspect you're thinking your mom would still want you to go and have lunch with your dad even if she can't be a part of it anymore."

"I hate him." A sob escaped me, and David held me tighter, whispering soothing words into my ear. "I'm honestly just not sure I can do it, David."

"Baby, you can do anything you put your mind to. I've seen you in action, and you're scary when you get like that." I laughed, and he joined me, still holding me tightly. We lay like that for a few more minutes, and as the tears dried on my cheeks I felt myself drifting toward sleep.

"Kate, I want to ask you something," David said, startling me out of my near slumber.

"Mmm-hmm?" I murmured, my lids heavy.

"Are you going to carry a baby for Hannah?"

It was as if he'd tossed a bucket of ice water on me. My eyes snapped open, and my breath caught in my throat.

"I... You said you wouldn't even consider it," I replied, my heart pounding under our hands. "You said it was a crazy idea, and that I was delusional. Remember that conversation?"

"I still feel that way," he said. "But I need you to be honest with me. If my feelings were a nonissue, and Hannah and Ben agreed to it, would you go through with it?"

"But your feelings do matter, David." I paused for a moment, trying to decide how to answer. I wanted to be truthful, but I wasn't sure exactly how blunt to be about it. "However, if it were just up to me, and Hannah and Ben were in, then, yes, I would. That is, if I didn't think you might leave me for it. Nothing is more important than our family, and I would never do anything to screw with that."

David sighed, scrubbing a hand across the shadow of a beard that magically appeared at night. "I wouldn't leave you. Ever. Not for any reason, Katie."

I nodded, my mind a tornado of thoughts.

"Because here's the thing," David said. "I love you more than the idea terrifies me, and I know you well enough to know that if you want to do this, I probably can't stop you. Or I shouldn't, because that's not how we do things, you and me."

"David, I would never—"

David put a gentle finger to my lips. "Let me finish, okay? This isn't about some power struggle or you getting your way whether I agree or not. We are a team, you and I. We've always supported each other, and that isn't something I want to mess with. So even though I'm worried—about you, and what could happen, and I'd be lying if I said those worries weren't keeping me up at night—how can I stand in your way when one of the things I admire most about you is how much you're willing to do for the people you love?"

I couldn't quite catch my breath. "So what are you saying?"

He turned me onto my back and shifted so he was looking down at me, his gaze intense. "I'm saying I'm willing to consider it."

"Really? What about the whole 'I'm making a baby with another man' thing? Or the 'giving a part of me away'?" That one had stung the most, probably because he had a point. While I was nearly positive I could separate myself from the idea of the baby being *my* baby, handing it over to Hannah with only joy in my heart, I wouldn't have bet my children's lives on it. So I asked him this genuinely, some part of me *needing* to hear him explain how it would be okay.

He shrugged. "It's Ben and Hannah." As if that explained it all. Which, to me, it did.

"So...is it okay if I talk with Hannah, then?"

He nodded. "But first I need to be sure you've really considered everything. There are a lot of complications... I don't want to see you get hurt."

"Fair enough. Tell me, what are you most worried about?" I had already written down a long list of pitfalls—the top of that list being not getting pregnant—but I wanted to hear what *he* was afraid of.

"It not working," he replied, as if reading my mind. "I'm worried what that will do to you." Then he paused, and I watched him, waiting. He frowned. "Or you having a hard time letting go of the baby once it's born. That's no small thing, Katie. This baby would genetically be yours. You told me when Ava was born that taking care of her, and loving her, felt instinctual. What if you feel that way about this baby, too?"

"I've thought a lot about that," I said, taking my time with my words to properly convey just how seriously I meant what I was about to say. "But no matter how many times I've tried to force myself into that scenario, to imagine what could happen if I became attached to the baby, I know that isn't going to happen. This baby would be Hannah and Ben's. I'd just be donating an egg and an oven. I've had my babies, and this already feels completely different."

David nodded. The air between us felt heavy, charged with David's worry and my determination to alleviate it.

"I have a big list of things that could go wrong. And when the sun comes up, and we have coffee in front of us, I'll show it to you. I want you to know I understand what this means, to offer this to them. I'm not delusional, despite what you may think." David rolled his eyes at that one and smiled. "I promise you I am going to be fine. Nothing bad is going to happen. I can handle this and anything on that list. As long as I have you with me, okay?"

I wrapped my fingers around his head and pulled him to me. In one quiet, warm breath he whispered into my ear, "Talk to Hannah. And we'll go from there."

24

HANNAH

The timer beeped, and I opened the oven door and peered into its depths. The cake was golden brown on the top, a thin ring of amber-colored liquid bubbling around its edges. Grabbing the dish towel I pulled the square cake pan toward me, pressing my index finger into the top and watching as the small circular indentation puffed back up a few seconds later. I turned off the oven and set the cake onto the cooling rack.

While I hunted for my grandmother's china serving plate, with the gold edge and blue rose pattern, I tried to keep the nerves from taking over. Kate had left me speechless when, over lunch at the little bakery that made the best clam chowder in sourdough bread bowls, she'd told me she and David had talked and that her offer to carry a baby for us was up for discussion. Real discussion. My speechlessness had quickly turned to a torrent of tears and so many questions I couldn't get them out fast enough. Kate had cried with me, saying she just knew it was going to work, if we agreed to it.

The gratitude had been overwhelming, imagining what her offer could mean if it all worked out the way she said she knew it would. Her confidence was intoxicating, and by the end of lunch I had no doubt it was exactly the right decision.

But now I had to talk with Ben. My stomach was clenched so tightly I wasn't sure if I was going to throw up or needed a strong drink, or both.

I turned the cake out onto the plate, drizzling the leftover syrup in the pan over the top of its warm surface. The rings of pineapple lay nestled in a thick layer of caramel, the result of butter and honey baked into a rich sauce, and I felt instantly relaxed, breathing in the sweet scent that reminded me of my childhood. Though I loved to cook, baking settled my soul in a way nothing else could. It was the precision of the measurements, the comfort of ingredients like flour, butter and brown sugar, and the rhythm of beating, stirring and folding.

When I graduated college—my intention to head to chef school next—my grandmother, who was half-Canadian on her mother's side, gave me her tattered copy of *The Laura Secord Canadian Cook Book*, from which she took the morning glory muffin recipe and the pineapple-upside-down cake that was now cooling on her serving plate. Even though it was old-fashioned and not a dessert you'd find in most people's kitchens these days, it was a favorite of Ben's. And today I needed all the help I could get.

The table was nearly set and dinner ready—sausage-and-pepper lasagna, perfect for the rainy cool temperatures that came with winter in San Francisco. I was placing the decanter of Syrah—which had been sent to the magazine by a Napa PR company—on the table when I heard the front door open. Luckily for me Shoana, *Femme*'s food director and my boss, only drank "white" things, like Chardonnay and gin, so anytime we were sent red wine I got to bring it home.

"What smells so good?" Ben came into the kitchen and dropped his messenger bag on the floor beside the table.

"Lasagna," I said, pulling it out of the oven and setting it on the stovetop. The blanket of fontina cheese was bubbled and slightly browned, ready for a sharp knife and hungry bellies. Ben pulled a string of crusty cheese off the edge of the glass dish and popped it in his mouth. "Can't wait," he said.

After pouring two glasses of wine from the decanter I handed him one and we clinked glasses and exchanged a smile.

"So what's up?" Ben sat down at one end of the table and swirled the wine in his glass. "Expensive wine. Lasagna. Pineapple-upside-down cake? On a Tuesday night?"

"How did you know about the cake?" I asked, sitting beside him.

He took a deep sniff of the air and winked at me. "Spill it. What's going on?"

"Can we eat first?"

After our plates were cleaned and cleared, I set a plate of cake in front of each of us and sat down, making little stabs at a pineapple ring with the prongs of my fork. Lost in thought, I jumped when Ben tapped his fork against my plate. "Hannah?"

"Sorry," I said, smiling before putting down my fork and pushing my plate away. "Just thinking."

"You can tell me anything, Hannah."

At this I nodded, though I broke eye contact. It was now or never.

"Kate offered to carry a baby for us."

When people say the silence was deafening, well, I now knew exactly what that meant. For at least thirty seconds, neither of us said anything or did anything. Ben stared at me, fork poised above his plate and a look of shock on his face. My heart fluttered and I looked down again, swallowing around what felt like a watermelon in my throat.

"Can you say that again?"

"Kate told me she wants to carry a baby for me. For us."

"That's what I thought you…" His voice trailed, as if he lost his breath partway through. "I wanted to be sure I heard you right."

"I know this is…unexpected. And sort of weird. And definitely uncomfortable? I have no idea what you're thinking. Can you tell me what you're thinking right now? Please?" Unlike Ben's slow and methodical response, the words flew out of my mouth like busy bees out of a hive.

"I'm thinking…" Ben shook his head, finally putting his fork down. Then he looked at me and grinned, and I felt discombobulated. Like everything had been turned upside down. "I'm thinking this is amazing."

"Wha— What?"

"Look, I have no clue if it's something we really should do," Ben said. "But after everything…after the meeting with Dan, I've come around to the idea that we might have to explore more unconventional options. My dad reminded me of that, actually, that night when I stormed away from dinner like a hormonal teenager."

"He did?" Ben hadn't said anything of that conversation, and I hadn't pried.

Ben nodded. "He told me there is no greater joy than being a father. And that if things weren't working—traditionally speaking—I needed to be willing to think outside the box. And this, well, this definitely qualifies as a nontraditional option."

"It certainly does," I whispered, feeling the weight and anxiety lifting, like tiny helium balloons floating up, up and away.

"Are you sure she means it?" Ben asked. "And what about David? How does he feel?"

"She means it," I said. "And she told me David is on board."

"Then so am I."

"Are we really going to do this?" I asked, taking a large gulp of my wine.

"Damn right," Ben replied, then pointed his fork up in the air to emphasize his point. "It's time for me to knock up your best friend."

I laughed so hard I spit my wine all over Ben's half-eaten piece of cake.

25

KATE

February

Hannah walked out of her building and shielded her eyes against the bright sunlight, looking around. I honked from where I was parked on the other side of the street—it was lunchtime and the streets were extra busy, which meant I hadn't been able to find a spot any closer. I hoped traffic wasn't too bad as we only had fifteen minutes to get to the clinic for our meeting with the social worker. David and Ben were meeting us there, and I felt a flutter of nerves swirl in my belly as I thought about the appointment. Hannah waved, waited for traffic to ebb and then ran across the street. She opened the passenger-side door and tossed her giant purse to the floor before getting in.

"Hi," she said, leaning over as she buckled her seat belt to kiss me on the cheek.

"Hi back. How was work?"

"Good. Fine. The usual." She pulled her purse—which was the size of an overnight bag—onto her lap and rummaged around in its depths, finally finding her sunglasses.

I wrinkled my nose. "What is that smell?"

She pulled out a large Tupperware container with some sort of deep red liquid inside. "Soup," she said. "We're doing this 'round the world, thirty dishes in thirty days' thing, and this—" she wiggled the smelly container between us "—is day fourteen. Russian borscht. Beet soup."

"But why is it in your bag, and now in my car?" The sour smell clung to my nose, and I opened my window a crack.

"Life of a recipe developer. I always have food in my purse," Hannah said, laughing. "Plus, it's dinner. Some of us like beets."

"Better you than me," I said, shaking my head. "What else have you got in there? Anything that doesn't stink?"

Hannah pulled out a small glass jar, filled with something pale yellow. "Creamed honey?" I asked.

"Goose fat. Want to try it?" Hannah went to twist off the lid and I took a hand off the wheel to stop her.

"Gross! Hannah Matthews, put that away."

"It's for day twenty, United Kingdom. Pork and onion pies with goose fat pastry." She smiled at my disgust and tucked it back inside her purse. "How about a chocolate macaroon?"

"Now you're talking." I took the chocolate-covered coconut ball she handed me and popped it into my mouth.

She sighed and stared out the window. "We made them with goose fat."

"You did not!" I stopped chewing, not sure what I would do if she wasn't kidding since I couldn't very well spit it out while I was driving.

"You're right. We didn't."

I swatted at her, and she laughed.

"Change of subject. Enough about goose fat and beets." I glanced in my vanity mirror while we were at a red light, wiping a small bit of chocolate from the corner of my mouth. "How are you feeling about this whole social-worker-meeting thing, and everything?" I didn't need to qualify what "every-thing" meant—Hannah knew I was referring to the surrogacy.

"I'm...cautiously optimistic."

"Does that put you closer to excited or terrified?"

"Probably right in the middle."

I nodded. "I know it's probably hard to believe this, but this is going to work, Hannah."

She looked out her window. "All my experience is with this kind of thing *not* working, so it's hard to imagine any-thing different."

"I get that." I glanced at her as she continued to stare out the window. "But I need you to at least try, okay?"

At that she turned quickly toward me. "Of course. I'm sorry—that sounded ungrateful."

"No, it didn't. And it's your turn for good news. It's your turn, Hannah."

"At least we don't have to rely on my body this time," she said, giving a short, sharp laugh that cut off nearly as soon as it started. "My uterus is like a garbage disposal."

I bit my tongue, wanting to tell her she was wrong and not to think like that—that she was beautiful and perfect in every way, even with her unreliable uterus—but I knew she wasn't fishing for a compliment. She simply needed to say it out loud. And while it made me uncomfortable to do so, I said nothing and let the comment hang between us.

I knew as soon as she told us this was a "safe space" that I'd be counting down the minutes until our session was over. Mina, the social worker assigned to evaluate our level of pre-paredness for the insemination and surrogacy, nudged the tis-sue box sitting on the coffee table closer to Hannah. With a tight smile and eye roll for my benefit, Hannah pushed it back to the center of the table. Mina missed the rebuff because she was pouring glasses of water for the four of us, chatting about the weather as is typical with San Franciscans. Laughter bubbled up inside me and I looked away from Hannah, trying to maintain some composure. Even though I knew this wasn't some pass-or-fail test, I didn't want to give "you're in a safe place" Mina any reason to doubt just how ready and committed we were to this.

"I know calling this 'mandatory' doesn't give the impression you have much choice in the matter," Mina said, handing us the water. "But you do. You always have a choice."

I nodded, while David murmured in agreement and Hannah said, "Right, of course." Ben smiled and took a sip from his glass, and I could tell it was just for show, his smile. None of us wanted to be here, but the fertility clinic required this meeting to move forward.

Though I had no doubts about carrying a baby for Hannah and Ben, I was finding the labels we had been assigned awkward and ill fitting. I thought of us as four friends, working together to achieve a dream. Simple. Beautiful. I did not relate to the term *surrogate*, and calling Hannah the "intended mother" felt formal and strange. She was just Hannah. Hopefully mother-to-be Hannah, if Mina ever let us out of here.

"So how does this work?" I asked, shifting in the overstuffed chair.

Mina watched me, leaning forward in her own puffy armchair. She was quite petite, and the chair practically swallowed her up. "It's normal to feel anxious," she said. She leaned onto her crossed knees and her feet barely touched the floor, giving the impression she was being held in place by only the tips of her toes.

"Oh, I'm not anxious," I said. While true, I also wasn't entirely comfortable with being evaluated. Mina smiled, and I smiled back. For a moment we both sat there, her tiny in the giant chair with a smile that displayed all her teeth, and me, leaning way back against the springy cushions, trying to appear as if this was all perfectly normal.

"Good, good," Mina said. "My job isn't to decide if you should go through with the surrogacy. That decision is up to the four of you. I'm here to talk through the potential challenges you might face with the process." She cleared her throat. "Especially in your situation, because this is an altruistic, traditional surrogacy. Most of the arrangements we deal with these days involve gestational carriers."

"Right, of course," Hannah said. She looked nervous, her fingers fiddling with a pen. Ben swirled the water in his glass, watching it as if it were the most fascinating thing he'd ever seen, and David's knees bounced up and down. We had agreed before going in that I would be spokesperson, in part because I had a bossy streak but mostly because I wanted Mina to know I was confident in this decision—that it had, in fact, been my idea. It felt important for her to understand that.

"I'm just going to come out and say it, Mina," I began. She nodded her encouragement. "But we—" I gestured to David, Hannah and Ben with a sweep of my hands "—we don't really see there being too many challenges. We've been friends for years. Decades, actually. And we've already talked a lot about this, separately *and* together."

Mina nodded, only the slightest of frowns playing across her mouth. I smiled confidently, certain she was about to say we clearly didn't need to be here and good luck.

"What if you can't get pregnant, Kate? Or if you do and then miscarry? I find many surrogate mothers experience a lot of guilt in that situation." I took a sip of water, my throat suddenly bone-dry. "Or if one side wants to keep trying while the other side has decided enough is enough?" When none of us answered immediately, Mina continued, "And what about your children, Kate and David? Are they prepared for this?"

I glanced at David, whose eyes were fixed on his knees.

"And though I know it's terrible to even imagine," Mina went on, "have you considered what you might do if there's a genetic abnormality with the fetus?"

"Well, I—" I hesitated, flustered by the sudden shift to the dark and tragic, and was grateful when Hannah interjected.

"Naturally we would support Kate's decision on something like that," she said, looking shaky and ill. Ben didn't look much better.

Mina nodded. "But this is going to be *your* intended child, Hannah and Ben. So while it might seem simple right now in this office, I promise you that a decision like that isn't always so easy if or when complications arise."

"We understand," David said, reaching over to hold my hand tightly. I had run out of steam, the conversation deflating me like a pin meeting the taut surface of a balloon. "We know things can go wrong. I'm a paramedic—I see terrible stuff every day. But we're ready." He smiled at me, because he knew how much I needed it at that moment. "We've talked to our girls and have been honest with them about what this means. And as for the what-ifs, well, we're just going to have to figure those out as we go. We love Hannah and Ben. And we want to do this."

I saw Hannah's hand reach out for the tissue box. I didn't look over at her, or Ben, certain if I did I would lose it entirely. Instead, I took a deep breath and locked eyes with Mina.

"What else do you need from us?" I asked.

"It isn't about what I need, Kate," Mina said. "I'm here to be a conduit between the four of you and answer any questions you might have. My job is to make your job easier, and to help make sure the relationship you have now stays strong and healthy through the process, and afterward, as well."

I nodded and pressed my lips together. "Okay," I said. "Then why don't we start over?"

"I think that's a great idea," Mina replied, shining another big smile my way. "Here are a few brochures that I think might be helpful..."

26

KATE

"This is more complicated than I thought," I said, watching David floss his teeth in the bathroom mirror, using one piece per tooth. I resisted the urge to yank the dental floss out of his hands and pull out a superlong strand and demand he use it. I was on edge, between our session with Mina and my subsequent meeting with the fertility attorney to go over the contract, the gesture I had been so excited about was turning into a giant ball of bureaucratic red tape.

David ran his tongue over his teeth, tossing another small white snake of floss into the trash can. "What is?"

Tapping my wet toothbrush against the side of the sink with perhaps a tad too much force, I added some toothpaste on the bristles. "Mina, our ever-helpful social worker. And Damon Cumberland, fertility attorney and fatalist." I popped the toothbrush in my mouth and attacked my teeth, brushing too hard for my sensitive gums.

He had another tiny piece of floss in hand, enough to wrap once around each of his pointer fingers tightly so his fingertips went bright red. His eyes met mine in the mirror. "Kate, they're just doing their jobs."

I scowled and then spit noisily into the sink. "I know that. Obviously I know that." I dropped my toothbrush into the holder and went into the bedroom. If I had to watch David floss one more tooth, I was going to lose it, and it wasn't his fault. But then I heard him sigh, which stoked the fire in my belly and made me angry about the floss all over again.

I noisily opened and shut my drawers, getting one of David's old T-shirts that I liked to sleep in, and was settled under the covers once he came out of the bathroom. He leaned against the door frame and crossed his arms. I scowled again. "What?"

He pushed off the door frame and lay on the bed beside me, propping his head up with his hand. "Are you sure about this?"

This time I sighed deeply, hoping the irritation I intended shone through, and rubbed some thick cream into my bare arms. The vanilla scent filled my nostrils and I took another deep breath.

"I'm just asking. This is a big deal, Katie."

Throwing back the covers, I got up and went back to the bathroom to pee. I didn't shut the door—we were long past that stage of things. "Why does it seem like everyone thinks I don't get that?"

"Maybe because you're the one getting pissed off whenever someone tries to help you?"

He said something else—something about how he didn't think our attorney, Damon Cumberland, was all that bad—but I flushed at just the right moment to block most of it out. Back in bed I tucked the duvet around the edges of my body and dropped my head onto the fluffy pillow a couple of times until there was a comfortable dent in the down stuffing.

"What's going on? I thought he was thorough and friendly enough."

I pressed my lips together, thinking about how to explain it. I wasn't sure I could pinpoint exactly what it was. Maybe it had to do with Mr. Cumberland's very expensive-looking suit and fancy office, which I knew Hannah and Ben's hard-earned dollars were helping finance because they insisted on paying for my attorney along with their own? Or the fact that we even needed an attorney, let alone two? More than likely it was how Cumberland had presented the terms of the contract. Everything from payment, which I insisted be removed from the contract, explaining this was altruistic and, no, I wouldn't take a penny from Hannah and Ben—that this was in every way a *gift* to them—to pregnancy termination, to health risks, to decisions about horrible, tragic things I didn't even want to consider. Yes, my current state of mind had a lot to do with the contract, a multipage legal document void of emotion that did nothing to showcase the love and motivation behind this decision. The entire process was starting to feel like a business transaction.

And, yes, that pissed me off.

"His suit was too expensive," I said.

"His suit?"

"Yes, his suit. And I bet he has a closet full of other suits just like it. And whatever exorbitant fees Hannah has to pay him will go toward yet another too-expensive suit."

"Kate, sweetheart, I—"

"Don't you get it?" I sat straight up and slammed my hands on either side of my legs, which were locked in the duvet's burrito-tight space. "This is something special and private. It should never have been typed out in boring black ink on legal-sized paper, where I'm called *The Surrogate* and you *The Husband*, and Kate and Ben *The Intended Parents*. And I don't care what Mina thinks about any of it, or what 'challenges' she feels so damned compelled to share with us. Or that Damon Cumberland is simply trying to 'protect my legal rights,'" I said, my fingers going up into air quotes around my last words.

I sighed and lay back against the pillows, letting David run his hand gently over my stomach. "Of course I'll take any medication the obstetrician recommends, and my vitamins, and I won't smoke or drink or use 'illicit' drugs. And no sex before or after the insemination, and I definitely would never abort this baby. I mean, what the fuck?" I put an arm across my face and closed my eyes, remembered the million other things I was contracted to do, or not do, my head swimming. "I wanted this to just be between us, you know? Me, you, Hannah and Ben. There are so many people involved, so many people telling me what to do, how to behave, how to feel."

"I know," David said. "I know this isn't what you were expecting."

I pulled my arm down and glanced at David. "No, it wasn't. And I really hate that Hannah and Ben have to pay for this."

"Kate..." He shook his head and looked away, and I knew it meant he had something to say I probably wasn't going to like.

"What?"

"Hannah and Ben are paying for this because they don't only need this contract...they want it. Ben said it was really important to Hannah."

I stared at him, not saying a word. Hannah had nodded and smiled and agreed with me when I ranted about all the legalese. Was she worried I wouldn't do what I said I would? I felt sick, and for the briefest of moments wondered if I really was sure about all this.

"The contract isn't just to protect your rights. It's to protect Hannah and Ben, too, and let me explain that before you say anything." He held up a hand, and I held in my argument. "Not from you, Katie. Hannah trusts you. Ben trusts you. But you heard the attorney. Even though our relationship with one another isn't complicated, what we're *doing* here is. So we need to make sure we're all on the same page."

"But we are on the same page, aren't we?"

"I believe we are," David said. "But these are the hoops, Kate. And if you want to do this for Hannah and Ben, you gotta jump through them."

"Stupid hoops," I replied, but my frown was a little less intense this time.

"There are so many things I love about you, but this?" He placed a hand on the left side of my chest, right over my heart. "This is the thing that I love the most."

"My left breast?" I asked, a smile overtaking the frown.

"Yes, Kate, I love your left breast more than anything else about you."

I nodded. "I thought so. You have a tendency to focus more on that one."

"Do I?" he said, rolling his body on top of mine. It was a bit hard to breathe like that, but I didn't want him to move. "Well, guess I should probably do something about that." He kissed my neck and I tilted my head back, then cracked one eye open and smiled. "Only over-the-clothes stuff, though, okay? Don't forget I'm on contract."

27

HANNAH

The nurse handed Ben a clear plastic bag with a blue-capped cup inside. Even though we had been here, done this, so many times over the past few years, Ben always held the bag as if it contained toxic waste—the zippered top pinched between two fingers and held slightly away from his body.

"Why does everything have to be see-through?" he murmured, looking at the bag in his hand as we followed the nurse down the hall. "I hate this part."

"But this is the best part," I replied, rubbing his back and trying to hide my smile. "Nothing like porn being prescribed for your 'procedure,'" I said, my fingers making air quotes for the last word. "Way better than anything I've had to do."

"This isn't a competition for who has it worse," Ben said, smiling as we sat down to wait until his name was called. "But you're right. Even if I have to go into a room right after another guy comes out of it, and the magazines are always the same ones, and everyone knows *exactly* what I'm doing in there."

I laughed. "At least they clean the rooms in between."

"Are you sure about that?" Ben asked.

"Let's talk about something else," I replied, grimacing.

"How about how you're feeling?"

"Really? Why not something more fun, or at least half-interesting?"

Ben gave me a look. "How am I feeling?" I took a deep breath and then let it out. "I'm feeling excited. And terrified. And so nervous for Kate." I chewed the inside of my cheek. "I can't stop thinking about what that social worker said, how Kate might feel really guilty if she doesn't get pregnant."

"That will be as much my fault as hers," Ben said, lifting the plastic bag up. "I'll try to get only the really fast swimmers in here."

I smiled, but my heart wasn't in it. "She won't handle it well. You know Kate—she'll blame herself no matter what."

"I know," Ben said, placing the bag-less hand on my thigh and squeezing. "So let's just hope it works."

"Ben Matthews?"

"Do they really have to use our full names?" Ben whispered as he got up, and I chuckled. "See you on the other side."

"Good luck, babe," I said.

He held up a hand in acknowledgment, following the nurse down the hall before going into one of the rooms.

My phone buzzed, and I looked at the screen. A message from Kate saying they were on their way. My heart fluttered as I typed a quick message back, wondering if today would be the day that changed my life.

"I got us something," Kate said, sitting up on the exam table. "Can you hand me the plastic bag in my purse?" She was gowned and ready, and we were just waiting for Dr. Horwarth and Ben's freshly washed sperm.

I grabbed the white plastic bag from her purse and gave it to her. "What is it?"

"You'll see," she replied, a goofy smile on her face. "Close your eyes and hold out your hands."

I did, and a moment later she placed something soft and light in my outstretched hands.

"Can I open my eyes now?"

"One sec… Okay, now. Ta-da!"

She had on a T-shirt, stretched tightly over her medical gown, with the words *Think Positive* written across the chest, an oval underneath the message with two pink lines in it—like you'd find on a positive pregnancy test. I burst out laughing, then instantly started crying looking at the shirt in my hands, which was identical.

"No, no, no. This wasn't supposed to make you cry!" Kate looked stricken and started to pull her shirt off.

"Leave it on," I blubbered. "I love it." With a quick wipe of my eyes with the back of my hand, I held up the shirt and read the words again. "I love it, really. It's perfect. Thank you."

"You're welcome." Kate jumped off the table to hug me. "I got one for Dr. Horwarth, too, in case you thought he might wear it?" She grinned and held out a larger T-shirt with the same message.

"He'll wear it for sure," I said, laughing at the image of the three of us in our T-shirts during the procedure.

"Good." Kate sat back on the table and smoothed Dr. Horwarth's shirt across her lap. "This is going to work, Hannah. I had a good long chat with my eggs this morning, and they know what's expected of them. They won't let us down."

I paused, running my fingers over the two pink lines on the T-shirt. "You know you won't be letting me down if this doesn't work, right?"

"It's going to work," Kate said, with a look that told me there was no point in arguing. "Now get your shirt on and get ready, because we're about to make a baby."

28

KATE

It had been eleven days since the insemination, and that morning I gagged while making scrambled eggs for the girls. Then I had the strongest craving for olives covered in melted American cheese slices—a particularly disgusting combination I had craved during my other two pregnancies. Sitting down on the closed lid of the toilet I glanced at the pregnancy test, knowing I still had thirty seconds to wait. Impatient, I rested my hands on my knees to keep them from grabbing the pee stick and bounced my toes against the penny marble floor. I couldn't wait to tell Hannah we were expecting. It was a moment that could only be topped by watching her face when her baby was placed in her arms for the first time.

A second later my phone timer beeped, and I grabbed for the stick, holding my breath. "Come on, come on, come on…" I repeated, my legs still bouncing. I flipped the stick over and stared at it.

There were two lines. I turned and looked in the mirror, a huge grin spreading across my face.

There were two lines.

In my haste to send David a text my phone slipped out of my hands and I grabbed for it before it could hit the ground. But in doing so I lost my balance and fell sideways, cracking my head on the towel rack. Dizzy, I quickly put a hand to the front of my head and was stunned when it came away covered in a lot of blood.

"Shit," I said, sitting down on the toilet seat again and grabbing a hand towel to press against the cut. I didn't look in the mirror because I was afraid I might pass out if it was too bad. Still pressing the towel to my head I bent forward to get my phone, my head throbbing. I called David's cell, even though I knew he had just started a twelve-hour shift, then hung up when I got his voice mail.

I didn't want to call Hannah because this wasn't how I wanted her to find out she was going to be a mother—in the ER, while I was forced to admit the pregnancy when giving a record of my medical history, some resident stitching up my head. No, it had to be special. Hannah deserved that moment.

Cora, David's mother, had gone back to Sacramento earlier in the week, and the mom I was closest to on the PTA had a houseful of flu-ridden kids. I could just call a cab, but I was going to have to call someone eventually—especially if the ER was busy and I wasn't going to be home to get the girls.

Once I was in the cab, a fresh washcloth pressed to my still bleeding head, I scrolled through my contacts and hit Dial.

"Hey, it's Kate. Could you do me a favor?"

Ben insisted on meeting me at the hospital even though I reassured him I was fine and was walking through the emergency room doors as I came out of triage.

He sat beside me on a waiting room chair and leaned in to get a look at my head when I lifted the wad of gauze the nurse had given me. "Ouch. How's the other guy?"

"I've always hated that towel rack. Now it's for sure getting ripped out of the wall." Ben laughed and leaned back, crossing one long leg over his knee.

"I forget how tall you are sometimes," I said. "Wonder if the baby will get your height."

He looked at me curiously but didn't say anything for a moment. "Do you know something?" he finally asked, his tone cautious.

I nodded, unable to hold in the grin. "The test this morning was positive. I was so excited I dropped my phone, then hit my head when I bent down to get it." Ben was still just staring at me, nodding as if I was telling him something that was only moderately interesting.

"Ben?" The nodding was disconcerting, and I wanted him to say something.

"You're pregnant?"

"I'm pregnant." I put my hand out for a high five, but Ben didn't acknowledge it. Instead he ran his fingers over his tight, dark curls and let out a jagged breath. "Hannah. I... We need to tell Hannah."

"No, not yet," I said, letting my hand drop. "I want it to be special, okay? And I've only had one positive test, so I don't want to get her excited until I'm sure there's something to be excited about."

Ben was back to nodding, and he looked a bit ill. "Yes. You're right. That's the best idea."

"Are you going to pass out on me? Because I think one head injury is enough for one day."

He leaned forward, his elbows dropping heavily to his knees, and cupped his chin in his hands. "We're going to have a baby." His voice was thick, and he was crying softly.

I felt a jagged surge of emotion hit the back of my throat.

With my free hand I rubbed his back, then put an arm around his shoulders. "This is great news, Ben. Are you okay?"

"Totally. I'm fine. You're the one bleeding all over the waiting room," he said, turning to look at me. "I'm supposed to be comforting you." I laughed. He shook his head, his eyes wide and bright with tears. "I'm just... I'm amazed. That's the best way to say it. This is amazing."

"Kate Cabot?" The nurse stood at the periphery of the waiting room, looking at the chart in her hand. She called my name again, in a monotone voice that suggested she was well into her shift.

Ben stood up when I did, keeping a protective hand on my back. "Do you want anything? A coffee? Shit, I guess you can't have coffee now?"

"Decaf is fine. That would be great, thanks." I told the nurse Ben was just grabbing a coffee and with a smile she promised to bring him back when he returned. Maybe she wasn't so miserable after all.

Fifteen minutes later, bored and hoping no traumas came in to bump me out of the queue, I heard the nurse's voice again. "She's in there." A second later the curtain was pushed to the side and in walked David, Ben behind him with two coffees in hand.

"What the hell happened?" David peeled back the gauze and inspected my head, his own forehead creased in what I knew was professional assessment tinged with a little personal concern. "Doesn't look too bad. Shouldn't leave much of a scar." He gently pressed the gauze back against the cut and held it there for me, then leaned down to kiss me.

"What are you doing here?" I asked, shifting on the uncomfortable stretcher. My butt was falling asleep. I touched my fingertips back to the gauze so he could let go. "How did you know I was here?"

"We had a patient transfer, and then I saw Ben walking through the waiting room."

Ben handed me my coffee. "Decaf," he said, grinning. "Also, I didn't tell him."

"Decaf?" David asked, crossing his arms over his chest. He frowned. "You never drink decaf."

"The test was positive." I said it as if I were announcing the most mundane thing—like that it was garbage day or that we were expecting rain overnight—but my face cracked into a smile so wide it actually hurt my cheeks.

"No kidding," David said, a smile slowly spreading across his face. "Guess scrambled eggs really are your litmus test, huh?"

Ben looked between us. "Scrambled eggs?" he asked.

"Not important," I said. "But what is important is me getting out of here so we can figure out how we're going to tell Hannah. I was thinking another T-shirt might be in order, maybe with a picture of an oven and a bun baking inside? Too lame? Or one that says, 'Does this baby make me look fat?' I think she might laugh if I walk in wearing that one. What do you think, guys?"

"I vote for number two," David said, kissing my cheek. "Now let me see if I can get you stitched and sprung so you can get to T-shirt making. Let me check who's on. I'll be right back."

After David left I held up my cup and Ben did the same. "Cheers to making a baby, Ben."

"Cheers," he said. Then without warning he enveloped me in an awkward hug, my one arm pinned against my body and the other still holding my coffee out to the side. Coffee sloshed from the hole in his coffee's takeaway lid, splashing onto the paper sheet covering the stretcher. Neither of us moved. "Thank you, Kate," he whispered, squeezing hard. "Thank you."

29

KATE

April

There was a knock and I lifted my head. "Mom?" Ava called out through the bathroom door.

I swallowed through the nausea and waited a moment to be sure I wasn't about to throw up again. "What is it, baby?"

"Do you know where my jean jacket is?"

"The hall closet, I think."

"Nope. I checked."

The wave of nausea swirled up through my belly, and I swallowed again, closing my eyes and feeling desperate for something, anything, to make this feeling go away. "Did you ask Dad?"

"He said to ask you."

Well, shit, David. Thanks for that. I had spent more time in the past two weeks with my head hanging in the toilet bowl than not, a particularly horrible side effect I hadn't experienced with either of my girls. Even though I was not one to suffer if I didn't have to—quickly reaching for my migraine pills or cough syrup for a tickle in my throat—I wanted to stay medication-free for this pregnancy. I had a newfound sympathy for every mother who had ever experienced morning sickness—or all-day vomiting, as was the case with me. It was horrible.

Feeling the wave of sickness starting to crest in my stomach, moving upward, I quickly told Ava I'd be right out and to check the closets again.

"Okay, Mom," she said, adding, "Feel better!" as I threw up again, nothing left in my stomach except for bile and the last sip of water I'd managed to get down.

A few minutes later I had brushed my teeth and washed my face and was fairly sure I could leave the safety of the restroom. As I opened the door I startled; David was right on the other side.

"Sorry," he said. "I made you some ginger and honey tea." I smiled gratefully and took the mug of steaming tea, the scent sharp and sweet and pleasing as it swirled into my nose. It was his mom's recipe, one she'd used through all her pregnancies—which she referred to as her four trips to "vomit-palooza"—and so far it was about the only thing I could stomach in the mornings.

"Ava said it sounded like you were throwing up your insides." He laid a hand on my hot cheek, and I leaned against it, the coolness settling me.

"She's not wrong," I said, taking a small sip of the tea. "That's about how it feels."

"Want me to reschedule the appointment today?"

I shook my head, then stopped quickly when the movement made my stomach lurch. "No. Even if I have to barf into plastic bags all through it, we're going." David laughed. "Did Ava find her jacket?"

"It was in the hall closet," David said. Then noting the look on my face he said, "She told me she looked there first."

"Mmm-hmm," I murmured, wrapping my fingers around

the mug. I had to admit my mother-in-law, Cora, was right about the tea; it did seem to help with the nausea.

"The tea's helping?"

"Maybe," I said, shrugging. I loved Cora, but she always made me feel a tad inexperienced—she had raised four boys, ran a successful business, could cook a gourmet seven-course meal with her eyes closed and oozed confidence.

The doorbell rang and Ava shouted up the stairs that their ride was here. "I'll go. You sit and regroup."

"Thanks," I said, going out on our bedroom's balcony. I saw our neighbor Darlene and her son, Henry, on the front steps and waved when she looked up, shielding her eyes from the sun. "Hey, Darlene," I called down. She waved. "Thanks again for taking the girls today."

"You bet," she said. "Hope all goes well at the dentist. Root canals are no fun."

"Thanks, sure it will be fine." We hadn't told anyone about the pregnancy yet, or that today was our ultrasound to see how many babies I had growing inside me. "I'll call you later. Bye, girls, love you."

Ava and Josie turned and waved, then followed Darlene and Henry down the front steps and to her car. A few minutes later I was shoving plastic bags into my purse and sliding my feet into my comfiest ballet flats, David pouring my tea into a travel mug.

"Think that will be enough bags?" David raised an eyebrow, watching me grab two more from under the sink.

"Better too many than not enough." I patted my purse and took the travel mug from him.

"Okay, last chance to reschedule. You sure?"

"I'm sure." My phone buzzed against my side, from inside my purse. I pulled it out and quickly glanced at the screen. "Hannah and Ben are on their way."

He opened the door and gestured for me to walk out ahead of him. "Let's go see what's causing all this vomit drama, okay?"

"Want to take guesses on one or two?"

"No need to guess." David shut the door and locked it behind us. "I know you have two in there."

"How?"

"Because you don't do anything half-assed."

30

HANNAH

I could tell Kate was ill the second I saw her, and my guilt kicked into overdrive.

"She looks *green*," I whispered, nudging Ben but smiling wide for Kate and David as they made their way to where we sat in the waiting room.

"Yeah, she does not look good," Ben whispered back; then his voice went louder when he stood up to give Kate and Ben hugs. "Hey, you two, long time no see."

I stood in front of Kate and held on to her arms, cringing when I asked, "How bad is it?"

She opened her purse. "I brought six plastic bags with me, and have one, two, three...four left. So, two bags in twenty minutes kind of bad." I must have looked horrified, because she pulled me close and hugged me tight. "It's fine. I'm fine. I'm hardly the first person to have morning sickness, and I'm actually feeling a bit better now."

I moved over a chair so she could sit between Ben and me. "I'm sorry if I smell like puke," she said, looking between us, a half smile on her face.

"You smell great," I replied.

"Only the tiniest bit like puke," Ben added. Kate and I each took turns punching him on his upper arms. "Hey, hey!" he said, laughing. David shook his head, keeping his eyes on the *National Geographic* magazine open in his hands.

"Ah, grasshopper Ben," he said. "One day you'll learn."

While Gerda, our ultrasound technician, got set up, a nest of nerves wriggled through my stomach. I took a deep breath, and Ben put a hand on my back. "You good?" he whispered. I nodded.

"What a fantastic story this is going to make," Gerda said, rolling her stool a little closer to the bed Kate lay on. "You have some best friend."

"I know," Kate and I replied at the same time, causing everyone to laugh.

"Let's see what we've got going on in here, okay?" Gerda said, turning the screen toward us. David, Ben and I simultaneously leaned toward the monitor, watching the strange and wonderful images flash across the screen.

"Looks like Dr. H was right," Gerda said. "You've got two babies in there."

"Holy. Shit." Ben put his hand to his mouth and exhaled loudly. David clapped him on the back. Kate turned her head toward me, and I tore my eyes away from the screen to look at her face, which was illuminated only by the monitor's glow, the rest of the room dark. She smiled, then did a fist pump with a "Yes!" I threw myself at her, and closed my eyes, hugging her tightly.

"Hannah, I love you, sweetie, but you're making it hard to breathe."

"Sorry, sorry." I released her. Even though I had been sure I would cry, my jeans back pocket packed full of folded tissues, I felt nothing but joy. This was the happiest moment of my life, and turning to Ben, I could see we were having a parallel experience. It was as if all the horrible moments we'd experienced trying to get to this point compressed into one tiny black dot, now too small to do any more damage. We grinned at each other, then started laughing, then held hands and jumped around the small room like children on a playground.

"Okay, see this first sac here? This is baby A, because she's closest to the cervix." Gerda pointed to a spot on the monitor. "And baby A is measuring...six weeks, one day, so right on track."

"Way to go, baby A," Kate said, gently patting her belly.

"And here's the second sac...okay, this is baby B. How big are you, baby B?" Gerda moved the ultrasound wand around under the sheet, and Kate sucked in her breath. "Sorry, sweetheart. You okay there?"

"Fine," Kate said. "Just a bit uncomfortable. How's baby B doing?"

"Baby B is measuring...five weeks, five days. Also, right on track."

"Is it okay if one is bigger than the other?" Ben asked, beating me to the question. I suddenly felt as though I were in the middle of an incredibly important exam I hadn't done a bit of studying for.

Gerda nodded, pressing a few buttons every now and then to take pictures. "Totally normal at this stage, especially in twin pregnancies. Okay, I think I'm done here but just going to check with Dr. H to see if he wants any other pictures. Hang tight."

As soon as Gerda shut the door behind her, the room filled with cheering, high fives and congratulations. "We did it!" Kate's voice was muffled, as we were all practically lying on top of her in one giant group hug.

"You did it," I said, pulling back to look her in the eyes.

"Hey, what about me?" Ben winked, and I kissed him—holding my lips to his longer than was perhaps appropriate given we had company.

"You both did it!"

"Without actually doing it." David smirked. We exploded with laughter, and if I'd known at that moment what the future had in store for us, I would have locked the door and never left.

31

HANNAH

May

"What else could I have said to her?" I turned to look at Ben. I felt sick to my stomach, but there were no tears. I was too worried about Kate to feel anything for myself. "She needs to know I don't blame her. That we don't blame her, not a bit."

"She knows, Hannah. She's just upset." Ben's jaw twitched as he tried to keep himself in check. "We're all upset."

"I know." I looked back at my hands, tightly clenched on my lap. We had been sitting on the front steps of our place for thirty minutes, barely speaking. "I was only trying to help. To somehow make it better for her."

"You can't. I can't. David can't. So just…just stop trying, okay?" And with that Ben stood up and went inside, and I stayed where I was, unsure if he wanted me to follow him or not.

Needless to say, things had not gone well earlier at our twelve-week ultrasound.

It started out fine, the four of us back in the same room as our earlier ultrasound, Gerda the technician doing her thing. But she took longer to turn the monitor toward us, and while the others joked about Ben having to break his no-minivan rule for sure now, I kept quiet—my eyes on Gerda who seemed focused on the screen and not at all on us.

"Is everything okay?" I asked, which shut everyone up pretty fast.

She squinted at the screen and moved the ultrasound paddle around on Kate's abdomen. "Here's baby A," she said. "Heart rate looks good and measuring...twelve weeks and one day. Perfect."

"That's great," Kate said. "Right? Hannah?" I looked at her, and her smile faltered, probably because of the look on my face.

I knew something was wrong. Had felt it when I woke up that morning, actually. I had tried to explain it to Ben, the shift I'd felt from when I went to bed—excited and confident about the ultrasound—to this morning, when halfway through my cup of coffee my stomach soured and a wave of anxiety moved through me. It had been the strangest thing.

"Just nerves," Ben had said when I told him what happened, kissing me atop the head and pouring my coffee into a travel mug so we wouldn't be late.

But I knew. Something wasn't right, which Gerda confirmed when she politely yet tersely excused herself to get Dr. Horwarth.

Foolishly, I had allowed myself to be lulled into the belief that because I wasn't the one trying to grow the baby, all would be fine. That I was the problem, and Kate being our surrogate fixed everything.

Kate was sitting up now and looked nervous, clutching my hands. "What's happening?"

Ben stared at the floor—because he knew, too—and David rubbed Kate's shoulders, his eyes on mine.

"I think Baby B may be hiding," I said, keeping my tone light. Kate squeezed my fingers, as if she were trying to pump them full of air, and nodded repeatedly at my words. "I'm sure Dr. H will figure it out."

But soon we all knew. Baby B was gone.

"Vanishing twin syndrome," Dr. Horwarth said, reassuring Kate especially it was nearly always related to an abnormality with the fetus. Kate had lain there so still, eyes on the ceiling and hands clasped over her slightly protruding belly, her mouth partially open as if she was on the verge of saying something but had lost the energy or inclination to do so.

"Kate, please look at me." She didn't. "Kate, look at me." My tone was harsher than I'd intended, but it did the trick. She turned toward me, her eyes glassy, vacant.

"I'm sorry, Hannah." Her bottom lip quivered and tears streamed down her pale cheeks.

And then we all started speaking at once. Well, at least me, David and Ben—Kate stayed disturbingly still and silent.

"There is nothing to be sorry for."

"You heard Dr. H. This was an abnormality with the fetus."

"There was nothing you could or should have done differently."

She turned away from us and looked back to the ceiling. "David, I'd like to go home."

When she sat up I stood in front of her, my hands firm on her knees. She still had the paper sheet covering her bottom half, and it crinkled under my fingers. "Kate, please. Tell me you're okay."

"I'm okay. Now can I get dressed?"

I opened my mouth to push her to tell me what was going through her head, but I caught David's look. I let go of her knees and backed up. "Sure, we'll just wait outside."

Ten minutes later we were heading to the bank of elevators outside the clinic, faces somber and no one speaking. Because I was the last one out the door, holding it open for the others, Gerda caught me before we left. "Hannah," she said, running up to me and handing me an envelope. "Here's a great picture of Baby A. I thought you might want it." After I quietly thanked her, I quickly shoved the envelope into my purse so the others—Kate especially—didn't see it. Down in the parking garage I hugged Kate before we went our separate ways, and she felt like a wet noodle in my arms. It terrified me, not only because I'd only seen her this desolate once before—when her mom died—but also because there was still a baby inside her. A perfectly healthy, twelve-week, one-day fetus that needed her to believe in it so one day I could hold it in my arms and tell it just how hard we fought to have it.

Now, sitting alone on our front steps, I pulled out the envelope and looked at the ultrasound picture. Baby A looked like a large kidney bean with tiny arms, nestled inside its black sac. And beside it was a second black sac—but this one was empty.

I folded the paper so the empty sac was tucked underneath the rest of the picture, using my nails to make the fold as permanent as possible. Later I would use scissors to cut the folded line so I didn't have to look at that empty sac ever again.

32

KATE

I felt terrible for how I'd left things after the ultrasound, for the look on Hannah's face when I walked away to get into the car, but I was in shock. Stupid, naive me—it never occurred to me that both babies wouldn't be fine, delivered naturally, on time, and the picture of health. That's what happened with Ava and Josie. I got pregnant the first time we tried with Ava, on our honeymoon, and after only three months with Josie, which at the time I had thought was torturous. Three whole months. Both pregnancies had been easy—my only complaint frequent migraines that were just slightly worse than my pre-pregnancy headaches—and over before I even had a chance to start hating anything, like my semiswollen ankles or inability to sleep because both girls liked to somersault in my belly at night.

Stupid, naive me.

When Dr. Horwarth said the twin had vanished—*how can a baby just disappear?*—things went into slow motion. And then the guilt came. Swift. Thick. Suffocating. Even though they all said it wasn't my fault, I had been tasked with protecting those babies, nurturing them with my body, and I had failed. That was on me.

So lying in that room, trying to absorb the terrible news, it occurred to me I had no business carrying a baby for anyone. I had been too cavalier, too confident, too certain of success. Mina, the social worker whom I'd basically written off as meddlesome and out of line, had been right—I was not prepared for bad news. And perhaps worst of all, I realized in the moments following the vanishing twin news how little I understood about what Hannah had been through. So facing her with this loss felt impossible, and I couldn't even look at her in that ultrasound room. I was supposed to be her salvation, her umbrella for the storm cloud she'd been under for years.

David had tried his best to pull me out of the fog. Reminding me there was another baby and not all was lost. The girls had been understandably sad, and Josie had cried when we told them. Ava sat very still, picking at a rough cuticle on her thumb and not looking at David or me, and my heart broke a little more. David and I had agreed we'd be honest with them in the event something went wrong, but it had all been hypothetical and I hadn't considered what it would be like to tell them such a thing.

Stupid, naive me.

Hannah had been calling and texting incessantly in the past forty-eight hours, and I knew I had to let her come over soon. To see that I hadn't completely lost the plot, and without a doubt to be reassured I was pulling it together for Baby A.

But I wasn't ready.

So I sat at the table with my full glass of green juice, which now after two hours had separated into distinct layers—the bottom murky green like swamp water, the top a pale green foam—and pushed my phone in circles, the text messages filling my screen. The house was quiet, the girls at school and David at work. I hadn't even turned the television on—I wanted no distractions for my guilt, planning to bathe in it a little longer.

When the doorbell chimed my fingers halted on making circles with my phone—stopping it upside down. I didn't get up, even when it chimed three more times. Then my phone buzzed, and I turned the phone to read the text message that flashed across the screen.

I'm outside. Open up.

When another couple of minutes went by without me answering the door, or the message, my screen flashed again.

I'm using my key.

A moment later I heard the front door unlock. I pushed my phone to the side and took a huge gulp of the juice, the now-warm, gritty liquid coating my tongue, and waited.

33

HANNAH

Standing outside Kate's front door I hesitated, my finger hovering an inch from the doorbell. It had seemed like a good idea two hours ago to storm over here, when Shoana confronted me about why the sorbet I'd made earlier was melting in the cupboard and the oven mitts were tucked in the fridge's crisper.

I had already burned onions I was supposed to be caramelizing for a Father's Day tart recipe, and then burst into tears when cutting up another onion—tears I tried to blame on the cut onion, but Shoana knew me better than that. I never cried cutting onion—I was infamous for it among my test kitchen colleagues.

Shoana tossed the sorbet, put the oven mitts in their drawer and pushed me gently onto one of the stainless-steel stools lined up at the kitchen island. In whispered tones, because I was afraid of how it might sound out loud, I admitted to having a hard time grieving the baby we lost. "Of course you are," Shoana said. "You've been through this so many times you've learned how to compartmentalize your grief, to tuck it away." With a jolt I realized how right she was, and that it wasn't the same for Kate. She had always felt things deeply, wearing her emotions like people wear name cards at social events.

"She won't call me back. And I'm trying not to push too hard, but...this is all such a mess," I said. "What am I supposed to do?"

"You're going to take those cherry vanilla bourbon bars from yesterday that are maybe the best thing you've made since you've been here, and go to her house. Don't tell her you're coming. Just show up and ring the damn doorbell."

"I'm not sure that's such a great idea."

"Of course it is," Shoana said with a dismissive wave of her hand. "The bourbon mostly burned off while it baked. I guarantee they are safe during pregnancy."

"That's not what I meant and you know it."

"Listen, I can't even imagine what this all feels like. For any of you. But leaving something to fester is never a good idea. You need to pull the splinter out, fast."

But now that I was at her door, a sweating pan of "mostly" nonalcoholic dessert squares in one hand and the other ready to ring the bell, ambushing Kate seemed a terrible idea. However, remembering Shoana's splinter metaphor, I jabbed my finger into the doorbell, the chime ringing inside. I counted to fifty in my head, then pressed the bell again. When that didn't do it, I sent her a text message that I was outside and to open the door.

Nothing. With a sigh I put down the pan and rummaged through my purse to find my keys. Then I waited another couple of minutes—expecting her neighbors to call the police any moment to report a suspicious loiterer—sent her another text and let myself in.

"Kate?" I called through the doorway. After kicking off my shoes, I padded down the hall, my heart beating fast. Looking around the empty kitchen I took in the half glass of green juice and Kate's phone, my last text message still illuminated on the screen. I called out her name again, then heard retching coming from the powder room off the kitchen.

Putting the squares into the fridge—clearly ginger ale was a better call at the moment—I dumped the rest of the green juice down the sink, cringing at the smell of it, and sat at the kitchen table to wait for Kate to be done.

The toilet flushed a moment later, and Kate came into the kitchen, pale and her face covered with a sheen of sweat.

She plopped down in a chair across from me.

I nudged the glass of ginger ale toward her, and she gave a small smile when she took it. "Are you all right?"

"Yeah. My stomach's off today."

"Not what I meant." I leaned my elbows on the table. "Talk to me, Kate. Please."

She looked at me, held my gaze for a moment, then dropped her eyes to the tabletop. "No. I guess I'm not okay."

"What do you need? How can I help?"

"I wish I knew, Hannah. I really do."

I thought about all the things I could say, maybe should say. Like how I wished I hadn't put her in this position. Or to reiterate that it wasn't her fault, and Ben and I didn't blame her for a second. Or how I understood how shitty it was to lose a baby and that, unfortunately, you never really get rid of the emptiness that leaves behind, and how sorry I was she had to know that. Or that it's okay to be pissed off about the whole thing. I didn't say any of those things, settling instead for what I thought might get her attention the most.

"Get over it."

Her head snapped up. "I'm sorry?"

"Get over it," I repeated.

Kate shook her head and sucked in her breath, then chuckled but in a this-is-so-not-funny way. "Wow. Okay, thanks for that, Hannah. You're right. I'll just 'get over it.' Brilliant advice." She tapped a finger to her chin and rolled her eyes up, as if searching for clarity in the air above her head. "Of course. Get over it. No idea why I didn't think of that. Thank you."

"Listen, I'm not saying that to be cruel or bitchy or insensitive—"

"You could have fooled me," Kate muttered, her fingers so tight on the glass of ginger ale her nail beds went pale. Her eyes were bright with anger, which is exactly what I was hoping for—I had to know if she had fight left in her.

"Seriously, I don't mean to be glib. But trust me—holding yourself responsible for this isn't going to help anyone, least of all you. You need to listen closely to what I'm about to say. Will you do that for me? Please?"

Her eyes were still angry, but she nodded.

"I have no idea why this happened, and I don't care. This isn't about a vanishing twin, or even the baby we have left—who is still very much healthy and growing and doing exactly what it is supposed to be doing, for what that's worth." Kate's jaw shifted back and forth, but she kept her focus on the glass in her hands. "I care about you. And I love you… so, so much for taking this on, for being selfless, for putting yourself through this for us, for me." She started crying, and I kept going. "I hate that this has happened. For so many reasons but mostly because I didn't want you to get hurt. You deserved an easy ride, Kate, and I'm sorry you didn't get it."

"I'm sorry I lost the baby." Kate's voice betrayed her guilt, and I wished again I could take it away from her.

"You did not lose anything," I said. "You have a baby in that gorgeous belly of yours. My baby, Katie. So, no, you didn't lose anything. You've fixed *everything*."

She smiled at me through her tears. "Thank you."

"You're welcome."

We sat together for a few moments, then Kate sighed deeply. "This still sucks."

"Yes, it does." I got up and went to the fridge, turning back to look at her when I opened the door. "How's the stomach?"

"Fine," Kate said, using her sleeve to wipe her eyes, leaving a black streak of mascara on the soft fabric. "I think about ninety-eight percent of my puking is a direct result of that juice."

"No more green juice." I pulled out the baking pan and grabbed two forks from the cutlery drawer beside the fridge. "Promise me."

"Promise. What's that?"

"This," I said, putting the pan on the table between us and handing Kate a fork, "is heaven in a pan."

Kate peeled back the tinfoil, then stuck her fork in and took a big bite of the dessert—vanilla cream layered on top of bourbon-soaked cherries and a shortbread cookie crust, all topped with melted dark chocolate—letting out a happy groan as she chewed.

"This is so much better than green juice," she said, taking another big forkful.

"Right?" I took my own fork to the hard chocolate top, cracking the glossy surface to reveal the pale yellow cream below.

I finished chewing. "Kate, it's going to be fine. You'll see."

"I know," she replied, sitting back and licking the cream from the fork. "But thanks for the reminder."

"What are friends for?"

"For telling me to get over myself and then bringing this to make up for it," she said, pointing to the dessert. We laughed and clinked our forks before burying them back into the dessert once again.

34

KATE

June

"I can't even believe it. A boy. *A boy.*"

"You say that like you've performed some kind of gender miracle," David said, chuckling. "There *was* a fifty percent chance, you know."

I pointed to my belly, eyebrows raised. "I don't make boys. I don't grow penises in here."

He laughed, saying obviously I did, and I linked my arm back through his, snuggling into his warmth. It was a beautiful day, full of sunshine and hope.

It had been nearly six weeks since Hannah and I had eaten the entire pan of dessert squares in my kitchen, and a lot had changed in that time. For one thing, the sickness was a distant memory, and the vanishing twin guilt barely a dull hum most days. Also, Hannah and Ben had become puppy parents to Clover—a mischievous little snow-white dog with a fancy breed name I could never remember—which was proving hilarious to watch. Hannah texted me every morning to tell me how many times she'd had to let the puppy out of its crate during the night, or how many household items it had destroyed in the previous twenty-four hours. I assured her on each occasion that babies were far easier to manage than puppies, which came out with sharp teeth and the ability to run.

"I think we should get your mom to come up for a weekend and we can go to that hotel up the coast—" David had stopped walking, and I turned back toward him. "What's up?"

"I am so proud of you."

I let him pull me back, drawing me tightly against his chest. My belly, which was bigger at this stage than I remembered from either of my other pregnancies, kept us ever so slightly apart. "Where did that come from?"

He shrugged and pushed a piece of hair back from my face, his finger resting on my cheek. "You're doing something not many people would. It's pretty amazing."

"Hardly," I said. "Though I'd like to tape this conversation and record it back the next time I do something to piss you off." I smirked, but he shook his head, not willing to let me make light of it.

"You're wrong. Who else would have done this for Hannah?"

Now it was my turn to shrug.

He put a finger under my chin and tilted my face up, and I squinted when the sun blinded me for a moment. "You are amazing," David whispered. "Don't forget it."

I pulled back and grinned at him. "Does that mean you'll make lunches tonight? So I can put these *amazing* feet of mine up for bit?"

"Done." David glanced at his watch. "We'd better get back. School's out soon."

I snuggled in deeper and groaned. "Do we have to? Can't they just take care of themselves?"

"I give you fifteen minutes before you're hungry and angry." He laughed and I scowled. But he was right—I was at the stage in my pregnancy where I had two helpings for every one of David's, sometimes three.

"Ah, yes, but I am always prepared." I reached into my purse and pulled out a chocolate chip granola bar. "See?"

He grabbed for it, and I tucked it behind my back. "Hey, this is my emergency granola bar! Are you really going to steal it from your pregnant wife?"

"Half?" David asked, then kissed me and pinned me to him while he reached behind me and yanked the bar out of my fingers.

Later that night, after the take-out pizza had been consumed and the girls were watching a movie, I lay on the couch with a cold pack on my forehead.

"Are you sure you don't want to go upstairs?"

I squinted at him, the light bright after having my eyes closed for the past twenty minutes. David sat on the ottoman, his elbows on his knees as he leaned toward me, a concerned look on his face.

"It's just a headache."

"Headache or migraine?"

"Okay, migraine," I admitted. "But it's not too bad. No tingling."

"Want something for it?"

"No. No drugs. The cold pack helps."

"Want me to rub your feet, Mom?" Ava turned to look at me from the other couch, her dark hair pulled into a messy ponytail. I tried to count back how many days it had been since the girls' last shower. Tomorrow. I'd make sure they showered tomorrow.

"Sure, baby, that would be awesome." I wiggled my toes and stretched as Ava came to perch on the arm of the couch. She tucked her legs up, sliding her toes into the space between the couch frame and the seat cushions, and squeezed her little fingers into the sole of one foot. "Ah, that feels amazing. Please, don't ever stop. You are my favorite oldest daughter."

Josie, who never missed a thing, turned from the screen and let out an annoyed, "Hey!"

"She said oldest daughter, stupid," Ava muttered.

"Not nice, Ava," David said. "Apologize to your sister."

"I'm sorry that you don't know how to listen properly." Ava smirked as she said it, back to rubbing my foot.

My warning glance was enough. Ava rolled her eyes and gave a short, but at least somewhat genuine, apology.

"Go to bed. I've got this," David said a few minutes later, his hand on my belly, rubbing in small circles. "I'll get their lunches ready for camp tomorrow and finish up here."

Smiling gratefully at him, I said I would. In truth the migraine was worse than I wanted to admit, and it worried me that they were happening more often. I'd had two the week before, both of which had come on swiftly and knocked me off my feet for most of the day. But I hadn't told David how bad they had been—there was nothing he could do about it, except worry and feel badly for me.

Trudging upstairs, the beat of my heart pounding painfully in my temples and my stomach churning with the seasick type of nausea that often accompanied my migraines, I repeated the mantra I'd started after I lost the twin. *This is temporary. This is for Hannah. This is all that matters.*

35

HANNAH

July

Kate got in the car and fastened the seat belt under her stomach, which at twenty-three weeks was cute and round and the belly I dreamed of having back when I used to think a pregnancy was in my future. Even though I had mostly accepted I would never carry a child, every now and then I'd have a flash of jealousy—and I had a feeling today was going to be filled with at least a few of those green-with-envy moments.

Clover whined and Kate whipped around to look in the backseat. "You're bringing the puppy?"

I sighed. It had not been the easiest morning so far. "I have to. Ben had to go to the office, some kind of emergency with one of their projects, and there wasn't time to figure anything else out. She can only be in her crate for like, an hour or two tops, or we have a seriously disgusting mess to clean up."

"Oh, man, Claire is going to lose it," Kate said, chuckling as she turned back in her seat. "I take it you haven't told her you're bringing the dog?" I put the car in Drive and pulled away from the curb.

"Easier to ask for forgiveness than permission," I mumbled.

"Besides, I'm sure it will be fine. I brought the travel crate, and she can't get into trouble when she's behind bars, right?"

"Famous last words, my friend. Famous last words." Kate turned around again and stuck her fingers through the holes of Clover's crate. "Hey, baby girl, you going to be good for your momma?" Clover whined again, and Kate laughed. "I'm thinking that's a no."

Fifteen minutes later we stood on Claire and Peter's front porch, and I rang the doorbell with my elbow as my hands were full with Clover in one and gift bags in the other, and Kate had a large two-tiered Tupperware container filled with lemon cupcakes. It was Claire's baby shower—she was due in about four weeks—and I was hosting. Which meant she organized everything and I showed up at her house with dessert.

The door opened to a flurry of brightly colored metallic balloons, which hovered toward us in a suffocating group. Kate looked at me and raised an eyebrow. *Balloons?* It did seem a bit un-Claire-like; her front hall was usually adorned with nothing more than a Mennonite bench, antique umbrella vase and dove-gray carpet runner. Perfect order, nothing out of place.

The she came out of the kitchen, and my jaw dropped. Admittedly it had been a few weeks since I'd seen her last. But she looked so swollen; everything was puffy, as if she'd swallowed the entire contents of a helium tank.

"Yes, I know I look hideous. Just get in here and stop staring at me like that." We stepped inside, and she shut the door behind us. "Nothing fits. Even my fingers are fat. Peter said I should get my wedding band resized, but why bother? I'm only getting fatter from here on out." She kissed me on the cheek, pressing her face to mine, and I smelled roses and onion. Then she kissed and hugged Kate, who awkwardly patted her on the back. They had never really warmed up to each other—

Kate felt Claire was a crappy sister, and Claire thought Kate was a bit "stuck-up."

"Claire, you look amazing," Kate said. "Pregnancy really suits you." I turned my head so Claire wouldn't see my smile, glad at least that Kate sounded genuine.

"Thank you, but I'm pretty much a hippo. I can't wait for this baby to come out. You look great, too. You're so tiny!" Then Claire looked at the crate I put down on the floor. "What's that?" Clover wagged her tail—which in turn made her whole body wiggle like jelly—desperate for some attention.

"Obviously that is Clover," I said. "I didn't have a choice. Ben had a work emergency." Clover let out a short bark, then started nibbling at the metal bars.

Claire frowned. "Fine. You can put her in the laundry room."

"Oh, yeah. That kid is going to be lucky to have her as a mom," Kate whispered, rolling her eyes, after Claire walked back down the hall.

"Hush," I said, steering Kate toward the kitchen. "She'll be fine. She may not be all warm and fuzzy, but she's organized and prepared."

"Perfect," Kate said, setting down the Tupperware and sliding off the lid. "Her kid will have monogrammed onesies and diapers, and her board books will be color-coded and alphabetized on the bookshelf."

I laughed as I set up the dessert tier, quickly placing the pale yellow cupcakes, iced with vanilla buttercream and topped with gold fondant polka dots, in rows.

"These are so pretty." Kate ran her finger around the inside edge of the container's lid, getting an errant smear of icing and popping it into her mouth. "And tasty." She leaned back against the counter, her empire-waisted maxidress resting over her belly bump. "Do you want cake or cupcakes for your shower?"

"I wasn't planning on having a shower." I busied myself with the last row of cupcakes, turning a few of them so the polka dots lined up.

"Hannah Matthews, of course you're having a shower!"

"But don't you think it's sort of weird? I mean, yes, I'm having a baby, but I'm not giving birth, so it feels self-indulgent or something. You know?" What I didn't say was that the idea of a shower freaked me out—not only all the attention that would literally be showered on me, my belly flat and baby-free, but also because I felt strangely superstitious about it. Even though I became more confident with every passing week of Kate's pregnancy, a baby in my arms still felt quite hypothetical.

Kate stared at me, her face a mix of concern and frustration. "This is *your* baby. I'm merely the oven here. And first-time moms get a shower. Period."

"Fine. This is my baby, and I will have a shower. Happy?"

"Yes." She nodded. "If it helps, we can do the shower after the baby's born. But it's happening. And you are not making your own cupcakes, no matter how good they are."

Just then a loud crash came from the hallway, and Claire let off a string of swear words unbecoming a mother-to-be surrounded by shiny balloons, crystal punch glasses and high-tea sandwiches.

I ran out into the hall to see what had happened, but I didn't get far. Clover came bounding into the kitchen, her now pale pink fur sopping. Kate put a hand to her mouth to cover her hysterical laughter and I chased Clover around the island, nearly slipping in the wet path she left as she ran. Claire stood in the hallway, watching it all, one hand on her belly and the other on her forehead. She did not look good, or happy. Finally I got a hold of Clover's collar and held on while she still tried to scamper away.

"How did she get out?" I asked, taking the paper towel Kate handed me and using it to mop up the punch from Clover's fur.

Just then Mom popped her head into the kitchen. "Has anyone seen Clover? I was going to let her out for a pee and poof, she just disappeared... Oh. Oh no."

"Yeah, let's just say we're going to need something other than punch to serve everyone," I said, picking Clover up. Keeping my arms outstretched so her wet pink fur didn't get near my dress, I plopped her into the laundry room sink. With a quick rinse and a towel dry with Mom's help, Clover was good as new in no time and snuggled back in her crate, oblivious to the path of destruction she'd left.

The doorbell rang, and I glanced at my watch. "Shit," I said, tugging on my dress to get everything back in place. "You stay." I pointed a finger at Clover, who was already snoring in her crate.

"This will be fine, just fine," my mom was saying in a soothing tone to an irritated Claire, while I went to open the front door to let the first guest in.

Soon the living room was filled with well-dressed women and a mountain of gifts, and Claire had a huge smile on her face as though being pregnant was the very best thing that had ever happened to her.

Everyone oohed and aahed over the gifts—beautiful hand-knit blankets, designer baby outfits and every kind of diaper cream you could ever need. By the time Claire opened yet another pair of sheepskin-lined baby booties—*why on earth would a baby here in this climate need slippers like that?*—I felt my stamina begin to chip away. I had been trying so hard to ignore the fact I wasn't the one carrying my baby, nodding when my mom said I wouldn't care about not being pregnant once the baby was born, or when Claire insensitively mentioned how lucky I was to skip the stretch marks and leg cramps. But at times the sadness and loss and envy was so intense, I felt like a puddle with nothing holding me together.

The last guest finally gone, I was in the kitchen helping Mom and Kate clean up when Claire poked her head in. "Hannah? Can you help me with the gifts?"

"Sure." I wiped my hands on the tea towel and walked out after her. I tried to ignore the ache still sitting in the center of my chest and managed to slap a smile on my face by the time we got to the living room. "Wow, there is a lot of stuff here. Lucky baby."

Claire stood facing the pile of gifts, arms crossed over her chest. I waited for her to tell me where she wanted everything to go, but she seemed lost in thought. "Claire? Want me to take these up to the nursery?"

"This should have been you, you know." Her voice was quiet, and surprisingly sad, and my throat closed up. "You were supposed to go first, Hannah. I'm sorry things didn't turn out that way."

"It's okay." I tried to laugh and failed. "It's not your fault I have a death trap for a uterus."

Claire turned to me then and, sensing how close I was to completely losing it, didn't acknowledge my comment, instead saying, "I have something for you." She walked over to the built-in cabinets beside the room's fireplace and opened one of the doors. After pulling out a flat rectangular package covered in poppy-red wrapping paper with a large silver bow, she sat on the couch and patted the seat beside her. I sat down and she handed me the package. "Open it."

"What is this?" But of course I knew what it was, and the tears came without warning.

She ignored the tears, for which I was grateful, and gestured to the gift. "It's a present for the baby. Open it."

With trembling hands I carefully untied the bow, then picked at one of the edges of the package, the gift paper thick and resilient under my fingers.

"For God's sake, Hannah," Claire said, laughing. "Rip the damn paper!"

I laughed, too, and grabbed an edge and pulled hard, the paper ripping straight across the package. Inside was a box, plain white with no markings. I glanced at Claire and saw she was grinning.

Opening the box I pulled the layers of crinkly silver tissue to the side and when I saw what was nestled inside, my breath caught. "Oh, Claire…"

She beamed at me. "He's going to love it as much as we did."

"But…but you should keep this!"

She shook her head. "No. This is for you."

I lifted out the book from the nest of tissue—an early edition of *The Velveteen Rabbit*, about a little boy who loved his stuffed bunny so much the bunny came to life—and opened the front cover, which was faded with age and use.

To Hannah and Claire, the greatest loves of my life. Dad xo

"I thought this was gone," I said, in awe of the gift in my hands. "How did you…? Where did you…?"

"After Grams died I went through some of the boxes in the attic, and I found it. I've been hanging on to it, waiting to give it to you when you had your first baby. And here we are."

I stared at the book, my hands caressing its surface, remembering how many times I begged my dad to read it to me, just one more time. "And here we are," I whispered. "Thank you, Claire. This means...this means so much to me."

"You're welcome. I know the way this is happening isn't your ideal scenario, and I'm sorry for all my bellyaching—literally—about my pregnancy. I'm sure you'd change places with me in a second..." She paused, busying herself with folding the tissue paper back up inside the box. "But once Kate has this baby and he's yours, you'll get to be just like every other mother—exhausted, sore nipples, covered in baby spit-up and never without an extra diaper and change of clothes in your purse...and happy for all of it."

"You're right." I closed the book and rested it gently in my lap. "I can't wait."

"Me, neither," Claire said, hugging me. "Especially because I'm going to need someone to complain to about the baby poop and nipple pain and sleeplessness. You know how cranky I get when I don't get my beauty sleep."

I laughed and hugged her back, holding her as tightly as her very round belly would allow.

36

KATE

I heard about what you're doing for your friend Hannah, and I wanted you to know I'm proud of you even if I don't fully agree with your decision. But I do hope you're feeling well—please let me know if there's anything you need.
With love, Edward McTavish

"What. The. Hell." I reread the last two lines three times, wondering who had told him. He didn't even know my wedding anniversary, so how could he know this most intimate detail? It didn't make sense—the only way he could have found out was if either me, or...

David. Shit.

I got so angry, so quickly, I couldn't catch my breath. With shaking fingers I ripped up the letter, the pieces fluttering to the table, then picked up my phone amid the mess of paper. Scrolling through my contacts I found the one for the ambulance dispatch. After two rings a woman picked up.

"Hi, this is David Cabot's wife, Kate? I need to speak with him...Yes...It's an emergency. Tell him to call my cell phone. Thank you." Still trembling, I put my phone down and leaned back, arms crossed on my chest. About four minutes later my phone rang, and I let it go three rings before answering.

"Kate, what's the matter? Are you okay?"

"No, I am not okay." I tapped my fingers on the tabletop, still fuming. With my other arm I swept the little bits of paper off the table and onto the floor, not caring that I'd just have to pick them all up again later. "I'm pissed off."

"What's wrong?" I could tell he was relieved. Also irritated and maybe a bit curious—having no idea what I was about to lay into him for—but no longer worried. "I only have a minute. Braden's waiting for me in the rig."

"What's wrong is that somehow Edward McTavish knows about the baby." David said nothing, but he did let out a long breath. "I don't suppose you have any clue as to how, do you?"

"Katie, I'm sorry. He tracked me down at work, wanting to make sure you got the letter about the wedding and to see if you were okay after your mom and everything. It slipped out. I'm sorry."

"It slipped out?" It felt good to yell at someone, so I kept going. "The man knows as little about my life as possible—on purpose, David. And of all the things you could have told him, this is what you choose? This?"

David paused, sighing again. "You aren't going to want to hear this, but he seemed genuinely concerned about you. About how the girls were doing without your mom around. Maybe you aren't ready, and maybe you'll never be ready to give him another chance, but it might be time to at least consider it. I really got the impression he wants to—"

"Stop. Stop talking." He stayed quiet, having been married to me long enough to know it was in everyone's best interest to do so. "Edward McTavish wants one thing—to alleviate his guilt. And I have no interest in helping him repent, David. Not by taking his money, or by filling him in on the details of my life so he can try to worm his way into it." I was shaking hard now, the adrenaline coursing through me and making me feel light-headed. Also, the headache was back with a vengeance, the tingling in my fingertips spreading up my forearms.

"I'm sorry. What else can I say? What's done is done, Kate."

"Yeah, thanks for that." Unexpectedly I started crying, which pissed me off even more. But the tears were at least quiet enough I could hide them from David.

"Listen, I really have to go. Can we talk about this when I get home?"

"Fine. Go." I was tired, the fight gone.

As much as I hated to admit it, I knew David had a point. Things were at a crossroads with my father, had been for a while—especially now that Mom was gone—and I had to decide if it was time to end this decades-long moratorium. But even if I wanted to thaw things out between us, I had loathed the idea of him for so long I had no idea where to even start.

Head pounding, I got up from the table and went upstairs, where I regretfully downed a couple of pills, knowing it was necessary, and crawled under the covers. I left the letter where it was, pieces scattered all over the floor under the kitchen table. David could clean it up later.

37

HANNAH

I rolled over and pulled the covers over my head, trying to drown out Clover's scratching and whining. "What time is it?" Ben asked from beside me, his voice rough with sleep.

Reaching my arm out from under the warmth of our bed, I grabbed my phone from the nightstand and pulled it under the duvet. I squinted at the brightly lit screen, then groaned and tossed the covers back. "Clover, it's only six o'clock."

"Want me to take her out?" Ben still sounded groggy, and I knew he'd be back asleep in thirty seconds.

"That's okay—stay in bed. Why should both of us suffer?"

"I love you." He patted my empty side of the bed with an uncoordinated arm.

I opened Clover's crate and gathered her warm, wriggly body in my arms. "Okay, let's go, you." She licked my face with so much enthusiasm I had to laugh, my frustration disintegrating. I let her outside to do her thing and brewed a big pot of coffee, then figured I might as well make the pie while I was up. Today was Kate's thirty-sixth birthday, and she had made one request: she wanted an apple pie and she wanted it all to herself.

With a glance outside to make sure Clover wasn't digging in the garden, I pulled the pastry out of the fridge to let it come up to room temperature while I peeled, cored and sliced the apples. Thirty minutes later the apples were nestled inside the crust, dusted with brown sugar and cinnamon and dotted with dollops of butter. After I braided the delicate pastry ribbons over the pie, brushing the top with melted butter and putting it in the oven, I hopped in the shower. Ben joined me a minute later, and despite my protestations that we didn't have time to do anything but shampoo and lather up, he said, "Come on. What better way is there to start the day?" I relented, which set us back ten minutes—but it was worth it.

With Clover snoring in her crate and the pie cooling on the kitchen island, we raced to the hospital for our breast-feeding class. After having to park in the secondary lot because the hospital was so busy, and another few frantic minutes of trying to find the right room for the class, we stood arguing in the hallway about possibly being on the wrong floor when we heard our names being called. "Hannah and Ben?"

Turning I saw a woman, early fifties with a stylish pixie cut—blond with a shock of hot pink on the front pieces—beckoning us into a room. "Thought that might be you. Come on in. We're about to get started."

"Sorry we're late," I said as we made our way toward her. She wore tight black yoga pants and a fitted long-sleeved shirt with the words *I make milk. What's your superpower?* written across its front.

"Like the shirt," Ben said as we walked into the room.

"Thank you! I have one for all the ladies." She stuck out her hand. "I'm Trudy, the instructor. Nice to meet you both." The room had a large conference table running its length, and Ben and I took the last two seats and smiled and said hello to the other couples already seated.

"Now that we have everyone," Trudy began, and I gave Ben a wry look that he pretended not to see, "I'd like to introduce you to someone." She pulled a soft-bodied doll out of a canvas bag from under the table and a murmur of laughter echoed around the table. "This is Sherry."

Ben nudged me and leaned over, whispering in my ear, "What sort of class did you sign us up for?"

I tried not to laugh, my frustration dwindling with his question and the appearance of the strange-looking doll. Sherry, a breast-feeding prop, looked like a cross between a handmade Cabbage Patch Kids doll and one of those "party" dolls you find at a sex shop. She was the size of a chunky three-month-old, bald with a single pink ribbon sewn to the top of her head, painted on eyes and a nose, and a hole where her mouth was—which made her look as though she was quite surprised to see you. I was afraid to ask about the mouth hole, and looking around the room and hearing the snickers I suspected I wasn't alone in that. Trudy seemed oblivious to the reaction Sherry had on the group, but I imagined she was used to it by now—either that or she really didn't see what the rest of us did.

Soon we were practicing our breast-feeding holds with Sherry, who as it turned out had a hole so we could "finger feed," which is basically taping a tiny tube to your finger to deliver pumped breast milk directly to your baby's mouth.

Though Sherry was supposed to put us at ease, that stupid doll made me worry more about my decision to induce lactation. The positions felt awkward, and no matter how many times Trudy said, "Line Sherry up against you, tummy to tummy, nipple to nose," I fumbled the holds. Ben, who seemed to be allergic to Sherry and the dust mites she probably carried inside her old stuffed body, started to sneeze, and both of us were soon miserable.

Three hours later we were on our way home, a top-of-the-line pump in the trunk of the car and a white T-shirt on my lap—the words *I make milk. What's your superpower?* emblazoned across its front in hot-pink puffy writing. Ben was still stuffed up and feeling like crap, and I was disheartened by my lack of success with Sherry, not to mention starving thanks to the lactation medication I'd been taking for two weeks.

"We need to leave in about fifteen minutes," I said, once we got inside the house. "I told David we'd get there a bit early."

Ben was preoccupied with the pump, trying to figure out what piece went where. "Did you see the instructions?"

I looked around halfheartedly, having no desire to worry about the pump at this exact moment. "Let's do it when we get home. I need to change."

"You go. I'm okay like this," Ben murmured, pulling out a plastic-encased brochure from the pump's carrying case.

I sighed but let it go. I needed to start pumping in a couple of weeks and knew he was only trying to help. Ten minutes later I came back down the stairs, dressed for the party and brushing out my hair, then stopped dead on the second to last stair, staring at Ben—who was shirtless.

"What the hell are you doing?"

He grinned and pointed at the suction pieces of the pump. "I'm testing it out." He turned on the pump, which was louder than I expected.

"You are not!" I laughed and stepped into the living room.

"What? You think you get to have all the fun?" He winked and picked up the cone-shaped suction cups that attached to the bottles. He placed them against his chest so his nipples were fully covered by the silicone cups. His eyes widened and he grimaced. "Holy shit." The pump made a rhythmic swooshing sound, and I could see his skin being pulled in and out of the cups.

I cringed and sat down across from him. "What? What does it feel like?"

His grimace turned to full-blown panic. "Get it off!" he shouted, but I was laughing so hard I had to keep my legs crossed so I wouldn't pee. He was trying to pull the cups off, clearly forgetting all he had to do was shut the machine down. I reached over and flicked the switch, and relief flooded his face. When he took the cups off, his skin had deep red circles surrounding his nipples, which made me laugh even harder.

"Do not tell anyone about this," Ben said, rubbing his chest. He pulled his shirt back on and frowned at the pump.

"Babe, trust me. I don't *want* to tell anyone about this." I snickered again, and he glared at me.

"I don't know how you're going to use that thing six times a day. It *hurts*."

I shrugged. "Whatever it takes." Opening the fridge, I pulled the cupcakes out and set them on the countertop. "And apparently a baby's suction is even more intense."

"I have no idea how that's possible," Ben said; then he lifted up the breast-feeding T-shirt from the couch where I'd dropped it. "You deserve this shirt. You should wear it everywhere you go, forever."

Smiling, I handed him the pie carrier. "Thanks, but I think I'll save that for sleeping. Not everyone in the world needs to know I'm lactating."

He glanced back at the pump and shuddered dramatically, and I laughed again as we headed out the door.

38

KATE

"Milk or OJ, girls?" I stood in front of the fridge, waiting for their answer.

"Juice," Ava shouted back.

"Milk, and one of Auntie Hannah's cupcakes please," Josie added. I grabbed the carton of milk and jug of orange juice, and kicked the fridge door shut with my foot.

"Your dad ate the last cupcake last night."

"Dad, no fair!" Josie pouted, crossing her arms over her little puffed-out chest.

"You've had so many you were at risk of turning into a cupcake," David said. "I *saved you* by eating that last one. *You're welcome.*"

Josie continued to complain, and I smiled as I poured her milk. Hannah had made two-dozen cupcakes, of which we'd eaten close to a dozen in the past few days since my birthday, and I didn't tell the girls I had the second dozen in the freezer. Those I was planning to use for bribes as needed.

"What's this babysitter's name again?" David asked.

A sharp pain moved across my forehead, and I gasped,

then put my hand to the spot and rubbed firmly a few times. Thankfully the pain subsided a moment later.

"You all right?" David asked, watching me.

"Yeah, fine. Babysitter's name... Jennifer. No wait, Janet? Shit, I can't remember. It's here somewhere." I went to grab my phone, lying atop the kitchen island, but for some reason my arm wasn't working right. It felt heavy and didn't want to move. "David, something weird is..."

"What?" David asked, but he wasn't looking at me now. He was reading something on his phone, his head down.

I tried to use my other arm to pick up my phone, and that's when the headache hit. Nothing like from a moment ago. This pain was blinding—bold and terrifying, like a thunderclap. I tried to tell David something was wrong, my skull was going to explode, but the words came out garbled and incomplete. His head snapped up and he looked at me in a way that scared me. I tried to speak again, but the pain made it impossible and I buckled to my knees, knocking the opened juice jug over in the process.

In a flash David was beside me, orange juice soaking into the knees of his jeans and the cotton fabric of my dress, which meant on top of everything else I would have to change before we went over to Hannah and Ben's. David shouted my name, repeatedly, telling me to keep my eyes open, to look at him. Someone was crying, maybe me. I hoped it wasn't one of the girls. I wanted to tell David to be quiet, because his voice was so loud and this was the worst headache I had ever had. But I couldn't speak, couldn't move, and then a thick black curtain moved across my vision and everything went dark.

39

Kate remains blissfully unaware of the frightening chaos her collapse creates. The whole time, she's unconscious. Through those frantic minutes waiting for the ambulance, while the girls sob and David desperately tries to get her to open her eyes, to wake up, to stay with him. Through the ambulance ride, which is scary fast with sirens blaring. Through the rush of the emergency room, where doctors explain to David in calm yet concerned voices she's suffered a ruptured aneurysm and has bleeding into her brain. Soon words like *subarachnoid hemorrhage* and *craniotomy* and *Glasgow Coma Scale* are tossed about in tense tones while Kate lies nearby, a plastic tube down her throat attached to a ventilator that keeps her breathing.

She misses the look of horror and disbelief on David's face when the doctors discuss the surgical options. The pregnancy complicates things, they explain, and the next twenty-four hours will be critical in getting the aneurysm secured. So while one surgery has a better outcome, it's riskier because of the amount of radiation involved—riskier to the fetus, the surgeon clarifies. Kate would be happy not to hear David ask if delivering the baby now, today, would help—she couldn't have forgiven him for making that decision without her consent, without considering Hannah and Ben's wishes, at only twenty-six weeks. Thankfully he's told probably not, and so the baby stays put.

"She's lucky," they tell David—about a third of people with ruptured aneurysms die instantly. When David asks about the other two-thirds, the doctors manage to hold eye contact when they say half of those patients die in the hospital. Unfortunately, it's impossible to say which of those last two groups Kate will be in, and David can barely stay upright when they tell him this.

Decisions are made, without Kate's opinion or consent. They will do the clip surgery—in the next few hours, or as soon as they can get an operating room prepped. It sounds dangerous, though leaving the aneurysm to continue bleeding into Kate's brain is the more dangerous of the two scenarios. They expect it will be successful, as she is apparently a good candidate.

For now the baby is safe, somehow unaffected by the storm taking place in Kate's body. They'll monitor him, too, and do all they can to minimize the effects. If Kate were awake and able to say it, she would thank them for thinking of the baby.

It's a precarious situation, and if Kate knew at all what was happening, her heart would break for David. Three hours ago they were getting ready to go to Hannah and Ben's for game night. Three hours ago she was a thirty-six-year-old pregnant woman whose biggest concern was a looming migraine that medication thankfully dulled, and who had an inability to remember the babysitter's name. Three hours ago she was a healthy and happy mom, simply trying to help her best friend experience the joy of motherhood. Three hours ago she had no idea the risk she had taken, or what it would mean for all their futures.

40

I haven't taken a proper, full breath since David's phone call from the hospital fewer than thirty minutes ago. In a rush Ben and I are out the door, chicken strips left half-cooked in the pan, a blender full of now half-melted ice, Clover left out of her crate in our haste to leave, front door unlocked and lights left on.

Upon our arrival, we find the ER jammed, as expected. We dodge the line like David told us to, pushing quickly through the doors that lead past the waiting room full of sick, bleeding and miserable people. I'm having a hard time catching my breath, the reality of what's happened strangling me. Ben holds my hand and tugs me forward, and I will myself not to cry. I don't want to cry in front of Kate.

And then I see David. His back is to us, but I recognize his close-cropped blond hair and the two roman numeral tattoos on the back of his neck, which represent his daughters' birth dates. He's standing before another set of doors, so still people trying to get by are forced to move around him.

"David!" He turns at the sound of my voice, and as he does,

I stop moving and my hand drops from Ben's. David's face is pale, in stark contrast to his eyes, which are red and swollen, the way Ben's get when he spends more than five minutes in a house with a cat. He looks awful. Ben gets to him first and hugs him, but David doesn't take his eyes off me. They are so green, so wet, the way lush grass looks after a rainstorm.

I still can't catch my breath. But I move forward until I'm standing beside them. *Kate.*

"Where is she?" Ben asks softly, close to David's face.

David gestures behind him, his arm waving around haphazardly, as if it has been deboned. "They took her."

"Where? Where did they take her, David?"

I stare at David, and I know. It's bad. He starts to cry again, and Ben holds on to him tightly to keep him upright, shooting me a panicked look over David's head.

"David, where's Kate?" My voice comes out loud. Too loud. Almost angry. But I'm not angry. I'm terrified.

"They took her. She's… They took her, back there. It happened so…fast." He sobs, then retches, but nothing comes up. Ben, looking stricken, keeps his grip on David.

My legs give out, and I fall to the scuff-marked linoleum floor, and though there's another question I desperately need David to answer—*What about the baby?*—I lose consciousness before I can get it out.

There's a lot of commotion. I'm being lifted, strong hands under my armpits and behind my knees. I can't focus on any one thing, so I don't bother trying. My eyes are still closed, but I can smell Ben. Or more specifically, his breath. Pungent with onion and jalapeño peppers from the guacamole, it tickles at the darkness behind my eyes as he calls my name, over and over. But I stay where I am, in this strange, oblivious place. Eyes closed. Remembering the first time I met Kate.

It's my third day of fifth grade, and the summer's heat is still going strong. It's so hot that teachers bring in fans from home, along with banana, cherry and orange popsicles for recess that melt faster than we can eat them. I'm at a new school this year, having moved during the summer, after Dad died. Mom is no longer able to take care of us without the help of my grandparents, who live in Marin County—Mill Valley specifically—in a house that feels as if it wasn't meant for children. So far I have made exactly one friend at my new school. A girl named Ruby Thoms, who wears thick glasses but has a kind face and really nice teeth. I'm waiting for Ruby outside the restroom, holding her backpack, when I see Kate.

She's short and curvy, which I notice first because I'm not, and pretty enough that she stands out right away. Big brown eyes and dark hair cut in a pageboy, with a silver elastic headband tucked behind her ears. I watch as she brushes a stray piece of bang back from her face, smiling at a passing teacher as she does. Because she's watching the teacher, and the hallway is busy with traffic of students coming and going to class, she doesn't see the boy off to her side, with a mirror crudely taped to a piece of a hockey stick positioned so he can see up her skirt.

But I do.

Before I even realize what I'm doing, I stride over to where Kate stands and with my hands on my hips, turn to the boy and very loudly say, "What exactly do you think you're doing?"

Kate, surprised by my arrival, looks at me before looking at the boy, who smirks at my question.

"None of your business."

"He's looking up your skirt with that thing," I say, pointing to the hockey stick and mirror, which the boy is trying to tuck behind his back. Two other boys flanking him on either side start to chuckle.

"Darren, you little pervert!" Kate shouts at him, which just makes the group of them laugh harder.

I see red, and my fingers grip tighter on Ruby's backpack straps.

Ever since my dad died, swiftly but painfully of pancreatic cancer, I've been having what the therapist—whom my mom forced me and Claire to see—calls "grief outbursts," but are really temper tantrums. However, "tantrum" sounds too juvenile for a ten-year-old, so the therapist and my mom agreed to a term they felt more appropriate.

"Not much to see, anyway," Darren says. "Except some pretty ugly granny panties covering a fat ass!"

Kate's face falls, and without thinking, I swing Ruby's backpack—which is heavy enough to set me off balance—hitting Darren right under the chin. He looks shocked for a moment, then his chin splits open—unfortunately for him, and I suppose for me once my mom finds out, it's the heavy combination lock Ruby keeps on her backpack's zippers that connects to Darren's face first—and blood pours swiftly onto his shirt. I stare at him, also in shock at what I've done but exhilarated at the same time.

Darren starts to cry, his friends crowding around him and shouting for help, and Kate grabs my hand and pulls me into the girls' bathroom. Ruby is washing her hands and looks surprised to see us burst in. I'm out of breath, dizzy from adrenaline and pretty sure I'm going to be grounded for a long time when I get home. But I don't care about any of that when Kate envelops me in a hug, squeezing so tight I can barely breathe. I feel more alive than I have in a long time, or at least since my dad died, and I don't want the sensation to ever go away.

"Thank you," Kate whispers, squeezing tighter. "You are now my best friend forever."

I have no clue how much time has passed, but I come to with a jolt. As if someone has tossed ice water on me. I'm lying on a stretcher in the ER, Ben hovering over me.

"What happened?" I sit up, then immediately fall back on bent elbows as a wave of dizziness engulfs me. My head hurts at the back, and my fingers find a small lump under my hair.

Ben puts an arm behind my back and eases me back onto the stretcher. "Just lie back. You're fine."

It all lands back into my consciousness. *Kate.* Something terrible has happened to Kate.

"Where's Kate?"

At this he pulls his eyes away from my face, and my heart rate speeds up. I'm trying to prepare myself for news I don't want to hear, but it's difficult to stay focused on Ben's face.

"She's alive," he begins, and a sound somewhere between a gasp and a sob explodes out of me. His eyes cut to mine quickly, stormy sky blue and worried. "David said she was fine and then just collapsed."

I have no idea how to deal with this. So many questions circle my mind, tornado-fast and impossible to pin down. "The baby?" My voice is thin, weak with fear. I clutch Ben's hands and hold my breath.

"The baby is fine," he says, the smallest of smiles coming across his face before quickly dropping away. "He's apparently just fine."

"But Kate..." My heart flutters uncomfortably.

He looks grim. "Kate is being taken care of. That's all we know for sure."

"Can we see her? I need to see her." I get up again, and this time things stay in focus. Ben holds my elbow tightly as I slide off the stretcher. He asks if I'm okay; I nod and repeat that I need to see Kate.

"I don't think we can yet. She's...she's unconscious. They only just let David go back with her." Ben watches me closely, keeping his hands on my elbows. "How are you feeling? You scared the shit out of me when you passed out."

"Fine. I'm fine," I say, irritation flooding my voice. How I'm feeling is of little importance right now. "What can we do? I can't just stand here waiting." I'm agitated, shifting from one foot to the other.

"David gave me his phone and asked me to call a few people."

A thought lands in my mind, and I nearly buckle again. "The girls, Ben. The girls."

"They're with the babysitter. He had to leave them with her when the ambulance came."

"They must be so upset," I say, pacing in the tiny room. "Here's what I'm going to do. You make the calls, and I'm going to look for David and try to find out what's going on. Okay?"

"Sounds good," Ben says, pulling David's phone out of his back pocket. "Hannah?"

"Yeah?"

"She's going to be fine."

"I know she is. Now go. I'll see you soon."

I watch Ben leave back through the doors leading to the waiting room, and then lean my forehead against the wall—the celery-green paint a surprisingly calming color when viewed so up close. Keeping my eyes on a tiny spot where the green paint has flecked off to reveal an apricot color below, I count to ten and try to find the strength to stand up straight again. I need to move, to find out where they took Kate, to see what David knows. But every ounce of energy has left my body, leaving in its place a deep sense of dread. Because no matter how many times I play the "Kate is going to be okay" track in my mind, my gut is telling me something different.

41

Growing up in San Francisco means living with the reality that the next earthquake could be the "big" one. In school we learned Southern California has about ten thousand earthquakes a year, which basically means you'd never hang any sort of picture or mirror at the head of the bed, and safely strapping table lamps to side tables is perfectly normal—as is having gallons of water stored in closets and under sinks. If you eat the supply of candy bars in the emergency earthquake kit, you're sure to be grounded for weeks. It's simply part of life, and generally you put it out of your mind.

But in the first few years after Dad died I became anxious about all sorts of things I hadn't worried about before. There were obvious ones, like getting cancer myself or having my mom or Claire or my grandmother die. But one unexpected thing that consumed my thoughts during that time was the risk of a devastating earthquake. I became obsessed with the screws holding the straps down—checking them every morning to make sure they hadn't loosened overnight. I timed how long it took to get from my bed to the closet, where I would hide if an earthquake struck while I slept. I quizzed my mom, sister and grandparents on the safest places in our house to take cover. They indulged me, even though I'm sure they talked in concerned, hushed tones about my mental state when I wasn't listening.

Later, when I looked back at that time in my life I realized it had a lot to do with lack of control—I mean, is there anything you have less control over than seismic activity? It's not that everyone doesn't talk nonstop about earthquakes when they happen, or worry about them, but it can't be an all-consuming anxiety. If it is, you're going to need to move somewhere else.

Technically, the quake that struck the October I was thirteen wasn't all that bad—a magnitude 4.9, which caused a feeling of the ground suddenly shifting underfoot, and the rattling of cups and dishes in my grandparents' kitchen cupboards. It was a Saturday, and Kate was over so we could work on our science project, which was due the following week. We were trying to power a clock with a lemon, and had just completed the circuit—to a round of cheering as the second hand started moving—when it happened.

At first I thought a big truck was going by—the vibration and rattle I felt through the wood floors into my bare feet didn't initially cause me to panic. But then the world tilted slightly, and our alarm clock attached to two lemons slid off the kitchen table, crashing to the floor. I screamed so loud my throat hurt, but I stayed statue still—fear locking up my limbs.

Kate, however, was quick and confident. She grabbed me by the shoulders—even though I was significantly taller than she was—and pulled down hard until my knees gave out and I fell to the ground. Then she dragged me under the kitchen table and while the table rattled and the kitchen came alive with sounds of dishes doing an earthquake dance, she shouted at me to hold one of the table legs and hang on tightly. I did as

I was told, the physical memory of clutching a table leg while crouched into a ball on the ground coming back to me—we had just done a "Drop, cover, hold on!" drill at school the week before.

I didn't realize I was crying until Kate let go of her table leg and came to crouch beside me—holding on to me instead of the much sturdier wooden table. "Shhhh, shhhh," she murmured into my ear while I sobbed. "It's almost over."

And in another ten seconds it was done. Everything stopped shaking. The kitchen quieted, and then got noisy again when my mom and grandmother came rushing down the stairs to make sure we were okay.

Kate didn't make a big deal out of what happened, simply asked my grandmother where she kept her broom and dustpan to clean up the smashed glass from the front of the alarm clock. Then she asked me to go out back and pick another two lemons from the tree and proceeded to sweep up the glass while excitedly telling my mom about how well the experiment had worked. My mom said she'd go get us another alarm clock at the store, and as I walked to the backyard to pick the lemons, I decided not to be afraid of earthquakes anymore.

Leaning against that celery-green hospital wall, I have the sudden desire to hide under a table or one of the gurneys. To have something solid to hang on to until the shaking stops— until I know Kate is okay, our baby is fine and life goes back to normal.

42

I compose myself and find someone willing and able to give me information, but all they can tell me is that Kate is with the doctors. David is nowhere to be found, and I expect it's because he's wherever Kate is. Heading back to the waiting room I find Ben sitting in one of the chairs, David's phone in his hand and the same bleak look on his face.

"Do you know anything else?" I ask.

He shakes his head, then puts his free hand on my knee when I sit beside him. "You?"

"No one would tell me anything except that she's with the doctors," I say.

"I called Cora. She's on her way to stay with the girls."

"Is the babysitter still with them?"

"She is. I just spoke with her and everything is okay there."

"I'm glad Cora's on her way, but maybe one of us should—"

"I'll go. You stay here." Ben gives me a quick hug and hands me David's phone. "But call me the second you know anything more. I'll come back after his mom gets there."

He kisses me, lingering for a moment and holding my face close to his once our lips part. "I love you."

"I love you, too."

"See you soon."

And then he's gone, back through the ER doors and sprinting toward the parking garage.

An hour later, Ben calls to let me know he's sent the babysitter home and is playing video games with the girls while they wait for their grandmother to show up. Kate has gone up to surgery, I tell him, and David and I are told it could take anywhere from three to five hours.

I've finally been able to get some information on her condition and that of the baby, thanks to the guardianship document Kate filled out with the fertility attorney—which essentially gives me and Ben medical decision-making power on the baby's behalf, as his intended parents. I've kept a copy in my purse because our attorney told me to, which seemed unnecessarily cautious at the time but something I'm now grateful for—without that document I'd still be cast out in the waiting room, panicking about Kate and the baby.

David sits opposite me in the surgical waiting room in a vinyl chair with wooden arms, one leg bouncing up and down, up and down. He leans his elbows on the armrests, and when he sits back I can see red groove lines on his forearms from the pressure.

We're currently the only ones waiting, but signs of people having been here recently litter the space—on one side table there's a take-out cup half-full of coffee with a deep pink lipstick stain on the rim, a candy bar wrapper lying beside it. Magazines are strewn across the other table, and I consider picking one up to try and distract myself. But then I see the magazine on top—a parenting issue with a cherub-cheeked, blue-eyed infant on the front cover holding a yellow rubber duck—and I turn away so I don't have to look at the happy baby.

Glancing at the clock on the wall I see another five minutes have passed, and I become irrationally angry at how slowly things are moving. I sense David feels the same, as he keeps staring at his watch and bouncing his knees. Then in a rush he's up and pacing the room.

"You okay?" I feel stupid as soon as I ask. "No, of course you're not."

"I should have pushed her about the headaches," David says, still pacing and seeming to have not heard a word I've said. "I'm a fucking paramedic. I should have known something wasn't right."

I stand up but stay put because his pacing is erratic—he's more circling the room than going back and forth now—and I don't want to make things worse by getting in his way. "David, there's no way you could have known about the aneurysm. Her migraines were worse when she was pregnant with the girls, too. Why would you think these were any different?"

He's mumbling now, hand running over his skull, pausing on his neck to rub the spot decorated by the tattoos. "Maybe if I had made her see the doctor, maybe they would have scanned her? Figured it out."

I put my hand on his arm and am nearly pulled over when he doesn't break his pace. "David, stop. There is nothing you could have done. Nothing anyone could have done. And even if you made her see a doctor, they would have never suspected an aneurysm. She's had migraines her whole life. They would have just thought these headaches were pregnancy related."

"Exactly, Hannah." He stops abruptly and stands in front of me, his eyes wild with worry. "Everyone would have thought they were pregnancy related. And maybe if she weren't pregnant, none of us would have written these migraines off. Maybe then she would have had a workup. Maybe then..."

Swallowing my own guilt, knowing exactly where he's

going even though he stopped just short of coming right out with it, I sit back down and duck my head. "No one could have seen this coming. No one. Not the doctors, not you, not me—"

"She did this for you!" he shouts, the room too small for the loudness of his voice. He's as far away from me as he can get, standing in a corner on the other side of the room beside a potted plant I'm fairly certain is fake. But I can see him quivering—with shock, fear or anger, I can't be sure. "She did this for you, Hannah."

I think about what I should do—apologize? Hug him? No, I'm too shocked to do anything but sit there, gaping at him. My instincts tell me to fight the accusation—to stand up for myself and tell him he's not the only one who's scared. That what's happening to Kate is not my fault. That she had been determined to do this. That it had been her idea from the beginning.

But the problem is he's said exactly what I've been thinking since I found out Kate collapsed. She did this for me. And here we are.

Before I can sort out the right thing to say David turns and walks out of the waiting room, smacking his palm on the door frame as he does, causing me to jump. A moment later I am alone with my thoughts and my guilt.

David still hasn't returned an hour later and I'm having a hard time sitting still. So I pull out my phone and make the call I probably should have made—to Todd & Associates and our attorney—the second we learned Kate was hospitalized.

It's only when her voice mail picks up that I realize how late it is. Nearly 11:00 p.m. She has likely left the office hours ago. I leave a message regardless.

"Hi, Annabel, it's Hannah Matthews calling." I pause for

a moment to try to figure out how to be brief with the message. "I know it's late, but I'm at the hospital. There's been a... complication and I need some advice. Could you call my cell as soon as you get the message? Thanks. Thank you."

I hit End Call and, still restless, grab some change from my purse and buy a soda from the machine. The sickly sweet liquid is cold and the bubbles burn the back of my throat when I take a sip. Then I sit down and finish the can as quickly as I can, knowing I need the caffeine and sugar to keep me going until Kate is out of surgery.

My phone rings a few minutes later. Glancing at the screen, I see "Todd & Associates."

"Hello?"

"Hannah? It's Annabel Porter. What's going on? Are you and Ben okay?"

"Thank you for calling me back so fast, Annabel." I resist the urge to burp from the soda, which I'm now regretting— the sweet, fizzy liquid sloshing in my otherwise empty stomach. "Ben and I are okay, but it's the baby and I'm not sure what we should be doing."

"What's happened? Is the baby okay?"

"He's fine. But it's...it's Kate." I take a deep breath. "She collapsed at home tonight from a ruptured aneurysm. She's in surgery right now."

"Oh, Hannah. I'm so sorry. How are you doing?"

"Not good, if I'm being honest," I say, sucking in another deep breath.

"Tell me, what do you need from me?" Annabel's voice is strong yet soothing, and I feel my shoulders relax.

"Is there anything we need to do, in terms of the baby and keeping him safe?" I cringe as I say it, hating that I can't just focus on what Kate needs right now, what David needs.

"Has a neonatologist been assigned to the case yet?"

"I'm not sure." I'm flustered and shaky. "Things moved pretty quickly once they brought Kate in. They—" My voice catches, and I try to swallow around it. "They're trying to save her life."

"I'm so sorry, Hannah."

I nod, ducking my head as the tears drop. "I gave the guardianship document to the nurse, which thank you for insisting I keep in my purse. I never could have imagined…well, any of this."

"Good, that was going to be my first suggestion. That document means the doctors will work with you and Ben when it comes to the baby's medical decisions. Now remember, Kate's needs will take precedence over the baby's, but at least you'll be privy to what's happening from here on out."

I nod again, not trusting my voice. "Let me pull out the contracts and sort a few things out, okay?" She pauses and I hold my breath, though I'm not sure why. "For now, focus on Kate and David, and take care of yourself. I'll talk with you as soon as I have more information."

"Thanks, Annabel. I appreciate it." After we hang up I go back to waiting alone, trapped with my own thoughts, longing for a distraction and hoping it comes in the form of good news about Kate.

Despite Mina's doomsday speech, and the horrifying scenarios we had to deliberate ad nauseam as part of the surrogacy contract, I never imagined this—waiting for news that my best friend, and my baby inside her, survived brain surgery. I suppose no one gives more than a fleeting thought to the fine print—like the zip-line waivers Ben and I signed on our honeymoon in Jamaica, which outlined a laundry list of risks we joked and laughed about, drunk on fresh love and so certain about the future.

"I'll still love you even if you fall and lose both your legs," I'd said.

"And I'll feed you soup through a straw if you break every bone in your body," he'd told me, kissing my bare, sun-kissed shoulder as he scrawled his name on the form.

Because when does the worst-case scenario ever really happen? It doesn't.

Except when it does.

I clutch the chair's armrests and take a deep breath. Then another.

Breathe.

I force myself to contemplate the worst-case scenario.

Breathe.

Kate doesn't survive her surgery.

Breathe.

We lose the baby.

Breathe.

I sit in the painfully quiet waiting room, alone—imagining David as he anxiously paces another hallway, and Ben as he stares at the television without really watching while the girls sleep, waiting for Cora, and Annabel Porter as she sends copies of our contract to the hospital administration and speaks with the neonatologist assigned to our case.

I keep breathing, because I can. Because while this horrible thing has happened, it hasn't happened to me. I am not lying on an operating table, a piece of my skull cut out and doctors' hands inside my brain trying to save my life.

I am still an intended mother. And our baby—trapped inside Kate's sick body, alive until someone tells us otherwise— needs me.

My next breath nearly strangles me, my eyes popping open in panic. With sickening clarity I realize my guilt isn't about Kate being on that operating table because she's carrying a child for me; it's because if I had to choose, right in this moment, from the deepest, most raw and honest corner of my soul, I would choose my baby.

I just make it to the trash can, beside the definitely fake potted plant, before I purge the soda from my guilt-racked stomach.

43

Four hours after they take her in, Kate is out of surgery. "Things went as well as they could have," her surgeon says, standing in front of the three of us in the waiting room. "We'll be watching her carefully, especially for the next twenty-four, forty-eight hours, but we did secure the aneurysm and stopped the bleeding. She's in recovery now."

"Is she awake? Can I see her?" David asks, relief flooding his voice.

The surgeon, whose name I can't remember, nods. "She's still unconscious, but you can see her. Just the husband for now, okay, folks?" He shakes David's outstretched hand, accepting his thanks with a warm smile, and is about to walk out when I stop him.

"How's the baby?"

He looks surprised the question comes from me. "The neonatologist will speak with you soon," he says, looking at David. "But I can tell you the baby is doing just fine. He's a fighter, like his mom." The surgeon smiles again, somehow unaware of our situation even though it should be written on Kate's file.

"I'm actually his mom," I say, my voice as steady as I can make it. "And we have a guardianship document that says all decisions about the baby are to be made by me and my husband." I see David visibly stiffen, and Ben shifts beside me. "So I would appreciate the updates about our son coming directly to us."

The surgeon's mouth opens, closes, and then he recovers beautifully with another well-timed smile. "I see. Well, as I said, the baby is doing well and the neonatologist will speak with you shortly." This time he holds my gaze.

"Thank you," I say, lacing my fingers through Ben's, which feel limp and disengaged.

David says nothing further as he follows the surgeon out of the room, and I sit down to wait for the neonatologist, my heart hammering in my chest.

"What are you doing?"

I look up at Ben. "What do you mean?"

"I mean, why are you making a thing of this right now. In front of David?"

My face pulls down into a frown, and I stand to face Ben. "Because I am his mother, and you are his father, and that is what we are supposed to do, Ben. We're supposed to protect him. To speak for him."

"Kate just got out of brain surgery, Hannah. She almost died. And we don't even know what's happening with her. So Kate needs us, too. She needs us to take care of David, not make this harder for him than it already is."

"How am I making things harder by asking about our child's welfare?" I am on the verge of collapse, of a breakdown I know I need but don't want to have.

"Because you didn't even ask about Kate," Ben shouts, incredulous. "You barely acknowledged the success of the surgery."

I square my shoulders and let the breakdown come. "I have

done nothing for these past three hours except sit beside David, who blames me at least in part for what's happening right now, and think about Kate. About how much I love her. And how badly I need her. And how horribly I've let her down. About how—" I can't continue, can't speak through my tears.

I take a jagged breath. "About how they might have found the aneurysm if she wasn't pregnant. David said it, and he's right. If her migraines were worse and there was no baby, then they might have checked into it. But the baby protected that aneurysm—don't you get it? She did this great thing for me, and it nearly killed her. And I can't do anything—*anything*—to change that."

Ben sits so quickly it startles me. His eyes are glassy and stare straight ahead. "I know," he whispers. "But I keep thinking, what would I do if it were you in there? How would I cope if your life were the one at risk? I want to be this baby's dad, to do the right thing by him. Of course I do. But I don't know him. I don't know what to do for him." He shakes his head and starts to cry. I drop to my knees in front of him and take his hands in mine. "Am I a dad even if he's not here yet?"

"Of course you are," I murmur, rubbing his hands and wiping my dripping nose against the upper sleeve of my sweater. "You were a dad the moment Kate got the positive pregnancy test."

He squeezes my hands and nods. "I'm sorry."

"For what?"

"For questioning you about all this. You're right. We can't help Kate, not exactly, but we can help our son. But we have to consider David, too, as we do that, okay?"

"Okay," I say, burying my face in his lap, feeling him lean down to hold me. We stay like that until a nurse comes to find us, saying Kate is settled in the ICU and we can see her now.

44

David stands over Kate's bed, his back to me, so I can't yet see her. I want so badly to turn and run away, back to my kitchen where a half-eaten dish of guacamole and melted margaritas and shriveled chicken strips that will now never become fajitas are waiting for all of us. Back where Clover is my biggest irritation, and waiting for the birth of our son my greatest anticipation. I'm terrified of what waits for me beyond the sliding glass panels that front Kate's room, unsure about what to say to David, how to apologize for earlier. And yet, where would I run to even if I could? This is the only place I can be.

I take a deep breath and knock on the door frame. David turns toward me, and then I see her. She's so tiny and pale in contrast to her dark hair, which now only covers half her head—the other half is shaved bald, with bandages thankfully covering some of the evidence of the craniotomy. There are tubes and wires crisscrossing her body and leading to an inordinate number of machines that surround her bed like a halo. And along with the ventilator snaking from her mouth, there's a drain tube coming out of her head that makes me squeamish to look at. I can't help it—my hand flies to my mouth and I choke back a sob.

"She's a bit swollen and bruised," David says, and I nod as calmly as I can. Her face and neck do look mottled and puffy, like she just had her wisdom teeth out or had an allergic reaction to something. "It's from the surgery."

And then I notice the bump of her belly, and the machine tracing the baby's heartbeat, and I start to cry. As relief floods through me I look back to Kate's face, feeling disloyal.

"I know it's hard to see her like this." David comes and stands beside me, leading me into one of the chairs against the wall. "But she's stable, and that's the best news we could get right now, okay?"

I wonder how he's holding it together so well. He sighs and scrubs his hands over his face, and then I know he's only holding it together because there's no other option.

"About earlier…in the waiting room with the surgeon—"

David stops me. "It's okay, Hannah. You had every right to ask about the baby."

"I hope you know I didn't mean to take anything away from…from what's happening with Kate."

He keeps his gaze on the bed, the tubes, his wife. "I know."

I look back at the bed, trying to find in it the Kate I know and love. But reconciling my vivacious friend with the frighteningly still figure, dwarfed by the medical equipment, is hard to do.

"It was just a migraine, like all the others. And she really seemed okay, Hannah. But then…she just wasn't." David's voice catches and I go to him, wrapping an arm around his shaking shoulders. "She was trying to remember the babysitter's name, and I was reading an email on my phone. And then she said something but it didn't make sense, it was gibberish. A second later she collapsed."

I nod, my heart beating furiously, imagining that moment. "Did you talk to your mom? How are the girls doing?"

"Very briefly. The girls aren't great. Ava is really struggling, she said, and they're both freaked out by what they saw, but they're hanging in there." Kate would be horrified to know her girls had witnessed her collapse, that they'd probably have nightmares now about the moment they watched their mom fall to the ground unconscious. I bite my lip, holding back another round of tears.

"And how about you?" I ask once I have control of myself again. "How are you doing?"

He shrugs, which is probably the best he can do. If it were Ben in that bed...well, I'd be on the floor and catatonic.

"Anything new from the doctors?" I ask, shifting my thoughts back to David and Kate.

"They said..." He exhales loudly, then tilts his head back, eyes closing. "God, they said so many things. And most of them aren't good."

I swallow rapidly, pushing back the bile that rises up in my throat.

"They keep saying they're happy with how well the surgery went." He rubs his thumb over the top of Kate's hand. "Which really tells me they didn't expect her to live through it." His shoulders shake, and I stare at the tattoos on the back of his neck before leaning in to hug him from behind. Kate was furious after he got the first tattoo, saying if he was going to forever mark his body, couldn't he of least have done it somewhere the whole world couldn't see? But I know she came to love those tattoos—it wasn't just ink needled under his skin; the tattoos were like love letters to his girls, proudly on display.

"They've blocked the bleed, which was our immediate worry. But we won't know how much damage—" David bows his head. "How much damage the blood caused. To her brain. And even though it's secured, it could rerupture." I don't ask what happens if the aneurysm starts bleeding again. I can only guess that would mean very bad things for Kate. "And she's at risk for all kinds of things, like a heart attack, bleeding disorders, stroke, brain swelling." He takes a deep breath. "It's a fucking mess, Hannah. She's a mess. Which is crazy because half a day ago she was perfect. Perfect."

I try to steer the conversation back to a place where I can remain even the slightest bit detached. "So what happens now?"

"Now we wait," he says, adding a moment later, "I can't believe this is happening."

"You and me both." I squeeze his shoulders again and try not to look at the tattoos. I can't think about Kate's girls right now. "Did they say anything about the coma? About how long they think she might be unconscious?"

David turns to look at me, and something in his expression makes my stomach drop. "Hannah—"

"People can recover from brain injuries," I begin, feeling panicky. "My uncle had a pretty bad stroke, and he's fine except for a little shaking in his one hand. And he's in his sixties. Kate's only thirty-six. There must be someth—" My throat closes and the word gets caught. "That has to count for something. Right?" And running through the back of my mind is the baby. What happens to the baby if Kate stays in her coma?

"They don't know if she's going to wake up," he says, so quietly I have to lean in to hear him over the monotonous whir of machinery currently keeping Kate's body working.

"They're wrong," I say, my teeth chattering with my own shaking. I've held it in too long. "They don't know Katie like we do. She's tough. She's going to pull through this."

"She is tough," David says, nodding. "But her body is under a lot of strain right now, with the surgery and…the pregnancy."

His choice of the word *pregnancy* versus *baby* sticks with me, leaving me with an uncomfortable feeling. It seems purposeful, and it makes my stomach hurt like I ate a too-spicy pepper.

"We need to talk about that," he says, his words slow and methodical.

"About what?"

"The pregnancy," David says.

The panic rises inside me like a tidal wave, but I try not to let it show on my face. "Why? Did they tell you something about the baby?" I'm instantly furious the hospital seems to be ignoring our guardianship documentation, and my request to be the first to know any updates on our son.

"Not exactly," he says. "The truth is they can't say for sure if it's making this more difficult."

"Making what exactly more difficult?" I'm confused now, my mind spinning. "I thought they said everything with the baby was fine?"

"The baby is fine," he says, staring back at Kate's face. I stare at her stomach, at the bulge under the sheet. "But I don't think the pregnancy is helping things, Hannah. Her body doesn't need any extra stress right now."

My hands drop off his shoulders, and I take a step back. I don't mean to do it, it just happens. Like I need to distance myself from him, from what he's about to say next.

"So I just wanted you to know we may need to do something about that."

45

And just like that, David goes from being…well, *David*, to a person I feel nervous around—like I'm suddenly standing outside the previously cozy circle of our friendship, unaware of what he's thinking, scared about the decisions he might make.

As soon as he says those words, *we may need to do something about that*, I back away from him and out of the room without explanation. I race past Ben, who stands in the hallway outside the ICU, talking on his own phone. My cell is already ringing as I press it tightly to my ear, ignoring Ben as he calls out my name.

Once Annabel picks up on the other end, I stumble and stutter around my words, panicking about the guardianship document but more so about my influence as the baby's mother. She assures me the document stands—Ben and I will make all medical decisions regarding the baby.

"I know, I know, of course, of course," I say when she reminds me Kate's needs take precedence, and David will make medical decisions for her while she can't. "It isn't about not wanting the very best for Kate. It's about also wanting the very best for my boy. Do the two have to be mutually exclusive?" I ask.

"Let's not get ahead of ourselves," she tells me, and I'm not sure how to take that.

There is a battle brewing, and though I feel it—like the change in an airplane's cabin pressure at the beginning of a descent—it's still fuzzy around the edges, so I can't see it clearly yet.

But it won't be long now.

After I hang up with Annabel I make another call.

"Cee-Cee?" I haven't called her that since we were kids, but it comes out without thought.

"Hannah? Are you okay? What's wrong?" Unlike my own, Claire's voice is strong, ready for action. The relief of hearing it is enough to make me slide down the wall of the hospital's corridor, my legs no longer able to hold my weight.

"No, I am not okay." I tell her everything that's happened. She listens, quietly, until I finish. Then she tells me what to do, and I've never been happier for it.

"Have you called Annabel Porter?"

"Yes. She's taking care of things from her end."

"Good. Okay, now as soon as you hang up with me you're going back to the ICU. You will remind the nursing staff of your guardianship document, and show it to them, okay? Do you have a copy with you?" *Yes*, I tell her, tucking my phone in the crook of my neck and digging through my purse. *I have it right here.* "Good, put it in front of them. They'll understand what that document means. And tell them your attorney has been in touch with your patient advocate. I have no idea if that's true yet, but it doesn't matter. Just say it."

I close my eyes and create the list in my head. *Show the nurses the document. Tell them about Annabel. Patient advocate. Make it clear I make decisions for the baby.*

"Walk back into Kate's room, hold her hand and tell her you love her and you are not giving up on her or the baby. Then find Ben and figure out how one of you can always be in the ICU in case you're needed. Take turns, get some sleep on a cot if you have to, but one of you must always be there. Got it?"

Yes. One of us must always be with our son. With Kate.

She pauses, and I hold my breath, feeling uneasy again. "It's going to be okay, Hannah," she said, her voice gentle and very un-Claire-like. I begin to cry softly and I long for my sister's arms around me. I am keenly aware of Kate's absence, lost without her. "And that's not me giving you platitudes, all right? You have done so much...so much for this baby. And Kate is strong. She's one of the most determined women I've ever met. I wouldn't want to compete against her for anything." I laugh a little, wiping my tears, imagining Claire and Kate arm wrestling or locked in a two-woman tug-of-war. "I know she's your best friend, Hann, but I'm your sister. And I will always be here for you."

Though I haven't left the ICU, as per Claire's instructions, I also haven't spoken with Kate in nearly three days. Well, that's not exactly true. I have been talking to her nonstop—telling her she needs to wake up, to push through, to come back to us—it's just that she hasn't said anything back. While, thankfully, she's still stable, she's not improving, either. And that has everyone worried.

In the past few days I've learned a third of the people in Kate's condition die immediately, where they fall, and am proud she's strong enough to still be here fighting, though her neurologist—a soft-bodied and soft-spoken man named Dr. Newman Voss, who has a penchant for very loud ties—

explains luck has as much to do with it as anything else. Phrases like *vegetative state* and *maternal death* fill her small ICU room during consults crowded with medical staff, David, me and Ben. It's all I can do to keep my lungs filling with air and not curl up in a ball on the floor as her doctors list the risks, complications and frightening statistics—of which there are many—but I stay steady beside Kate, and our boy, the entire time. However, each time they mention the pregnancy, never calling it a baby like I wish they would, David glances at me, his expression difficult to interpret, and I have to look away.

Dr. Voss, when probed by David in those first few hours postsurgery, said Kate could have a slightly—and by slightly he reiterated we were talking an incremental, probably insignificant percentage—higher chance for a positive recovery if she weren't pregnant. When I push him on what a "positive recovery" means he's noncommittal. In gentle tones he says we need to prepare ourselves; the damage to Kate's brain is likely extensive and traumatic. But David hears something quite different. Despite his medical training and everything Dr. Voss has been telling us and Kate's lack of improvement, David becomes convinced if we deliver the baby, Kate will wake up and be *his* Kate again.

And while I want nothing more than for Kate to wake up— to hear her complain about how I let her eyebrows grow in and didn't read her the latest celebrity gossip magazines and spent far too much time crying at her bedside—I understand what Dr. Voss is trying to tell us.

It's highly unlikely we'll ever get *our Kate* back again.

46

Clinging to the idea that a nonpregnant Kate might fare better like it's a life raft, David pushes for a C-section and we suddenly find ourselves crammed into her ICU room, discussing our options.

Our neonatologist, Dr. Emma Swartzman, has the look of a cookie-baking grandmother—gray hair pinned back in a low bun and rose-framed reading glasses hanging around her neck—but she rarely smiles and is all business when it comes to delivering news. "Dr. Voss and I have discussed this at length and, medically speaking, delivering the fetus—"

"Baby," I say. "Please, can we call him a baby?"

She nods, looking slightly irritated to be interrupted. "Of course. Delivering the baby today, or even in the next few days, is unlikely to change Kate's condition but most certainly will complicate things for the baby." David shakes his head and walks over to the small window in the room, hands on hips and back to the rest of us. I have no idea what he's thinking, and it terrifies me.

Dr. Swartzman continues, "We're just shy of twenty-seven

weeks right now, which gives him about a seventy percent chance of survival if delivered today. As you know, at this early stage we're most concerned about his lungs."

Ben and I nod—one of our first acts as parents was to sign off on the corticosteroid shots to speed up the baby's lung development, and Kate has already been given one course.

"Now, if we can give him another week or so? Maybe two? We're looking at ninety percent in terms of survival and fewer postbirth complications. We'll likely give another course of steroids even if we make it two weeks, but for now the best thing we can do is to leave him put."

I look at David's back, trying to comprehend how we've ended up here—where David and I seem more like strangers fighting each other for control versus grieving friends supporting each other. My eyes still on David, who has yet to turn around, I say Ben and I would like to give the baby his best chance for survival—so we want to hold off on the C-section. Dr. Swartzman nods, saying that would be her recommendation as long as Kate remains stable. David says nothing, still facing the window, hands still on his hips. I want to scream at him to engage, to talk to me, to tell me what he's thinking, but instead I thank the doctors, then sit back down in the chair at Kate's bedside.

Now, two days later, I spend an inordinate amount of time at Kate's bedside silently willing her to hang on, to get better and for our boy to grow. I'm terrified David will push for the C-section again—even though, at least for now, he seems to have accepted Dr. Voss's assurances that the pregnancy is not harming Kate—and so I choose my words carefully when we're together, which is beyond exhausting.

David has gone home for the afternoon to see the girls, and

Ben is checking on Clover and meeting briefly with his dad, so much to my relief I'm alone with Kate for a few hours.

Squeezing some of Kate's favorite cream into my hands, I stand at the end of her bed and pull back the thin sheet. Her toenails are covered in polish—a reddish hue called Pinking of You—though the pedicure is starting to grow out, a tiny half-moon peeking out from under the polish at the base of her nails. It reminds me time is moving forward even if it doesn't feel like it most days, and running my fingers over the smooth, still glossy polish it's hard to believe she can't just walk out of here. Rubbing my hands together to distribute the cream, which releases the heady, sweet scent of vanilla into the otherwise antiseptic-smelling room, I start with her left leg.

This has become a twice-a-day ritual. She's retaining a lot of the fluid they're pumping into her, and one of the nurses suggested some massage could help with that, so I've been rubbing her feet, her legs, her arms. Secretly I hope she'll spontaneously wake up and laugh, the way she does when getting a pedicure. She's incredibly ticklish, especially her feet, and has a tendency to kick if the tickling gets too intense.

"That intern was here again this morning. Remember the one I told you about? Young—he must be some kind of boy wonder—Ken doll hair and very white teeth and dimples? Anyway, he said he's on for the next twenty-four hours so he'll be back. You may want to open your eyes the next time he's here. Promise it will be worth it." Making my way up to her ankles, her calves, I massage gently, working her putty-like skin under my fingers. I try not to focus on the indentations the pressure of my fingertips leave, something known as "pitting edema," and instead think about asking the nurse if I can shave Kate's legs. She would hate the stubble that now covers her calves.

"Also, Ben is bringing a whack of food from his mom. She

made those Jamaican patties you love, the ones with beef and cheese inside. I'm sure we can sneak you one if you're up for it." I watch her face for any sign she's hearing me—Dr. Voss said many patients in comas report being able to hear what's happening around them—but her expression stays lax underneath the ventilator keeping her breathing, her eyelids closed thanks to the clear tape the nurses use to prevent dryness.

Moving to the other leg, I squeeze out another glop of cream and rub my hands together again. "The baby is doing well," I say, my fingers kneading Kate's skin. "He's strong, like you." I lose my breath with the words, the tears close.

At moments like this one, I'm conflicted about how to feel—about how to behave as Kate's best friend *and* as the intended mother of the baby inside her. Through the awkwardness of teenage years, to the fun of college, to the excitement of weddings, to the joy of babies, to the heartache of funerals, I have known Kate—loved Kate—for nearly three decades. She has been such a constant fixture in my life, a tether to my past, that I can't even imagine the chasm left behind if she's no longer part of my future. By contrast, I have known this baby for fewer than six months, and only on a two-dimensional ultrasound and by the sound of his heart on the Doppler at our appointments. And yet, imagining the deep, dark hole he will leave if he doesn't survive leaves me trembling.

It has become impossible for me to separate Kate from the baby, and the baby from Kate. So when I'm alone in the room with Kate, I talk to him, too.

"Hey, baby boy," I begin, watching the speed at which the tiny heart icon on the monitor flashes. "Keep at it, my love. You're doing some really good growing in there." I take one hand and place it on Kate's belly, rubbing gently the way I would if it were my own stomach bulging with life. "But make sure you look after Kate, too, okay? She needs to rest so she can get better."

I'm used to the machines now, barely noticing the noises they make, and find the rhythm of the beeps and whooshes relaxing. When the alarm first goes off, I'm so confused by the sound it doesn't immediately occur to me to panic. Until Kate's room suddenly fills with people and I'm shoved roughly to the side as the medical team begins working on her, their voices tense yet controlled as they crowd around her bed.

Moving out of the way so quickly I underestimate how much room I have, the back of my head smacks into the wall and I see a meteor shower of stars behind my eyes. But the pain barely registers because all I'm thinking is that I'm watching Kate die.

47

"We need to update you on Kate's condition," Dr. Voss says, the corners of his mouth turning down in a sad way that belies the happy yellow polka dots on his gray tie. Dr. Swartzman sits beside Dr. Voss at the end of the rectangular table, an even more serious look than normal on her face. The family meeting room where we've congregated has too many chairs and no windows and smells faintly like lemon and rubbing alcohol. I don't like that we're meeting in here instead of Kate's room—the change in routine is disconcerting and it feels as if this is the place where people get bad news, but based on what just happened in Kate's room I'm not sure what other kind of news I can expect.

"Kate had a stress-induced heart attack. As we've discussed, it was one of the risks but one we'd hoped to avoid." Dr. Voss leans forward in his chair and looks at us, and I flinch under his stare, which is compassionate and tells me what he's about to say I'm not going to want to hear. "We did manage to get her stable again, but unfortunately we think it might be difficult to keep her stable. We need to see this as a significant setback."

David's father, Tucker—who drove David back to the hospital when I called to say Kate was in trouble—is a replica of David aged about thirty more years. He wraps his arms around his son as if trying to protect him from the latest news. David is stone-faced, and I suspect he's in shock again. I'm having a hard time swallowing, and my head pounds painfully from where I hit it against the wall. I glance between Dr. Voss and David, trying to digest the significance of this news.

"What does this mean?" I'm seated, Ben standing behind me, the warmth of his body making it suddenly too warm. I can't breathe. I can't think. I want to leave the room and pretend that none of this is happening. Ben's hands gently massage my shoulders, but I shrug him away. "Dr. Voss. Please. What does this mean?"

"It means Kate had a heart attack, Hannah. And the chance of her coming out of this is not good," David says, his tone sharp. "You like to toss around statistics, so let's call it a ninety-nine percent chance Kate isn't going to recover. Clear enough for you?" He yanks his body out of his dad's embrace and strides out of the room. Tucker follows him, which leaves Ben and me, the two doctors, and an uncomfortable silence.

The wall clock ticks loudly. Ben is crying softly. Dr. Voss clears his throat.

"Hannah, Ben, we do need to talk about the baby," Dr. Swartzman says.

I wrap my arms around my belly and rock forward, not sure if I'm going to throw up or pass out. "Are you okay?" Ben asks softly, leaning down to my ear. I feel tears from his face transfer to my temple.

I nod, then whisper, "Excuse me."

Thankfully there's a washroom next to the family room, or else I would have vomited right in the hallway. It's violent and painful, and leaves me a shaking mess on the bathroom floor. But somehow it also clears my mind. I can't deal with the news about Kate, not now. I have to tuck that away, because in order to get through this I need to believe I'll hear Kate laugh again, and feel her arms around me, and get one of her "I'm having a bored stay-at-home-mom moment—want to play hooky?" texts. If I have to face any other scenario right now there is a 100 percent chance I will never make it off this bathroom floor.

Ten minutes later I'm back in the room, and Ben hands me a bottle of water and rubs my back. David and his dad are still missing, and Dr. Swartzman is now standing. "Sorry about that," I say, sitting down and taking a long sip of water. "Please tell us about the baby."

Dr. Voss sits on the edge of the table, and his shirt expands to accommodate his ample belly, making it look as though he's wearing a white fabric-covered inner tube. "As I said, our tests this morning show Kate's heart did endure damage. How much remains to be seen," he says, as if anticipating my question. "But we can still allow the pregnancy to progress, at least for the time being, and the baby is doing well."

Ben sits beside me and grabs my hand. It's clammy, but I hold tight. I ignore the first part of what Dr. Voss has told us, focusing on the second part. "And how long can we do that for? How many weeks should we realistically be aiming for at this point?" I sound better than I feel, and glancing over at Ben—with his head bowed and eyes closed—realize I need to be strong enough for both of us. "I mean, can Kate...?" I swallow around the pain in my chest.

"As long as Kate is stable we can support her to thirty weeks gestation." He looks at Dr. Swartzman, and they exchange a look I don't understand.

There's something they aren't telling us, or are hesitant to say, and now I'm not only sad and devastated and worried—I'm nervous.

"I wanted to wait for David to be here to talk with you about this," Dr. Voss says, glancing at the door. Then he sighs and crosses his arms over his chest, covering the bright yellow polka dots of his tie. I wish he hadn't done that—the sunny polka dots were the only cheerful thing in the room. "Hannah, Ben, David wants to go ahead with the C-section."

My mouth opens, but nothing comes out. I look between the doctors and at Ben, willing him to do something other than stare at his lap. "I'm sorry—what did you say?"

"David has requested that the fetus—baby—be delivered in the next day or so," Dr. Voss says.

"But it's too soon!" Any control I have evaporates. I am frantic, desperate, and I rip my hand out of Ben's before standing quickly. "Why? He told me he would wait. And you told us the baby isn't hurting Kate, right? Even with what happened today? Besides, I know Kate wouldn't want him delivered so early if he doesn't have to be. I know she... Well, I know her. And what about what we want? We make decisions for our son, not David, and this is definitely not what we want."

Ben rises beside me. "Hannah, David's just thinking about Kate first, which is exactly what he should be doing. He's not doing this to hurt us."

I want to slap him and tell him to shut up, that this baby needs us now more than ever. And while what he's said is true, I'm infuriated he's not thinking of our child first. But unleashing a torrent of anger on Ben isn't going to help anyone at the moment, least of all me, so instead I ignore what he's said and focus on the doctors. "Please, please don't do this. This baby is our son. And he's the last..." I choke on my words, clear my throat, try again. "This child matters. Not just to us. He matters to Kate, too. I know he does. Please."

Dr. Voss is sympathetic, but he explains there's little they can do. As per Kate's health care directive, which she updated as part of the surrogacy contract process, David makes all medical decisions about her care. And even though Dr. Voss and his colleagues still don't feel the pregnancy per se is making her condition worse, the heart attack has changed the landscape—it lends more strength to David's position, he explains, because without question, Kate is sicker than she was a day ago.

"But what about the baby's rights? What about our rights as his parents? We have guardianship. We make the decisions for him, not David." The numbness is creeping in, threatening to shut everything down to protect me from the emotions trying to take over.

"Unfortunately the fetus isn't recognized as a person with rights until it's born, and even with the guardianship document David's decisions for Kate's care take precedence at this stage," Dr. Swartzman says. "Especially because at twenty-seven weeks gestation, with a full course of steroids, your baby has a decent chance of survival. I'm sorry, Hannah, Ben, but our hands are tied here."

I nod, anger building back up. I allow it to fill me, because I'm going to need all the fight I can harness. I need to let go of my grief for Kate. I can only focus on one thing: our baby boy, who didn't ask for any of this and deserves the best chance we can give him. It's most definitely selfish of me, and convenient to believe it, but I know Kate would want me to stop this C-section. If I can't help her, she'd want me to help the baby.

"I need to make a phone call," I say, stepping away from the table. Ben looks at me curiously, but I don't explain. "Thank you for the information."

Ben follows me out of the room, and I pick up my pace.

"Hannah," he calls out, but I don't stop or turn around. "Hannah! Where are you going?"

I whip around and put my hand out in front of me. "Don't," I say, my voice shaky but strong enough to draw the attention of a couple of people walking past us. "Do not say another word."

Ben exhales and lowers his head, shoving his hands into the pockets of his jeans. I can tell he's frustrated with me, with how I'm behaving, but I don't care.

"She's his *wife*. The mother of his kids. I will not crucify him for this, Hannah, no matter how much I wish he would make a different decision. But I'll talk to him, maybe I can help him see—"

I shove my hand out again, which silences him immediately. "She's *my* best friend. I love her. And I also love David." I walk backward a couple of steps so the distance between us is even greater. "But it's time to pick sides, Ben. I know how that sounds and I *hate* myself for saying it, more than you know, but you have to choose. It's time to choose."

"What the hell are you talking about? *Pick sides?* This is David and Kate and Ava and Josie. Are you suggesting we turn our backs on all of this, on all of them? She's *dying*, Hannah. What's wrong with you?"

This time instead of retreating I take quick steps toward Ben, until I'm standing directly in front of him. In soft tones, one hand resting gently on his chest, I say, "Yes, she's dying. And after we save our boy I will collapse into a heap and grieve for Kate, and David, and the girls. But right now? Our baby could die, too. And he's the most important thing, Ben, no matter how callous that sounds. So I should be asking you the same question. What's wrong with *you*? How the fuck can *you* not see that?" I let my hand drop and back away from Ben, continuing out of the ICU, the hiss of the automatic doors shutting off anything Ben has left to say. He doesn't follow me, and once I'm outside the hospital I pull out my phone and sit on an empty park bench.

With shaking fingers I find the number in my contacts. The phone to my ear, I close my eyes and let the sun warm my face. It's late in the afternoon but the sun is still strong, and it revives me ever so slightly.

"Annabel Porter, please... Yes, Hannah Matthews," I say, waiting for the receptionist to put me through. A moment later a familiar voice comes onto the line.

"Hannah, it's Peter. Is everything okay?"

I try to speak, but everything I've been holding in bursts open and I'm sobbing, unable to get the words out.

"Hannah, take a deep breath. It's going to be okay." He murmurs his support for a few more moments, then carries on. "Listen, Annabel is in court this morning. Tell me, what's going on?"

I'm a snotty mess, but I'm at least able to speak now that I've calmed down a bit. "Peter, Kate..." I dip my head, the sun warm on the back of my neck. "Kate had a heart attack. Things aren't looking good."

"Jesus, Hannah." I can hear him exhale deeply. "I'm so sorry. Jesus. Are you okay?"

"No, but I don't have time to worry about that right now." I wipe my face with my free hand, then wipe my hand on my pants to get rid of the dampness. "I need your help."

"Of course, anything you need."

"David has demanded a C-section. In the next day or so."

"How many weeks again?" Peter's voice has shifted into professional mode, which relieves me to no end. I need to back away from the emotion of the situation and focus.

"Twenty-seven weeks right now. He's too little, Peter. He needs more...time."

"And David is unwilling to allow the pregnancy to progress any longer?"

"It appears so," I say. "At least according to the doctors. I haven't spoken to David yet. Kate is stable, but I don't get the impression they expect her to stay that way. "

"What does the neonatologist say about the baby's risk?"

"She said he has a 'decent' chance at survival right now. But if we can get to twenty-eight weeks, his chances jump to ninety percent."

"So we need to keep him in there for at least one more week." He's opening a drawer, rustling papers around.

"Yes," I say, my voice so soft now I hope he can still hear me. "God, yes, please."

"Okay, Hannah. Here's what we're going to do…"

48

By the time I get back up to the ICU I'm ready to speak with David, to convince him to wait one more week for the C-section. Peter said that should be step number one, to try and solve the issue between us first. If David is unwilling to wait, then we ask for a second opinion…and then maybe a third opinion, which will buy us and the baby some more time. In the meantime Peter will have Annabel file an application for an injunction, which will prevent the hospital from taking further steps and delivering the baby until a judge has ruled. I'm horrified at how quickly things have unraveled, but I'm prepared to do whatever I have to.

As I approach the nursing station, one of the charge nurses looks up and smiles. "Hi, Hannah, you're going to have to wait a minute. She's got two visitors in there right now." Thinking maybe Ben beat me to it and is already talking with David, I lean against the far wall so I'm out of the way of passing medical staff and visitors. I feel jittery on the inside, keyed up with adrenaline, but my outsides are exhausted and I'm grateful for the solid wall behind me.

A few minutes later a man walks out of Kate's room, his arm around David's shoulders. His tanned and sun-spotted forearms tell me he's older, likely my mom's age or so, but because his head is bowed—the two men in deep conversation—I can't clearly see the stranger's face. But I do see a quite round patch of bald skin in the middle of his crown, a bull's-eye in his otherwise dark, gray-flecked hair. David's nodding at what the man is saying, and wiping his eyes, and it's only a few seconds later when the man looks up that I realize who he is.

Edward McTavish. Kate's dad.

I've never met him in person, but did once see a picture Kate had buried deep in her chest of drawers, when I was sleeping over at her place and had forgotten to pack my pajamas. Before I can even stop myself I've pushed off the wall and the words are out. "What the hell are you doing here?"

"Hannah." Ben suddenly appears, and I wonder where he's been all this time. His voice delivers the warning I surely need: *Be calm. Don't make anything worse.* But I can't abide by his warning tone or my own good sense, because Kate would not want this at all.

"Hello, Hannah, I'm Edward," he says, extending his hand, which I ignore. Kate would hate that I'm thinking this, but she really does look like her dad. "Nice to finally meet you, though I'm sorry it's under these circumstances."

"I know who you are." I cross my arms over my chest and glare at him. "But what I don't understand is why you're here."

Edward pulls his hand back and clears his throat, looking uncomfortable.

"It's okay, Ed," David says.

"'Ed'?" I say, turning on David. "Why did you let him come here? Kate would have a fit, David."

I can feel Ben's anxiety coming off him in waves, and David's look and tone tells me I'm pushing my luck. "You don't speak for Kate, Hannah."

I'm exasperated, disbelief etched on my face. "She would not want this, David, and you know it."

"He is her father. And he deserves to be here."

"*Deserves* to be here? You've got to be kidding me. She hates him. You know it. I know it. Hell, he probably even knows it." I gesture wildly toward Edward, who still looks as though he wishes to be anywhere but in this hallway. "How can you do this to her?"

"You're crossing a line, Hannah." David's face is pinched, his expression one I've never seen before.

"I'm sorry, but she would not want this," I say, my voice and shoulders dropping simultaneously. Any hope I had of finding common ground with David is quickly evaporating with every exchange we have. "She would not want him here."

David takes two quick steps toward me, fast enough that it catches me off guard and I stumble back into Ben, who rights me, keeping his hands on my arms in a way I hope he means to be comforting. "I guess she didn't tell you, did she?" he says. "So much for the best friends who tell each other everything, huh?"

"David, come on," Ben says, and all I can do is stare at David, wondering where this is going.

"They had lunch about two weeks ago. Patched a few things up, apparently. We were planning on going to his wedding."

I'm too shocked to respond—pained that Kate didn't tell me she met with Edward and wondering why not.

"Is it okay if I say something?" Edward asks. David, Ben and I don't respond, so he continues. "Hannah, I know the relationship I have with my daughter is complicated. And I wish it were different. I wish we were…close. I hope we can get there." He runs a hand through his hair, stopping on the bald spot to rub the skin for a moment. "But no matter what has happened in the past, I love her. She'll always be my daughter, and I'm only here to support her, David and my grand-daughters."

I try to find compassion for Edward, to accept what he's saying and reconcile that with what David has just told me—that Kate had reached out to her dad. But all I can hear is Kate's childhood voice, shaking with emotion as she told me she wished her dad had died like mine had instead of simply leaving—that at least he'd have a good reason for breaking her heart.

I don't know why Kate didn't tell me about lunch with her dad, maybe because she wasn't sure it was going to stick, this mending-fences thing; maybe because even if we had been best friends for all these years, there were still some things we didn't share with each other. But my need to protect her while she lay nearby unable to speak for herself, to say the things no one else is, takes over and my compassion evaporates.

"I don't care that you had lunch with Kate, *Edward*. Or that you're sorry. And I'm not sure why she reached out, but you being here feels wrong. So why don't you leave and offer your support from a distance? You're good at that from what I hear." My tone is malicious, and I try to stop myself, but I can't. It feels too good to have a landing pad for my anger. "Why don't you just get your secretary to type her a letter and enclose another check she'll never cash? She doesn't want anything from you, Edward. *She doesn't need you.*"

When David shoves me I think we're all shocked. I'm not physically hurt, because he didn't use much force, but now we're in even murkier waters—a line has been crossed on both sides, and I'm not sure how we can come back from it. Ben holds on to me, staring at David in disbelief. "What the hell, man?"

Edward continues standing in the same spot, his eyes sad. But David is furious. I've never before seen him like this; frankly I didn't think he had it in him.

"Like I said, you don't speak for Kate." David's face is lit up with anger, nostrils flaring, mouth tightly drawn, eyes narrowed. "I do. And if I can't, then Edward does."

"David, I don't think now is the time," Edward says, and I wonder what he knows that I don't. What does David mean, that Edward "speaks" for Kate?

David sees the confusion on my face, and continues, agitated yet eager to share what comes next. "I suppose you didn't know that, either, huh? She listed Edward as her alternate agent on her health care directive. Not you, Hannah. Edward."

I am speechless, trying to comprehend what he's telling me. There's no way Kate would have given her father decision-making power on her behalf. *Is there?*

"Get out of here, Hannah," David says, barely opening his mouth to get the words out. "Leave. Now." Edward puts a hand on David's back, tells him to calm down, that this isn't necessary, but David shrugs him off and steps closer to me.

In response Ben steps partially in front of me, a worried look on his face as he tries to talk David out of what he's suggesting. "Look, we're all upset. This is not going to help."

"It's okay—I'll go." I place a hand on Ben's arm to have him stand down. I turn to walk through the doors, tears streaming down my face, and I choke back a sob when I hear David's next words.

"I don't want you back here, Hannah. I mean it."

Past the automatic doors I collapse against the wall, sobs racking my body. "I'm so sorry, Kate. I'm sorry."

Ben comes through the doors and frantically looks left, then right, seeing me against the wall. He walks over to me and gathers me in his arms, and I allow myself to fall apart. He holds me up, kissing the sides of my face, the top of my head, murmuring all the right things at just the right moments so I can really hear them. After a couple of minutes I pull back and give him a questioning, desperate look.

"Were you able to talk with him? About the baby?"

Ben shakes his head. "I tried before...before all that. He's so overwhelmed, Hannah. I honestly don't think he knows what he's doing. This whole Edward thing." He sighs. "Are you okay? He didn't hurt you, did he?" Now I see the anger on Ben's face, and I run my fingers across his forehead to erase the worry lines.

"No. But I have to tell you something, and I need you to listen without getting mad."

He looks at me for a moment, his eyes searching mine for a clue, then nods. "Tell me."

Things escalate quickly and it isn't long before I'm wondering if we've done the right thing. After Ben and I ask for a second opinion from an expert in Los Angeles—which Peter figures buys us at least another seventy-two hours—Annabel applies for the injunction to keep the C-section from happening until at least thirty weeks, and ever positive, Ben tries to reassure me things can still have a good outcome.

But everything is a mess—I'm barred from the ICU thanks to David, told by the very uncomfortable head nurse, who has clearly never been placed in this situation before, that they will have to call security if I try to see Kate. Annabel is working on it, referencing the guardianship document and the fact that I'm the baby's intended mother to try and overrule David's decision. Ben is still allowed to visit, but he mostly stays outside Kate's room and receives updates about the baby from the nursing staff and Dr. Swartzman.

I go to call David's cell a dozen times, wishing I could

somehow make him see none of this was meant to hurt him or his family—I merely want to give our baby the very best chance at life. But I never get further than letting his name flash up on my screen, my finger hovering over it. Besides, even if I find the courage to call, there's little chance he'll talk to me after learning about the injunction application.

And through it all—the endless calls and texts between Peter, Annabel and us, and Ben's updates from the hospital—I miss Kate so desperately I have to press my hands hard to my chest to dull the sharp pains that radiate from shoulder to shoulder and throat to stomach.

The days somehow pass, and we make it just past twenty-eight weeks. Because the judge has yet to rule on the injunction application, and the second opinion determined that delivery would likely not improve Kate's condition and could increase complications for the baby—the ethics board confirms the hospital cannot perform the C-section David has requested. Yet I know that even if we "win"—making it to or beyond thirty weeks—we'll still have lost so much.

49

The first time I heard about David I couldn't have guessed he would become Kate's whole world. At the time he was merely a Good Samaritan, who happened to be in the right place at the right time.

We were both students, Kate starting her final year of a business degree, and me finishing a bachelor of science, with a focus in nutrition. I was between relationships, recently dumped by a guy on my rowing crew who felt I was interfering in his bid to become a world-class rower. Kate was dating Jackson Harris, a fellow biz student who at least on paper seemed like the perfect catch. The problem with Jackson, however, was that he was notoriously bad at reading Kate—for her twenty-first birthday he got her a very expensive cashmere sweater that made her itchy, and tickets to see a famous comedian who was on tour and just happened to be in San Francisco for two shows. But Kate hated cashmere and hated stand-up comedy even more; two things Jackson should have known after dating her for more than a year.

So another year later, on Valentine's Day, when Jackson told

Kate he had something special planned, she was sure it meant a ring. When my phone rang around dinnertime that night I was deep into a *Sex and the City* marathon and a take-out container of chow mein, and had to press the handset tight to my ear to hear her furious whispers.

"Who gives his girlfriend of two years a fucking key on Valentine's Day?"

"Kate?"

"Of course it's me. You aren't going to believe this. He gave me a key. A key!"

"Where are you?" I took a bite of the noodles, slurping them up before responding.

There was a pause. "Turn off *Sex and the City* and put down the chopsticks, Hannah. I need your full attention."

"How do you what I'm watching?" I asked, pausing the show. But I kept eating. I hated cold food.

She sighed, irritated. "Because it's Valentine's Day."

"It's off. Okay, so what happened?" I asked.

"You know how he said he had a 'special surprise' for tonight, and I thought maybe he was going to propose?"

"Yes." We had fully debated and analyzed Jackson's "surprise" multiple times in the past week. She flipped back and forth between hoping it wasn't a ring and wishing it might be. I had done my best to play devil's advocate, knowing she liked Jackson a lot but worrying that marrying him wasn't going to make her happy long term—they really were so different, and not in the way that can balance things out in a relationship.

"Well, he did not propose marriage. And guess where we are? We're at the fucking Outback—the *Outback*, Hannah, on Valentine's Day—I mean, does it get any less romantic and uninspired than that?" I laughed a little, and she let out an irritated sigh. "He *proposed* us living together, in his disgusting apartment where the toilet seat is always covered in urine."

I laughed again, until Kate told me this was serious and not even a bit funny.

"Sorry. You're right. So where are you now?"

"I'm in the restroom. And I have to go back because our steaks and the clichéd Bloomin' Onion Jackson apparently loves are probably out and I need to break up with him immediately."

"Wait. What? You're going to break up with him on Valentine's Day? At the Outback steakhouse? All because of a key?"

"Not just because of the key." She sounded exasperated. "The key is just the final nail in this relationship coffin."

I rolled my eyes. She did always have a flair for the dramatic. "Okay, fine. Go eat your steak, break up with Jackson and then come here. I have lots of Chinese and bad TV."

When Kate didn't come over, or call me to fill me in on how Jackson took things, I figured the steak came out and she lost her nerve. Or that the breakup was dragging long past the steaks and into the early morning hours. Until the phone rang at two in the morning—startling me awake on the couch, the container of cold and greasy chow mein crumpled in my armpit. It was Kate: she was in the hospital, being kept overnight for observation.

Seems the breakup didn't go quite as planned.

She'd gone back to Jackson and her filet mignon and double-baked potato, and was mulling over how exactly to tell him he could keep his key and everything that came with it, when a mouthful of meat got lodged in her throat. Jackson panicked, slapping her on the back repeatedly while she choked, her eyes rolling back in her head just before she dropped to the floor beside their table. David, on a similarly bad Valentine's date two tables over, jumped up—and with the help of the Heimlich and his chosen career path—saved her life.

Kate didn't break up with Jackson that night, or for two

weeks afterward. But when she called David to thank him—
after tracking his phone number down from her ER admitting
report—she asked him if she could buy him dinner to show
her appreciation. "Anywhere but the Outback, okay? I think
you should avoid steak for a while," he joked. She broke up
with Jackson right after the phone call, and that dinner was
the beginning of Kate and David.

But David couldn't save her this time.

There was no maneuver to fix her brain, to reverse the
damage the aneurysm had left behind. He was like Jackson that
night at the steakhouse, panicking and flailing and useless—
standing by as he lost his wife, his life, a little more each day.

50

I'm sitting at the kitchen island with a coffee and a store-bought muffin my mom dropped off, with neon-purple dots I can only assume are blueberries, when Ben comes downstairs. Clover is at his feet, barking and jumping in circles. I smile at her enthusiasm, and Ben smiles at me.

"That's nice to see," he says. He picks Clover up and then comes into the kitchen and hands her to me. She turns in circles on the top of my thighs, then burrows deep into my lap with a happy sigh. "Is there more coffee?"

I nod yes, my mouth full from my last sip. I run my hands over Clover's toasty warm body, her silky fur lacing between my fingers. "So I'll drop her off to get groomed. Then I'm going to pop into the office before heading to the hospital," Ben says.

I murmur that's fine, then laugh when Clover nudges my hand because I've stopped petting her. "Okay, okay," I say, resuming my stroking. "But I have to drink my coffee, too." She lifts her head to look at me, then lets it drop back down and closes her eyes.

"What do you have on today?" Ben pours himself a mugful of coffee before leaning back against the countertop. I know what he means, and it certainly isn't as if I'm planning to get to the grocery list or head to work to catch up for a few hours. What he's really asking me is, "So, how are you going to make it through today?" I push the muffin toward him, and he takes a bite, oblivious to the fake blueberries.

"I'm having lunch with Shoana to go over a few things for the next edition, and then I'm meeting Peter and Annabel to get an update."

Ben nods, looking at me critically. "Do you want me to meet you there?"

"That's okay. You have enough going on today. Besides, I'd rather you go see Kate."

It's been nearly two weeks since David shoved me and told me to stay away from Kate's room. Two weeks more we've been able to keep our son inside Kate's sick body. Two weeks since Kate's heart attack. It has been the longest two weeks of my life.

"Okay," he says, pushing back from the counter and wiping crumbs from the front of his shirt. He holds out his arms, and I set Clover into them. "Call me after you see Peter."

"I will." I kiss him goodbye and get Clover's collar and leash, then wave as I shut the door behind them.

After lunch with Shoana, where she tries to stuff me full of pasta carbonara, garlic bread and panna cotta, declaring me so skinny I'm practically waiflike, she tells me everything with work is fine and she'll call me if she needs me. "I don't want one iota of your energy going to this magazine," she says, pushing the creamy panna cotta toward me until I relent and have another bite. "I'm not kidding, Hannah. You need to focus on you, and your family, okay? We're fine, I'm fine, and your job is going to be here when you come back."

After thanking Shoana another few times for lunch and her reassurance, my phone rings just as I walk out of the restaurant. My heart drops when I see the caller ID.

"Hello?"

"Mrs. Hannah Matthews?" The voice is young, cheery and doesn't sound the least bit concerned about anything. This should set me at ease, but I'm too far down the rabbit hole of worry to notice.

"Yes, I'm Hannah Matthews."

"Oh, good. It's Lucy Smithson, over at San Francisco General. I'm glad I was able to catch you. It's about your husband…"

Ben. Oh, my God.

"He's down in triage and you're listed as his emergency contact so I thought I'd—"

I have no idea what Lucy says next, because I hang up and sprint down the street, frantically waving my hand for a taxi as I do.

I call Ben's phone repeatedly while I'm in the taxi, but it keeps going to voice mail. I'm a mess by the time we get to the hospital a few minutes later and don't see the commotion at the front entrance because I'm frantically digging around in my purse for money for the fare.

"What's going on here?" the driver says under his breath, as he brings the car to a stop just short of the entrance. I stop rummaging the depths of my purse and look up to see at least two dozen people walking back and forth in front of the doors, holding picket signs and blocking the entrance. There's also a news truck and a few bored-looking reporters and camera people standing to the side.

As the group walks past my window, I read the signs.

I am the voice for those who cannot speak.

God is Pro-Life.

Every Life Matters.

But it's the last sign I see that makes me gasp.

Save Baby Matthews.

The driver is clearly reading the signs, too. "Ah, right.

There's a pregnant lady here in a coma, and some sort of issue with the baby. I heard something about it on the news earlier. You hear anything?"

"No," I reply, my voice hoarse. *The news? How did they find out?* I temporarily forget why I'm at the hospital, the shock of the signs, the picketers overwhelming me.

But then the shock fades and I'm out of the car, tossing a twenty into the front seat. I keep my head down and walk quickly past the picketers, and am shaking like a leaf by the time I get through the emergency department's entrance.

"My husband, Ben Matthews? Please, where is he? What's happened?" I lean heavily on the triage desk.

"Hannah?"

I whip around and there's Ben. A large white bandage on one hand and a surprised look on his face.

The relief is so sweet I start laughing. "Ben."

"What are you doing here?"

"They called me." I gesture to the phone in my hand. "I thought... Well, it doesn't matter what I thought." I took his hand in mine, holding it gently. "What happened?"

"An incident at the groomers. No big deal. Clover got freaked out by another dog and bit my hand when she tried to get away."

"She bit you? Are you okay?"

"Two stitches and a tetanus shot. I'm fine. Here, sit down. You look worse than my hand."

I sit heavily and drop my bag to the floor, spent from the rush of adrenaline.

Just then a nurse comes into the waiting room and hands Ben a piece of paper. "Okay, Mr. Matthews. Here are your discharge instructions. And your insurance form went through— it was just a missing number apparently."

"Thank you. Also, do you know who called my wife?"

"No one from down here. Maybe accounts receivable, for the insurance form? They might have called your emergency contact. Anyway, you're all set. If you notice any reddening of the skin or have significant pain or swelling, come right back, okay?" She turns to go, then notices me sitting there beside Ben.

"You okay, hon?"

"Yeah, yeah, I'm good. Thanks."

"Okay, then. Might want to put a muzzle on that dog of yours." She smiled, and Ben thanked her again before sitting down beside me, an irritated look on his face. "An insurance form mix-up hardly qualifies as an 'emergency.' Sorry they called and freaked you out. That's the last thing you need to—"

"It's fine. I don't care, now that I know you're okay. But have you seen... Have you seen the signs, outside the main entrance?"

"Yes." His expression darkens, and I know the signs affected him as deeply as they did me.

"How do they know about any of this?" I ask. "How do they know our last name?"

He sighs and leans back in his chair, resting his bandaged hand gingerly on this thigh. "Edward talked to a reporter."

My mouth drops open. "Why? Why would he do that?"

"I have no clue. Seems he told them about Kate. And the injunction. Maybe he thought it might help David? Gain some sympathy for him and for, and I quote, 'the hell Hannah and Ben Matthews are putting my daughter and family through,' end quote."

Leaning forward on my knees I rest my forehead in my hands and close my eyes. "Shit. What are we going to do?"

"I understand you're probably not thrilled about this being aired in the local media, and Kate's father is probably regretting it by now, but this is actually really good news for us," Annabel says. The four of us—me, Ben, Peter and Annabel—are sitting in Peter's office, going over the latest developments—specifically, the protesters outside the hospital.

"How so?" I ask. "It's hard to see any of this as 'good news.'"

"Because pro-lifers tend to be strong, determined groups," Annabel replies, tapping her pen against the folder on her lap. "And now that they've decided to intervene, our case is even stronger."

"Intervene how?" Ben asks, looking as confused as I feel. "They don't know us. They have no ties to the baby, or to Kate."

"True," Peter says. "But they don't need to have any relationship with you or even the child in question." He flips open a file and releases a paper from the clip holding the stack together. He places the paper on the table in front of us, and I glance at it, trying to understand what I'm looking at. "Essentially they've filed a motion to intervene with the courts. They're asking to become a party to the suit."

"But what happens now? What does 'intervene' mean exactly? We'll still have full guardianship rights for the baby, won't we?" I ask, nervousness tickling deep into my stomach.

"Yes, guardianship remains with you and Ben," Annabel says. "The best way to think about it is as a stall tactic. It will buy us time. And time is what we need."

"So what happens next?" Ben asks.

"Now a briefing happens, and we prepare a memorandum of the points and authorities of the case. And the other group does the same. And then we wait for the judge to make a decision." Peter sits back in his own chair and pushes his glasses on top of his head. He looks at least ten years younger without his glasses, having one of those baby faces despite his forty-two years. "The way we see it, we have two choices. One, we can wait it out. I suspect this pro-life group is only going to increase their presence, and it won't be long until this is a national story." He leans forward and riffles through some papers on the table. "And when that happens, things will get locked up for a while because the judge will want to proceed very carefully, which again will be to our benefit. These cases don't happen often, and we're talking precedent-setting stuff here."

The thought of being involved in something "precedent setting" makes me nervous. I only want our baby to get stronger; I have no interest in forcing any of us into a courtroom and subsequent battle.

"And what's the second choice?" I ask.

"The second choice is to withdraw the application," Annabel replies. "You allow David to make whatever decision he wants, which as we know from Damon Cumberland is to move ahead with the C-section. Without our application to anchor the case, the other group probably won't move forward. Or they'll try, but a judge will be less willing to consider it after the intended parents have withdrawn."

I take a deep breath. "Can I ask a question?"

"Please," Peter says.

"Is it true that Kate put her father down as an alternate on her health care directive? After David?"

Peter pauses before replying. "Yes, it's true," he finally says. "I know you're wondering why you aren't on the list, Hannah. But in this case there's a good reason for that, and it has nothing to do with your relationship with Kate."

I look at him, tears in my eyes. "She would have been given legal advice to not name you on her health care directive," Peter explains, his voice gentle. "For a situation exactly like this. It's a conflict of interest, because of the baby." I nod.

"Hannah, we're at twenty-nine weeks and one day," Peter continues. "Dr. Swartzman feels your baby has an *excellent* chance at survival if delivered right now, as does the other expert we spoke to yesterday."

I look up at him, then Annabel, and take a sip of water. "I still want to wait until at least thirty weeks. We're so close. Please, let's keep moving forward."

"Hannah, be reasonable," Ben spits out, frustration spilling out with his words. "David is devastated. This is killing him. And now he has to walk past those signs every time he leaves the damn hospital."

"And whose fault is that?" I let out a short, harsh laugh. "He has his ever-helpful father-in-law to thank for that."

Ben shakes his head, looking at me as if he isn't sure who I am, or maybe, who I've become. "You haven't... You haven't seen him lately. It's bad, Hannah. Really bad. Don't you think we've pushed things enough?"

"No, I don't!" I shout, twisting in my chair to face him. "Until we're sure our son can be delivered safely, no, we haven't pushed things enough."

Peter clears his throat. "Look, the hospital can't perform the C-section until the judge rules or we drop the application, or God forbid, something happens with Kate that makes it absolutely necessary for delivery to happen. And I know this is hard. David is grieving, he's suffering and he has to make decisions and think about things no one should ever have to. But that's your baby Kate is carrying. And I believe you do have a responsibility to ensure the safety of your son, however you can."

Ben doesn't respond to Peter, glaring at me instead. I glare back, and an uncomfortable silence fills the office.

"Why don't we give you two a minute?" Peter says, he and Annabel standing, barely disturbing the heaviness of the room. A moment later they close the door behind them and it's just Ben and me—a boulder of anger and hurt resting between us.

"He is our friend, Hannah, our best friend, and he is fac-ing the very real possibility of a life without Kate," Ben says. "Please, let's not forget *everything* that's at stake here."

I clear my throat, trying to compose myself so the fury doesn't take over. "Why do you always feel so compelled to take David's side?"

"Oh, so we're back to this whole fucking 'taking sides' thing? There are no sides here, Hannah. And even if there were, I am not taking David's side…" He bows his head, shak-ing it slowly.

"Yes, you are. Every time you push back that's *exactly* what you're doing."

"I have no idea how to talk with you about any of this!" This explodes out of him, and now he has my full attention. "You've pulled away from me, and it's *exhausting* trying to figure out what to say, what not to say and what you want from me."

"What I want from you?" I narrow my eyes, mentally push-ing the boulder of anger closer toward him. "*Complete strang-ers are trying to protect our child, Ben*. Why aren't you fighting as hard as I am for our baby?"

"You want to know why?"

"Yes! Please. Enlighten me." Without question our shout-ing is seeping past Peter's office door, but we're too far gone to care about anyone hearing us.

"Because that could be you in that bed! That could be you buried under all those machines, only alive because of a ven-tilator. That could be *you*, and that's all I see when I walk into Kate's room. I want this baby, so desperately I can't even take a deep breath when I think about him. But I can't fight David anymore, Hannah. I don't want to fight him. So please, stop asking me to." His shoulders roll forward, and I know what I'll find if I tilt his face up to mine—heavy tears and a desperate need for me to remember that we are stronger together. But I keep my distance, because as heartbroken as I am about every last detail of this situation we're in, I must be single focused; I won't survive any of this otherwise.

"I can't," I whisper. "I'm sorry, but I can't."

His head lifts, his face betraying his disappointment and worry, along with what I think is a hint of disbelief, and it occurs to me Ben and I may not make it out of this in one piece, either.

51

The next morning when my phone rings at 7:00 a.m., I'm sitting on the living room couch—where I slept the night before—putting together the breast pump, Clover snuggled beside me. Things are still icy between Ben and me after our argument in Peter's office, hence the couch, and even if I knew how to fix it, I'm not sure I have the energy to do it.

"How's my very pregnant little sister?" I ask, putting my phone on speaker so I can finish assembling all the parts. I've been pumping religiously since Kate's collapse—even though technically I wasn't supposed to start for another two weeks—worried about being ready to nurse whenever the baby was born. Six times a day, including once in the middle of the night. It's draining and disheartening, and despite Trudy warning me that at first I'd be lucky to get drops of milk after a twenty-minute pumping session, I push each session to thirty minutes. I've been meticulously collecting the milk and transferring it with a dropper into a test tube, which is in the freezer. After eight days I have exactly a quarter of an ounce and raw nipples.

Claire lets out a long breath before drawing in a few short ones. I drop the bottles and pick up my phone, taking it off speaker.

"Are you okay?" I ask.

"Oh, I'm better than okay," she says, breathing deeply again. "I'm finally in labor, and determined to have this baby before six p.m."

I stand up so quickly I knock the pillows off the couch and Clover startles out of her deep sleep, barking nearly the instant her eyes open. "You're in labor?"

"It was the Scotch bonnet sauce that finally did it. Thank Ben's mom for me, would you? Her hot sauce is hotter than hell, but looks like it did the trick."

"You're in labor."

"For the second time, yes," Claire says, laughing a little. "We're heading to the hospital. I wanted to let you know it's okay if you want to wait until after the baby's born, when we're home, to come by."

I know she's thinking about the pro-life group and their signs, and how both have grown significantly in only twenty-four hours. And that I'll have to walk past them to get through the doors, and more importantly, that her having her baby today when our situation is so tenuous may be more than I can handle.

"Don't be crazy." I throw the pump pieces back into the carrying case. "I'm on my way." I sprint up the stairs, Clover right at my heels, and burst into the bedroom. I toss my phone on the nightstand, then wriggle out of my shorts and pull on a pair of jeans and a long-sleeved cotton shirt.

"Ben," I say, loudly so he wakes up. Clover helps by jumping up on the side of the bed and letting out three short barks. "I'm going to the hospital. Claire's in labor."

He sits up quickly, trying to rub the sleep out of his eyes. "Claire's having her baby? Like, now?"

"Yes, like now," I reply.

He watches me as I race around our room, trying to keep from stepping on Clover while I do. "I'm coming with you."

I pause, take a breath, try to figure out if I even want him there. "Fine. I'm leaving in five minutes," I finally say.

"Okay. I'll be ready." He grabs a pair of jeans from where he dropped them on the floor the night before and a crew neck T-shirt, which he pulls over his head in one move. "Hannah, are you sure you're okay?"

"Why does everyone keep asking me that?" I grumble, grabbing my toothbrush and speeding it over my teeth. I spit in the sink and watch him from the bathroom mirror. He looks worried, and it makes me antsy. "I'm fine. This is my sister and my niece we're talking about, and so, yes, I'm sure. Now get dressed or I'm leaving without you."

Once we arrive at the hospital I understand Claire's hesitation. The group has more than tripled in size, to the point where it's hard to see a space to walk between the protesters and their signs. There are also police out front now and more news crews scattered about.

"Oh, my God." I have visions of David walking past this group, these signs, every day. Of Ava and Josie somehow seeing this, and understanding what it means. I suppose I could thank Kate's dad for bringing this fight here, for unknowingly giving our baby a voice in this terrible situation, but all I feel is a pit of gloom in my stomach.

I'm sure every time David sees the *Life Is Precious* sign circling around, all he thinks about is Kate and how the preciousness of her life is under threat. These signs, their messages, have reduced her to a body in a bed—a vessel for something more important. And by forcing David's hand to keep the baby inside her, we are also forcing him to relinquish the pathetic kernel of control he has left: his ability to make a decision when it comes to Kate's care. My stomach churns, and I feel hot and light-headed.

Ben presses his lips together, the way he does when he's trying to keep something to himself. "Let's go through the emergency room doors."

My body betrays me, and I start to shiver despite how warm out it is already. I'm grateful Ben's beside me—no matter what has happened between us. He leads me through and away from the circus, and we're almost past the worst of it when I hear "Hannah Matthews?"

Suddenly a microphone is shoved in my face, held by a pretty young woman with a perfectly styled bob and long, mascara-heavy eyelashes. I'm standing in front of her, mute, trying to figure out how she recognizes me...until I see the copy of *Femme* in her other hand, the magazine held open and displaying my photo and byline. Ben shoves me forward, trying to get me away from her microphone, but the crowd has swallowed us. Now there are other microphones and tape recorders and outstretched arms all around me, and I open and close my mouth a few times, feeling claustrophobic and desperate to escape. The questions come rapid-fire.

"What's the status of the baby, Hannah?"

"What's Kate Cabot's condition? Is she still on life support?"

"When do you expect the judge to rule?"

"How far along is the pregnancy?"

"No comment," Ben says, grabbing both my arms and pushing me forward hard enough I stumble a bit. I can't draw a full breath and am grateful when Ben's determined shoving somehow breaks us out of the group. He grabs my hand and tells me to run, and so we do, making it through the emergency room doors a moment later, which the media are blocked from entering by security.

I'm hyperventilating, and I try to focus on what Ben is saying instead of how hard it's become to breathe.

"Hannah, they can't get in here. Breathe. Out through your mouth, in through your nose." He forces me into a chair and pushes me forward so I'm chest to thigh, my head between my knees. "There. Better. Keep breathing."

It takes ten minutes, but soon my breathing has evened out and I don't feel as though I'm going to faint. And after I've managed to sit up, I clutch Ben's jacket to hold him tight to me and I know it's not worth it—I can't fight Ben, too. Somehow I have to find a way to fix all of this, to heal the damage we've endured and, in some cases, done to each other—before it's too late.

I'm feeling steadier once we've made it up to the labor and delivery floor, where we find Peter at the nursing station.

"Peter," I call out, and he turns. He's wearing jeans, a simple plaid button-down and tennis shoes, and away from the law firm and without his glasses on, I'm struck again by how young he looks—more like a first-year associate than the firm's founding partner. He smiles and comes toward us.

He hugs us, smelling fresh-from-the-shower clean, his shirt carrying the slightest hint of some kind of cologne. "Claire will be happy you're here. She's in room 201." He points to the right down a long hallway. "I'm just off to grab her some ice chips, so I'll meet you back there." He pauses, watching us carefully. "You guys doing okay?" I nod, an embarrassed flush threatening my cheeks when I think about our shouting match in his office the day before. "Good, okay. That's good," Peter says, turning to head down the hall. "I'll see you in there."

As Ben and I walk toward Claire's room, I suddenly remember the pump. Sitting on the kitchen island where I forgot to grab it in our haste to get here. "Shit," I say, stopping so quickly my rubber-soled espadrilles squeak on the linoleum.

"What? What's the matter?" Ben stops a step ahead of me, and looks back with concern.

"I forgot the pump at home."

"Do you need it?" Ben sounds irritable, and I try not to let it bother me. After what happened on our way in here of course we're both still on edge.

"I didn't get a chance to pump this morning, and I don't want to screw up the schedule. It's okay. I'll just run home and get it." But the thought of crossing back through the crowd of reporters and picketers makes me weak.

"No, you stay. I'll go back and get it—you go in with Claire."

"Thank you," I reply, relief washing over me.

"Sure," Ben says, a hesitant smile on his face. "I'll be back as soon as I can, okay?"

We kiss goodbye—quickly and without fanfare, the way we used to before heading to work back when life was simple—and I wonder if I should have held him to me longer, as if that alone could erase whatever still held us apart.

But he's gone before I can do anything about it, and so I head to Claire's room, which is large and cheerful with huge windows and pale lavender paint on the walls. I'm struck by how different this room feels compared with Kate's, which is white and clinical and lifeless.

Claire is pacing in front of the windows, one hand held to her belly and the other on her phone. She looks beautiful and relaxed—her hair up in a smooth and taut ballerina bun, all held in place with a thin black fabric headband. Her face is bare, which allows the smattering of freckles across the bridge of her nose to stand out. I'm swept back to when we were kids, spending lazy summer days making watermelon-and-mint popsicles with Grams and swimming in our grandparents' pool, which had been original to the house and always had a thin layer of slippery green algae on its rough stone sides.

"You look too beautiful to be in labor." I hug her, her belly pressing between us. "How goes it?"

"It goes," she says, grimacing slightly through a contraction. I hold her hands, which tightly squeeze my own, and breathe with her until her face relaxes again and she stands up straighter. "You are so lucky you don't need to do this," she says, taking in a deep breath. Then, seeing the look on my face, she starts apologizing profusely. "Shit, that was the most insensitive thing I could have said. I'm so sorry, Hannah. I didn't mean—"

"No, it's okay. I know what you meant."

But Claire's guilt is still etched on her face. "Can I blame my stupidity on the pain of my uterus trying to eject itself from my body?"

"You don't need to apologize. You're right. There are definitely pros to outsourcing labor." I smile and change the subject. "Where's Mom?"

"She's making calls out there somewhere, telling everyone she's ever known her first grandchild is coming." Surprisingly this doesn't hurt me, though I would have expected it to as I—the eldest—was the one who was supposed to give Mom her first grandchild.

"I would have thought she'd be attached to you."

"She has been—trust me. I had to get Peter to practically drag her out of our bedroom this morning when she was trying to help me get dressed. I mean, I may be in labor but I can still put my underwear and bra on myself, you know?" She rolls her eyes, then closes them as another contraction moves through her.

"Those are picking up, huh?" Peter asks, coming to stand behind her and rubbing her lower back in swift circles. He glances at his watch and back at Claire's face, which is still scrunched in pain. A minute later the contraction subsides and Claire is back to normal. She takes my hand and squeezes. "How are you?"

"I'm fine. Stop asking me and worry about yourself, okay?"

"Where's Ben? Didn't he come with you?"

"He went home to grab my pump. I forgot it in the rush." Claire starts pacing again. "Sorry, I have to keep moving. It's like someone is pounding on my spine with rubber mallets. Or something equally as horrible."

I walk beside her, linking my arm through hers while she uses her other hand to balance herself against the window's long ledge.

"How's the pumping going?"

I shrug. "It's fine. I'm making about enough to feed a baby hummingbird breakfast at this point."

Claire laughs at that, and a moment later a doctor—who I think looks a bit old, with his donut of white hair and crinkled skin, to still be practicing medicine—arrives and says it's time to check Claire's progress.

At that point I leave and wait outside the room, hoping Ben gets back soon. I see my mom coming down the hall, her pace quick and frantic but just shy of a jog. It's sweet how excited she is, and I find myself smiling.

"Hannah!" she says, her tone enthusiastic and a good match for her pace. "When did you get here? Where's Ben?"

"About half an hour ago. And Ben just ran home to get something I forgot."

"Okay, good," she says, craning her head toward Claire's room. I probably could have said Ben was headed to hunt moose in Canada's far north and she would have responded the same way. "What's happening in there? How's Claire?"

Before I get a chance to respond Peter pokes his head out the door. "She's ready to start pushing," he says, his grin stretching so wide it takes over half his face. Mom practically leaps toward the door, then as an afterthought, reaches back to hug me. "That's my cue," she says. "See you later, honey."

I give Peter a look. "Claire asked your mom to be in the room for the delivery," he says, answering my unspoken question. "Trust me—I was as surprised as you look. I figured even I'd have to grovel to be allowed in there." He chuckles, then glances back into the room when my mom calls his name. "There's a waiting room just down the hall. I promise I'll come and find you the moment I can, okay?"

I'm glad my mom will be there with Claire and Peter, to see her grandchild born. I'm grateful it's not an experience she has to forgo. Fighting tears I make my way to the waiting room, then send a text to Ben to let him know where I am. I try, unsuccessfully, to ignore the truth about my own child—it's likely with all that's happened I won't be present at his birth. By the time Ben gets back with the pump I'm a mess in the corner of the waiting room, clutching a box of tissues a kind stranger—a to-be grandfather—hands me when my weeping becomes too obvious to politely ignore.

I try to tell Ben why I'm so sad, which he blames on Claire's labor—something I want so desperately to experience but never will—chastising himself for not insisting we stay home until after the baby is born. I'm too tired to explain so instead lay on Ben's lap, my feet curled up on another chair, and cry softly while he holds me. Soon the tears ebb and a while after that Peter comes in to tell us it's a girl. Amelia Ellen Todd. Born at 5:51 p.m., seven pounds, two ounces, with a headful of dark hair. Mom jumps repeatedly as she hugs me, saying over and over again how she tried to dissuade Claire and Peter from using Ellen—a name she'd always felt wasn't feminine enough—as baby Amelia's middle name, but I can tell she's thrilled.

I sit with my family, fawning over the baby like everyone else does, letting her tiny fingers wrap around mine as her navy blue eyes take this brand-new world in. And while I smile and laugh and coo at her, the jealousy inside me rages like a wildfire burning out of control.

52

Claire's nurse has found me a room so I can pump, and I'm ten minutes into my thirty-minute session when there's a knock at the door. She told me no one would need the room and put a sign on the door so I wouldn't be disturbed, so I'm irritated by the knock. I need to pump, but more than anything I need a few minutes alone.

I glance down to make sure the cover-up is doing its job before saying, "Yes? Hello?"

The door opens a crack, and my mom pokes her head in. She looks rumpled—which is quite unlike her—blouse untucked and one of her white tennis shoes untied, the lace dragging behind as she comes into the room. She also somehow looks younger and older all at once—her brow wrinkles deeper but the rest of her face smoothed out by joy.

"Hi, Mom. I'd get up, but I'm a bit busy here." I smile, and she smiles back, the whooshing sound of the pump filling the moment of silence between us.

"You're already such a good mother, Hannah, for being so diligent with the pumping."

A lump forms in my throat. "Thanks, Mom," I whisper,

and she gives me a kiss on my forehead. "How's Claire doing? How's baby Amelia?"

Mom pulls a chair up beside me and sighs deeply, happily. "Claire is great. And Amelia is a little slice of heaven. Babies just have the most beautiful scent to them, like roses and sweet milk." She inhales as though that will bring the smell back, and then her smile falters as she glances at me. "But I want to know how you're doing, Hannah."

"I'm good. Great," I say but drop my eyes from my mom's, knowing I can't hide the truth from her.

"I know you put on a brave face for your sister and maybe even Ben, but you don't have to pretend for me."

"I'm not pretending. Not exactly." I glance at the wall clock. I'm strapped to this contraption, and therefore trapped in this conversation for fifteen minutes more. "I'm happy for Claire and Peter. And Amelia is...well, she's perfect."

"She really is, isn't she?" Mom grins and nudges my shoulder gently. "But apparently they're going to call her Ami, with an *i* for heaven's sake, which I for one think is unfortunate. Amelia is such a pretty name. So feminine, but strong, too."

"You know Claire, Mom. She knows what she wants, and she does what she wants."

"I know." Mom sighs again. "You were always the easier child."

I laugh. "I definitely won't tell Claire you said that."

"Well, it's true, and she knows it. Claire was the fireball. Explosive. Determined. Unpredictable. The one who could have just as easily ended up selling marijuana, albeit very successfully, out of a camper van with a boyfriend named Forest."

I nudge her back with my shoulder. "And me? What did you expect me to do?"

She looks at me, her eyes scanning my face—as if she can read the subtleties in my expression, can see right through my smile to what lies underneath it. "I expected nothing."

"I'm not sure how to take that," I say, laughing again. "I think I'd prefer successful marijuana saleswoman."

She shushes me. "It means I never had to worry about you. I knew you would always make good decisions." She rests a hand—warm though a bit rough probably from all the hand washing required in the hospital—against my cheek. "You are so much like your father that way."

Tears suddenly threaten, and I hold my breath, feeling the burn in my throat.

"Roger was fearless," she says, pride and love filling her tone. I don't remember that about my dad, though in fairness I only saw him from a child's eyes. He was the man who read us stories at night long after we should have been asleep, and helped us put our bicycle chains back on, and who had magic tweezers to get rid of even the tiniest of slivers. "Even though things didn't always turn out as he hoped, he took it in stride. Never complaining, just focusing on what had to come next and loving his family." Mom's hand tapped against my cheek a couple of times, as gently as butterfly wings, and I leaned into it. "Remember what he said, after the doctors told us there was nothing else they could do?"

I shook my head.

"Did I never tell you this?"

"I don't think so."

"Well, he said, 'Time to squeeze those lemons dry.' And he booked that vacation to Hawaii the next day, even though he was quite unwell by that time and we didn't have the money."

I remembered that vacation. It took Claire and me by surprise, as it came only a week after spring break, which we had spent at our grandparents'—where I tried to be on my best behavior because they had a pool and Grams made lemon-iced cake every day and I wanted to be invited back even though they were strict and didn't let us stay up late to watch television. I wouldn't know until later that was the week Mom and Dad got the devastating news the cancer was winning, and Dad didn't have much time left.

Our surprise Hawaiian vacation was full of sun and warmth and the sort of activities you never forget, like swimming with dolphins, zip-lining over treetops and taking a helicopter ride over a volcano. Dad and Mom held hands often enough that Claire and I snickered about how gross it was, but it made me happy to see—a sure sign they weren't headed for divorce like some of my school friends' parents had. And though Dad was pale despite the sunshine and sick enough to stay in bed one day, we believed him when he said he must have picked up a bug on the plane.

So even though my precious little world came tumbling down when they sat us in our sunroom and told us Dad was sick—the kind of sick no one can fix—the week after we got home, waterlogged and buzzing with stories of our exotic adventures, at least I had enough of a suntan left to remind me maybe life could be good again.

"I don't think I'm like that, Mom," I say. "I wallow in the lemons until they rot. I've complained a lot, trust me, and I'm not sure the decisions I've made recently would count as good ones. There are days, Mom…" I take a deep breath. "There are days when I'm sure I'm making everything so much worse."

"Honey, what's happening to Katie is not your fault."

"But what's happening to David is. And what's happening between me and Ben is."

Mom doesn't say anything for a moment, and I take her silence as agreement. "There is nothing more instinctual, more important than protecting your child, Hannah. So while you have had to make a very difficult choice, you made the right one. Don't lose sight of that. Ben may not be able to say it now, honey, but he will thank you. He loves you too much to let this come between you in any permanent way. And David will forgive you. You'll see."

"I don't think he will forgive me, Mom. How can he?" My voice is gruff with tears, and the reality of what I've said hits me in the gut like a wrecking ball.

"He will." She nods vehemently. "David is grieving right now. He's dealing with the loss of the life he knew, the wife he loved. Katie is fighting as hard as she can, and we can only hope she pulls through this to be the Katie we remember and love. But while David is praying for that, he's also preparing for the worst. Trust me—I know what that's like. There's very little room for anything else or anyone else's feelings."

For the first time I see my mother as a woman who loved her husband deeply, and then had to let him go far too soon. Before now I've only considered the loss as one for our family—that Claire and I lost our dad too young, and we went from a happy family of four to a still functional but less happy family of three.

"Go to him, Hannah. Share his grief, his fear, his worry. Unburden him, and let him know you're there for him and for Katie, no matter what happens."

I shake my head and tears fall onto the cover-up. "He doesn't want me there, Mom."

"He needs you there," Mom replies, grabbing a tissue and wiping my eyes for me like she did when I was a little girl. "He's not mad at you, sweetheart. He's mad at what's happening to Katie. To his family. And he has to stay in fight mode, so he can be strong for the ones who need him most. His anger is about survival more than anything else." Her voice softens, and she turns my chin toward her. "This isn't about you, honey."

I nod, letting her wipe away another stream of tears. "Okay," I say. "I'll try to talk to him."

"That's all you can do. The rest is up to David."

53

As it turns out it wasn't up to me after all. Or David, for that matter.

After I talk to Mom, I speak with Ben—who is relieved when I say it's time to drop the injunction application and give David back the right to choose what happens next with Kate. But before we call Annabel we consult with Dr. Swartzman, who assures us the baby is strong and doing well; his lungs have matured thanks to the steroid injections, and she feels we may be reaching the point where he's going to do better out of Kate's body than in it.

A few hours later we're back home, and I sit at my kitchen island, trying to get up the nerve to call David and ask if I can come by and see him, and Kate, while Ben bustles around me doing dishes, walking Clover a couple of times and taking a work call. I want to ask him to leave me alone for a while, but I don't. And he stays close by, the way I know he will.

As I sit, my phone in hand and gaze unfocused, I run over in my head what I want to say to David when I finally call. Starting with how sorry I am. I'm so lost in my own thoughts

I jump when the vibration tickles my palm, and my heart rate speeds up when I see the caller.

David Cabot.

I drop the phone on to the island. "Ben," I say. My voice is shrill, and Ben's beside me quickly.

"What? What's wrong?" He looks at me, then at the phone vibrating across the counter. "Are you going to answer it?"

I shake my head, my breath coming so fast I'm feeling dizzy. Ben looks at me again, a question on his lips; then he picks up my phone.

"David? Hey, it's Ben. What—" He listens for a moment and I feel as though my heart is going to burst out of my chest. Then he drops to the chair beside me without saying a word, my phone tightly clutched against his ear, his head bowed.

And I know.

I didn't know when David called the night Kate collapsed, never could have imagined what news waited for me on the other end of that handset.

But there was only one reason David would call me now. Something has happened to the baby.

I'm in shock. There's numbness throughout my body I'm grateful for, because it keeps me from feeling any pain. At least for now.

It's not the baby. It's Kate.

She had a massive stroke about an hour ago. While I sat at the kitchen counter worrying about what to say to David, Kate's brain was drowning in blood. It doesn't look good, David tells Ben. Kate's showing signs of significant brain damage, but they won't know more until after the tests are complete. But the baby is okay, for now. Somehow, he is still fine.

David is alone at the hospital, Tucker having left to go home not long before the stroke to relieve Cora and to spend some time with the girls. David is frantic, desperate for answers he's not getting, fearful about what those answers will be when he gets them...and in the midst of it all he called me.

He called me.

And all I can do is sit at the kitchen island feeling comfortably numb while Ben tries to hold the last pieces of our best friends' former life together. He soothes David, calmly telling him to breathe, to sit down if he feels as if he might pass out, and that we're on our way. He promises he won't hang up the phone, but he'll hand it to me so he can drive. The whole time I sit catatonic on my stool, and when Ben shoves the phone in my hand I hold it limply against my leg like I have no idea what to do with it.

"Hannah. Talk to him." Ben's tone is harsh, and I draw my eyes to his face but everything is in slow motion. "Now, Hannah. Put the phone to your ear and talk to David. He needs you."

I nod and do as I'm told, hearing nothing for a moment. Ben grabs me by the arm, and we're out the door, my mouth open and ready to speak when I finally come up with the words.

"Hannah?" David is crying, and I press the phone so tightly to my head as I get in the car that it starts to hurt my temple. I feel confused, like the time Claire threw a baseball harder than either of us thought she could right into my forehead—even though she was aiming for the bat in my hands—giving me a concussion. My mom and Grams had taken turns waking me every hour throughout the night.

My breathing isn't right as I settle into the car, and I wonder if I might be having a heart attack. Ben looks at me impatiently, and I realize he's waiting for me to buckle up. When I don't, he reaches across my body and fastens my seat belt, at the same time whispering, "Kate would do this for you. Talk to him."

At the mention of Kate's name something inside me snaps, and though the flood of pain is so intense I have to bend at the waist and lie on my lap so I don't scream, it clears my head. With Ben's hand on my back while we drive, I stay doubled over and talk to David.

"David. I'm here."

"Hannah...it's bad."

"I know. We're almost there, okay? Ten minutes. So just listen to my voice. Keep talking to me."

"Okay." He doesn't say anything else, but I know he's still on the line. I can hear his breathing, shallow and punctuated by the white noise of the hospital.

"Did Kate ever tell you about the summer we went to that camp in Canada?" I ask.

Still nothing from David except for his breathing, though it doesn't sound like he's crying anymore. I sit up and rest my head against the window, watching the dark night fly by. "There were all these blueberries. We ate so many by the end of that month, Kate joked we were going home a pale shade of lavender." I smile, remembering how Kate had developed a severe aversion to blueberries by the end of our vacation, to the point where she would gag if she tried to eat one.

"She still hates blueberries," David says softly, and I nod though he can't see me. I have tried over the years to sway her with my homemade blueberry muffins and cobblers and pies with sweet whipped cream, but she'd always turn her nose up, telling me blueberries were evil and should be left to the bears and birds.

"Well, along with all the blueberries, and mosquitoes, and mice running around the cabins, there was this cliff..."

54

The summer Kate and I were fourteen I was invited to join her and her mom for a monthlong vacation to Canada. Rena was helping her college best friend, Susan, who was recently divorced and who had decided the best way to take charge of her newly single, middle-aged life was to spend her ex-husband's money and escape. So she packed up her life in California, bought a little campground in Ontario's cottage country and convinced Kate's mom she couldn't do it without her. Rena McTavish was nothing if not a loyal friend, who also understood how hard it was to find your way once your identity as a Mrs. was gone. It was decided together they would set up the campground, get the dozen or so cabins fit for guests, and at the same time give Kate and me a fun summer-break experience. Having never traveled beyond California state lines, except for our one family trip to Hawaii, I had my bag packed the moment my mom agreed—two months ahead of time.

What Rena didn't know was how run-down the campground would be—mice had set up nests in nearly every cabin, along with a few red squirrels and the odd raccoon, and the whole place was in desperate need of some elbow grease and vision. The dismay on her face when we arrived was evident, and her quiet, "What have I gotten us into?" as we drove up the pine-needle-covered driveway, surrounded by a forest of trees, made me worry we'd be turning around and heading back to California before even getting out of the car.

But despite its lack of aesthetic appeal, the campground was set on a beautiful lake, whose deep green water hid a rocky bottom and loads of fish to catch. The mosquitoes were fierce, there was no running water at first and Rena mentioned more than once that perhaps we should go home—she had promised my mom a fun adventure, and I think was worried I might report no such thing. But after a few days of hard work the cabins started to show signs of their former campground glory, and Kate and I begged her mom to stay the whole month.

One of our favorite ways to spend the day, while Rena and Susan painted the cabin exteriors, covered in mosquito repellent and sticky brown paint, was to head down to the lake to swim and stuff our faces full of the blueberries that grew wild.

There was one day in particular, probably about a week into our stay, which I will never forget—likely because it was the first time, though not the last, when Kate showed her fearless side and left me giddy with the desire to be just like her. Perhaps it was because my dad died so suddenly and so young that I felt more protective of life, less willing to take risks. Or perhaps I was always that way; stepping out of the familiar and comfortable wasn't easy for me.

On this afternoon the sun trickled through the leaves, illuminating the white birch bark that surrounded this part of the lake with a silver sheen. It was hot, hotter than it had been since we'd arrived. Even with the canopy of trees protecting us from the sun's rays, it was that sort of oppressive heat where you would shed your own skin if that would offer relief. Kate and I lay practically naked in the coolest place we could find, a flat rock a few feet from the lake that was shadowed by a large tree. We lay spread-eagled on old cabin beach towels, dressed in bikinis that were already grungy from a week of lake swimming. I let out a sigh, grumbling about the heat. I felt lazy, almost as if the sun had melted away my motivation as it melted me to my towel. Kate, having flipped to her stomach, turned her head toward the water and cracked open an eye. She seemed to contemplate taking a dip, but then closed her eye and rested her head back on the towel.

It was a good day. We were fourteen and doing exactly what we wanted to be doing on a lazy summer day—absolutely nothing. "I'm hungry," I said, sitting up. "You hungry?" Kate shrugged, not opening her eyes. "More for me, then." I grabbed a handful of the wild blueberries from the bucket beside me and shoved the tiny, slightly sour fruit into my mouth. I took another handful and pushed those in, as well. Kate sat up and took her own handful, her jaw moving slowly as she chewed and stared out at the water—which looked as if it had diamonds dancing on its surface thanks to the brilliant sunshine.

With our cheeks bursting with blueberries—looking like the forest chipmunks who would run across our feet to get the peanuts we held out, somehow stuffing nut after nut inside their ever-expanding cheeks—the giggling started, which soon turned into uncontrollable laughter. Blueberry juice dribbled from the corners of our mouths, staining Kate's bathing suit and my towel. I looked at Kate and gave her a big toothy grin, knowing my teeth were purple and filled with the fruit's dark skins.

Laughter burst out of her, along with a few half-chewed berries, which hit me smack on the forehead. Laughing so hard we could barely catch our breaths, we held our stomachs, squeaking out pleas for each other to stop. I felt as though my muscles were about to snap, or that I might actually die from laughing too hard. We finally lay back on our towels, heaving and panting and grinning. An instant later Kate stood up and started running up the hill toward the hanging cliff we always talked about jumping from but as of yet, hadn't found the courage. Scrambling off my towel, I ran after her, shouting for her to wait up.

We burst through the trees on the massive overhanging rock. Kate was a few feet ahead of me, her head held high to the sun. "What do you think?" she asked, not turning around. "Is it time for us to conquer this cliff once and for all?"

A second later, before I could answer her, Kate started running toward the edge and launched herself off the cliff. The sound of her jubilant shout bounced off the rock face as she fell to the water below. I was frozen to my spot, holding my breath, until I heard the splash. Then, trance broken, I lay down carefully to peer over the edge into the long drop to the water. The pine needles stuck sharply into my bare skin, but I barely noticed.

"Kate!" I shouted. "Kate! Are you okay?" I scanned the water, looking for a sign of her white-and-red-starred bikini.

Then I heard "All good!" from the water below. I rushed back down the hill, stumbling a little in my excitement and haste to make sure she really was okay. Kate was dripping wet on the shore, a small gash bleeding on her leg, but with a look of absolute joy on her face.

"You're crazy," I said, shaking my head and frowning at her leg, which now had a rivulet of blood stretching the length of her shin. "And you're bleeding." I pointed to her leg, which she then dipped in the water to staunch the blood. A small dot of red appeared almost immediately, but the rivulet it created was much shorter and paler this time.

"Now it's your turn. Let's go." I protested but allowed Kate to pull me toward the hill. "You won't believe how good it feels to jump off. Just aim a bit left to miss the rock that got me."

I felt scared but also thrilled as I clambered up the hill behind her. The sun settled on my face as I reached the top of the cliff again, and she grabbed my hand, making sure we stood side by side. Despite the heat, I was shaking hard enough my teeth chattered.

"On the count of three," Kate said, her eyes shining and her cheeks flushed.

"*One...two...three!*" We ran the length of the rock together—hands held tightly—me screaming and Kate whooping gleefully. I felt the rock under my feet disappear, and we were suddenly suspended in the air, hands still clutched together, whooshing down toward the dark, deep water below.

55

As we near the hospital's parking garage David has to get off the phone. The doctors are there, and they need to speak with him. I hang up and give Ben a stricken look.

"Don't go there," he says, clutching my hand. "We don't know anything yet, okay?" Minutes later we're speeding past the news crews, and the pro-lifers and their signs, and through the entrance, the doors opening automatically but slowly enough I'm practically pressed up to the glass in my haste to get inside. In the lobby we're hit by fluorescent lights and scuffed linoleum, the stale smell of cigarette smoke wafting in from the overflowing ashtrays standing guard on each side of the entrance. And the whole time I'm running, I'm thinking about that cliff, and wishing we could go back—before marriage and babies and the aneurysm threatening to take away the person who understands the only way I will jump is if she jumps with me. I trip as we round a corner and am falling until Ben grabs my arm and yanks me up, tugging me forward so we keep our momentum.

Finally we're in the ICU and we have to adjust our pace,

but the adrenaline makes it difficult to slow down. As the nurse directs us to the family room—the same room as before, still with too many chairs and no windows and the pervasive smells of lemon and rubbing alcohol and bad news—my legs feel restless, longing to still be running somewhere.

Dr. Swartzman is in surgery, so it's just me, Ben and Dr. Voss, who assures us the baby is okay for the time being. I ask if David's joining us, having expected him to be in the room, too.

Dr. Voss shakes his head. "No," he says. "He's with Kate." I hold my breath, not liking the look on Dr. Voss's face.

"What can you tell us? How is Kate?" Ben leans forward onto the table, nearly putting his elbow into a sticky ring of some kind of spilled and dried liquid. By the color and tackiness of it I'm guessing it's cola. I can't tear my eyes away from the ring, which has bits of lint stuck in it, and wonder how long it's been there—how many elbows have rested into it— and why no one has bothered to wipe it up yet. I put my hands in my lap, far away from the grimy table.

"Unfortunately Kate's had a stroke," Dr. Voss replies. "Her aneurysm reruptured, and the bleeding into her brain was extensive."

He clears his throat and I clench my hands more tightly on my lap, my fingertips digging painfully into the tops of my hands. "Like I've explained to David, cases like this generally do not have a positive outcome. The blood is toxic to the brain tissue, and the damage is typically irreversible."

"What are you saying?" I whisper, though I know the answer. Knew it the moment he told us David was with Kate, instead of in here with us.

"We've done two separate sets of tests, and both show Kate has no brain activity. I'm very sorry."

"What do you mean 'no brain activity'?" Ben asks, the table

squeaking as he applies more pressure on his elbows, leaning toward Dr. Voss.

"It means Kate is brain-dead, Ben. She's never going to wake up," I say.

Ben looks at me as if the words I'm speaking are a foreign language. There is no understanding on his face, or panic, or grief. No, that will come later. For now it's simply confusion. Disbelief. I long to go back to the shock, to sit in this lemon-scented family room and rest my arms on the table right in the middle of that sticky, lint-littered soda ring, oblivious to the reality of what this means.

Kate is dead. Machines are keeping her body going, Dr. Voss goes on to explain, but it won't be long before her body begins shutting down. *But what about the ventilator? What about her life support?* Ben asks, still trying to absorb the news. Dr. Voss says life support can keep a body functioning for some time, but eventually the body will start shutting down, organ by organ, system by system. There's simply nothing more they can do.

Kate is dead. I say it again in my head, but it still isn't registering.

"What about the baby?" Ben asks, and I gasp, which draws a concerned look from Dr. Voss. For one brief moment I forgot about our baby trapped inside Kate's lifeless body.

"We'd like to deliver him as soon as possible," Dr. Voss says. "We've scheduled the C-section for nine a.m. tomorrow morning, so everyone has a chance to say goodbye to Kate first."

I check my watch. It's nearly eleven. Ten hours.

In ten hours David will lose his wife. Ava and Josie, their mother.

In ten hours I will become a mother. And at the same time, will lose my best friend and the woman who made it so.

56

I hear Kate's voice, as clear as if she were in the room with us—just another audience member present for Dr. Voss's terrible news.

Time to go throw some eggs, Hannah.

Without explanation I'm up and out the door, sprinting away from the reality of Kate and the stench of rubbing alcohol and to the bank of elevators. But the elevator takes too long so I run to the stairwell, racing down the stairs to the lobby as quickly as I can. I know Ben isn't far behind me. I can hear his voice echoing through the stairwell as he calls my name, his footfalls on the concrete stairs loud as he tries to match my speed.

I stumble out of the stairwell into the lobby and am out the front doors an instant later, my heart pounding. Then I launch myself into the crowd of protesters, grabbing the first sign I see and throwing it across the sidewalk.

"Get out of here!" I shriek, ripping another sign out of a shocked protester's hands and tossing it into the fountain at the front of the hospital. I am creating a scene, and the crowd has stopped moving in its circle, curious and wary of what

I'm about to do next, wondering who might stop me if I don't stop myself.

"Go away!" I shout at them, spinning wildly in circles and pointing fingers into surprised faces. "We don't need you! We don't want you here. So take your fucking signs..." As I scream I try to break one of the signs by standing on the rectangular piece of cardboard and yanking on the wooden stake handle, but it's surprisingly resilient. I feel the sharpness of the stake's edge bite into my palm, and look down to see a deep line of blood in my palm. Using my other hand I heave that sign into the crowd, causing a few people to quickly disperse to avoid getting hit. Someone yells back, "Hey! Take it easy." Someone else is shouting about the police, but I don't stop. Can't stop. "Leave. Now!" I shriek.

For another minute or so—though it feels much longer—I yell at and into the crowd, my words and actions wild. "Don't you see you're making things worse?" I sob out, trying to pry the *Save Baby Matthews* sign from the determined fingers of a middle-aged woman wearing a flashy coral scarf. "Stop... it... Give it...to me." But she refuses to hand it over and sets her stance wide so she can pull back against me. We're in a tug-of-war, her telling me to let go, me screaming at her to shut up and give me the sign—and then suddenly, I'm pulled away as strong hands grab me.

I kick and fight but am overpowered and being carried away from the crowd, and then the owner of these strong hands—a police officer—presses his fingers into my scalp so I'm forced to duck, making sure I don't hit my head when he puts me in the back of the cruiser.

I see Ben standing a few feet away, straining against the bulk of another police officer who is keeping him from getting to me, his hands on either side of his head and a panicked look on his tear-streaked face.

★ ★ ★

"You're lucky. They aren't going to press charges," Peter says from beside me in the back of the cruiser.

I nod. "Well, I guess that's one good thing." My voice is hoarse from all the yelling, and there's a horrible pain behind my eyes. I rest my head back against the seat and take a deep breath. "I'm sorry you have to be here. You should be up with Claire and Amelia."

"Don't worry about that. They're both fine. But you are clearly not. What happened, Hannah?"

"I just needed to throw a few eggs," I whisper, closing my sore eyes. Then a little louder I say, "I lost it, though I guess that's fairly obvious. Kate is dead, and I totally fucking lost it."

He says nothing for a moment, the silence of the car punctuated only by the chatter on the cruiser's scanner. "I'm sorry about Kate. I can't imagine what any of you are going through right now. But you need to hold it together, okay? Ben is having a coronary, not literally of course, but he's as stressed as I've ever seen him. Plus, there's a baby that needs you. He needs you to hold it together."

"I know," I say. "I'm sorry."

"You don't need to be sorry." Peter puts a hand on my arm, and I turn to look at him. "You're free to go. But if you want to take another minute here before you head back upstairs, to get yourself together, take it."

"Thank you," I say. "Please don't tell Claire or my mom what happened, okay? They don't need to worry about this."

"I can't promise they won't find out," Peter says. "After all, I expect you're making tonight's news, but I won't tell them for now. Promise." He smiles and I lean into his embrace.

"Can you ask Ben to come in here?"

Peter nods, knocking on his window for the officer outside to open the door. "You bet."

I take another deep breath as the fresh air wafts into the cruiser through the open door, and a moment later Ben leans in, concern sketched across his face. "Hannah." He lets my name out in one long breath, and I start to cry. Softly, without drama this time.

"I'm sorry. I'm so... I don't know what happened."

Ben sits down on the seat and leans on his knees, his tall frame awkward in the cramped backseat. "I just need you to answer one question for me, okay?"

I nod, our eyes meeting.

"Do I need to worry about you? Like, really worry about you?"

I shake my head. "You do not need to worry about me."

"Okay, because..." He sighs and runs a hand over his face. "Because what just happened out there, well, I'm worried, Hannah."

"I promise. You do not need to worry. I'm okay. *I'm okay.*" I reach out and press my palm against his cheek, and he takes another deep breath. He takes my hand and turns it over, lifting the piece of bloodstained gauze the officer gave me and looking at the cut in my palm. "You should get this checked out. It looks deep."

I close my hand, his fingers trapped in my fist, and wait until he looks at me. "It's fine. I'm fine. Now, how about you knock on that window and get us out of here?"

Ben smiles, then with his eyes still on mine, raps his knuckles against window.

"I need to see Kate," I say. "And David."

"I know you do." Ben holds the car door for me. Then he wraps an arm around me, taking some of my weight as we make our way back into the hospital.

57

I see Edward as soon as I walk through the ICU doors, lean-ing against the wall outside Kate's room, looking thin and tired, his arms limp by his sides and the wall clearly holding him up. I pause for a moment, unsure if I should walk right past him without a word or wait until he's gone, but then he looks my way and I know what I need to do.

"I'll be right in," I say to Ben. He looks at Edward, then back at me, and nods before heading into Kate's room, pausing to rest a hand on Edward's shoulder. I sit in one of the chairs by the nursing station and wait. Edward joins me a moment later, sighing deeply as he settles into the chair beside me.

We're silent for a moment, and then I do the thing I never would have expected a few days ago: I grab his hand and hold it tight. He looks down at our hands, surprise etched on his face, then begins to sob. Though his body shakes, he is quiet aside from the occasional intake of breath. I hold his hand tighter, keeping my eyes straight ahead and letting my own tears stream down my cheeks unencumbered.

"It isn't supposed to happen like this," Edward says, when he's able to. "A father is not supposed to bury his daughter."

I nod but can't speak. And for one selfish moment I hope I never know what that pain is like.

"How can I... How can I ask for forgiveness now, Hannah? It's too late. It's too late." He bows his head, and I turn my body so I'm facing him. I soften my voice, let him see my own tears.

"You know something, Edward? I think she forgave you a really long time ago."

He shakes his head. "That's kind of you to say, but you were right the other day. She hated me, has ever since she was old enough to understand what happened. And all I ever did to try and fix it was write those goddamned letters and send checks. As if that would somehow make up for everything. I was so, so stupid. So stupid." He wipes a shaky hand across his eyes, and I notice again how much Kate looks like her father. "I didn't know what else to do. I love her so much, but I didn't know how to be a father."

"She did not hate you. She was angry and upset and wished things were different, but I promise you, Edward. She didn't hate you." And as I say it, I know it's true. Kate had a complicated, fractured, distant relationship with her father, and he hurt her no question, but hate had no part in it.

"You know, when we had lunch a few weeks ago she told me it was the baby that finally made her come to meet me," Edward says. "She said she would not infect your baby with any of her anger, because she wanted him to be pure and perfect for you, and she decided it was time to let a few things go."

I'm not surprised when he tells me this—it sounds like something Kate would say, a decision she would make. I'm overcome with gratitude for her willingness to put my son first.

"I'm sorry about all of this, Hannah. About the reporter and everything that came after that. Please also tell Ben, would you? I really thought I was helping." His voice is low, his tone regretful, and I'm suddenly filled with compassion for a man who only days ago I hoped to never see again.

"You shouldn't be sorry," I say, remembering what my mom said after Amelia's birth. "You did what you thought was best for your child. You were trying to protect her, like a good father would. Don't ever be sorry for that. She would be grateful, Edward. I know she would."

He nods. "Thank you. Even though David said you don't speak for Kate, I really believe you do. You knew her better than anyone else, have always been there for her." He smiles, and I return it the best I can. "I am indebted to you for taking care of her when I couldn't."

And with that Edward squeezes my hand one last time, then stands and walks out of the ICU, not looking back once.

David is sleeping in a chair in Kate's room. Ben is outside making calls. Cora and Tucker will bring the girls—who are mercifully asleep, tucked in under matching princess-adorned Pottery Barn quilts—to the hospital early in the morning, so they have a chance to say goodbye to Kate before the surgery.

I'm relieved when David finally closes his eyes, not only because he needs the rest but also because his rapid pacing of the room and his grief-fueled outbursts have left me emotionally and physically wrung out. I try, but my words, my arms can't help him. Not right now. It's been a slow, painful goodbye, and there is no peace yet—not for David. He's still very much in fight mode, even though there's nothing left to fight for. And the realization of exactly what he's losing—the gritty, horrific, unbelievable reality of Kate being erased from our lives—is starting to take shape, to set up space in David's mind and body. He is barely holding it together and though

I don't want to witness any of this, I vow not to turn away when he needs me most.

After I assure David I won't leave the room, won't leave Kate, he finally settles into the chair and within minutes his eyelids droop and his breathing deepens. I try to picture what life will look like now, with Kate's absence. But it's too hard to fathom, my brain not allowing the images to load, and so I stop imagining life without her.

There are tubes and wires and very little room in Kate's bed, but I crawl in beside her regardless, tucking my body up against her still form. Her chest rises and falls in a mechanical rhythm, the perfection of her breathing disconcerting and reassuring all at once.

Her belly is round under the sheet, and I put one hand on it, feeling the fetal heart rate monitor strapped around her middle. I rest my head beside hers, the edges of the tape holding her ventilator in place scratching against my cheek.

Looking at Kate's face now, I try to remember that girl who jumped off the cliff without a moment's hesitation. But she's not here anymore. Impossible to find amid the tubes and bruising and frightening stillness. Leaning in close to her ear, which still holds the diamond stud her mom gave her for her eighteenth birthday, I whisper, "I just threw a very big egg, Katie. You would have been proud. And whenever you're ready to jump off that cliff, you jump. I'm going to take care of everyone for you. I promise."

58

David's in the hallway, shouting for help. Something about the baby. I've stepped out of the room to call my mom, and hang up midsentence.

Machines beep incessantly at the nurse's station where Ben and I stand, and the sound mingles with David's frantic voice. Two nurses are on the move, heading for Kate's room, and Ben is at their heels. But I'm a few steps behind, sluggish with fear, terrified of what's happened to make the machines make these noises.

Kate lies in bed, looking essentially the same as she has since I first saw her here—serene and pale and motionless except for the rise and fall of her chest. Alarms are screaming, the baby's monitor is flashing and David stands in the corner, tears streaming down his face and hands clasping the sides of his head as he watches helplessly as the medical team works around Kate. Dr. Swartzman rushes in and scans the continuous stream of paper that prints from the machine measuring the fetal heart rate. Ben and I stand outside the room, trying to stay out of the way, holding our collective breath while we wait to find out what's happening.

The nurses start moving about hastily and Dr. Swartzman looks over at us, speaking quickly but calmly. "The baby's heart rate is dropping and he's in distress. We need to get him out right now." Her voice is urgent but steady. I feel as if all the oxygen in the room has disappeared.

"But this isn't supposed to happen until later," I say, my voice squeaking out. It's only five in the morning. "We need time." I feel faint and lean against Ben. David drops to the ground in a crouch, burying his head in his arms. I look at Ben, and he knows what I'm thinking. *Help him.* A moment later he's beside him, crouched down and speaking quietly into his ear, his arms holding David's shaking shoulders.

Dr. Swartzman stands in front of me. "It's amazing, all things considered, that we made it to this stage, Hannah. Your baby has an excellent chance at survival. But we can't wait any longer. I need to get him out."

"What about Kate?" I whisper, trying to breathe through the sob that racks my chest. "We're supposed to have some more time. We need some more time with her. The girls aren't even here yet."

She puts her hand on my arm and squeezes. "Kate has done the most incredible job at keeping your son healthy and giving him time to grow."

I know what she's not saying; it's time to say goodbye.

The operating room is bright and cold, even with the gown overtop of my clothes. Spotlights come on as Kate is wheeled into the room, a nurse bagging her, as the ventilator is temporarily unhooked to accommodate the move to the operating room. Staff in masks, gowns and gloves move about the room in coordinated chaos, hooking up machines, reattaching the ventilator, draping the table to keep me from seeing exactly what's happening below her neck. I'm told to sit on a stool at Kate's head, and ask if I can touch her face. The nurse says that's fine, and so I lay my hand against her cheek, her forehead, telling her what a great job she's done. What an amazing mother she is. How much I love her. How much we all love her.

David, despite his devastation at knowing his moments with Kate are numbered, insists I be the one to go in for the C-section. He wants me to be the first person to see the baby, saying Kate wouldn't have wanted it any other way. I am overcome when he tells me this, and for as long as we can we cling to each other, our foreheads pressed together, our arms around each other, the tears falling between us.

David and the girls will wait outside the operating room until after the baby is born, and will then have a chance to say goodbye to Kate before she's removed from life support. But I can't think about what happens after the baby is born beyond the logistics of it, because if I do it will consume me and I can't fall apart now—our boy needs me.

Dr. Swartzman peers around the sheet and tells me things are about to get under way. She adds that my son will be out in fewer than twenty minutes, and so instead of focusing on the loss I know is coming, I try to prepare myself for imminent motherhood. A neonatal intensive care team is waiting off to the side, an incubator ready to whisk the baby away as soon as he's born—Dr. Swartzman tells me she'll do her best to give me a moment with him, but it depends on how he's doing when she gets him out.

A moment later she's made the incision. I focus all my energy and attention on Kate, knowing Dr. Swartzman has things under control. I whisper favorite memories into Kate's ear, like the time when we were fifteen and drank a bottle of my grandfather's cherry whiskey after cutting class, only to spend the rest of the night so sick our parents decided that was punishment enough. Or the first time I babysat Ava, and was so proud of myself until we realized I'd put the diaper on backward—thanks to a stream of runny, pea-green baby poop that escaped the incorrectly positioned diaper and ran all over Kate's brand-new beige couch. I laugh softly while I recount some of the more memorable moments we've shared, and I kiss her forehead every few minutes. Then I tell her the secret ingredient in my guacamole, wishing now I'd told her the first time she'd asked, and promise I'll teach Ava and Josie how to make it.

I'm so focused on Kate it takes me a moment to come back to the present, to understand what Dr. Swartzman is saying. "It's a boy," she says, but her voice doesn't carry the excitement one expects in the first moments after a baby is born. She sounds tense as she says it, and my heart rate speeds up. But I stay on the side of the curtain like I've been told to, too afraid to ask questions or move—there is no baby crying, no one is talking, but there's plenty of movement. I can hear the squeak of rubber-soled shoes shuffling across the floors. Then, finally, "Hannah, would you like to meet your son?"

I nod and push the stool back so the nurse can place the tiny bundle in my arms. She doesn't fully let go of the baby, who is wrinkled and quite red. "Happy Birthday, baby boy," I whisper. Staring into his face I see some of Kate right away, and I turn back to her to tell her how beautiful he is, how perfect he is, and then he's gone. Whisked away to the incubator and the doctors who will work to keep him here with us.

I look again at Kate, her face blank, and wish desperately she could meet him. That she could see the moment I became a mother, because of her. And though I know it's unlikely she can hear me, that she's probably somewhere far away now, I kiss her cheek and whisper "Thank you" over and over until my voice grows hoarse.

59

October

I meet Ben in the hall, just outside our current hospital room. After eight weeks in intensive care, Cole has been transferred to a step-down room from the NICU, which means soon we'll be able to go home, a family of three.

Our boy had a variety of medical issues early on—requiring round-the-clock oxygen support and a plethora of medication—but has since grown strong, his face and body filling out thanks to formula and my breast milk. Nursing has been both a wonder and a challenge. I never made enough milk to satisfy Cole's needs, but the feel of him suckling at my breast, his tiny fingers hanging on while he drinks, eyes closing in contentment, moved me in a way I wasn't expecting. Somehow, it made him mine.

"David's with him," Ben says before I can ask why he isn't in the room with Cole.

I nod, my heart fluttering inside my chest like a butterfly caught in a net. Though David knows he's welcome anytime, he hasn't visited Cole yet. To know he's here, sitting with our son, fills a hole inside me I hadn't realized was there. I hand Ben his coffee and gesture with my head toward the room.

"How is he?" I ask. Ben knows I mean David, not Cole.

"He seems okay," Ben says. "I told him to stay as long as he wants."

"Good, good." I notice how tired Ben looks this morning, his eyelids heavy and his face sagging. "Why don't you go get something to eat, to help wash this coffee down?" I smile at him, and he returns it.

"Want anything?" Ben asks, heading down the hall to the locked doors of the unit.

I shake my head. "I'm good, thanks."

"I'll get you a muffin or something. You haven't eaten anything since last night." He pushes the button beside the doors to unlock them. "Be back soon."

With another sip of my coffee I walk toward our room. David sits in the rocking chair beside the crib, Cole bundled and in his arms. I hear David's voice, low and soft, and at first I think he's simply talking to Cole, but then I notice the book in his hands—my tattered copy of *The Velveteen Rabbit*—and I take a quick step back, watching with tears in my eyes. Once David turns the last page and sets the book down, I wipe the tears away and knock on the door frame, smiling gently when he looks up.

If I think Ben looks exhausted, he has nothing on David, who is almost unrecognizable. My heart lurches, seeing the marks grief has left on his face. It has been nearly two months since I've seen him, at the funeral, and much like then all I want to do is hold him and tell him it's going to be okay. We're all going to be okay. But I stay by the door, waiting for David to decide if he wants company.

At first he stares at me as if he's trying to place why I seem so familiar; then he smiles before looking back at Cole. I take that as an invitation and walk into the room. "He looks like Kate," he says. "His eyes. Do you see it?" David's own eyes come back to mine, and I hold his gaze while willing myself not to cry.

"I saw that right away." I keep my voice soft, small so as to not scare him away, then sit down in the chair beside him.

"I hope it's okay that I'm here," he says, eyes back on Cole, who is staring wide-eyed at David as though he knows exactly who he was.

"It's more than okay," I reply, rubbing his arm with my free hand. "I'm glad you're here." Then I notice a rectangular-shaped bandage on the back of his neck, just below his hairline. "What happened?" I ask, gesturing to the bandage.

"I got another tattoo."

I press my lips tightly together as tears fill my eyes again. I don't have to ask of what. I know what's underneath that bandage—three tattoos, all sets of Roman numerals. Two are older, representing the dates of Ava's and Josie's births, and the other—the date of Kate's death and Cole's birth, I presume—is probably just starting to scab over.

We sit in silence for a moment and I don't try to hide my tears, my hand still on David's arm while he rocks back and forth, back and forth. When he finally speaks it startles me, and my hand drops from his arm. "The autopsy came back," he says, his tone flat. "It confirmed Kate had an AVM that ruptured, which is what we already guessed, but it was good to know for sure."

I nod, Annabel having already told me the results. That Kate's brain bleed was the result of a ruptured aneurysm, this so-called AVM, which she'd probably had since birth and that was possibly responsible for her migraines. Kate had a ticking time bomb in her head that no one knew about and that could have exploded at any time. There was no indication, Annabel said, that the pregnancy in any way caused that bomb to go off.

"Thank you for letting me name him," David says, so quietly it comes out nearly in a whisper. "Did you know we thought Ava was a boy?"

"I remember that." David had been thrilled to have a boy, Kate less so. She said she had no idea how to raise a boy, with all the stuff that came along with that. But turns out the ultrasound technician had gotten it wrong, labeling the umbilical cord a penis. Ava had been a huge, welcome surprise.

"Kate had finally conceded to Colton. It was my grandfather's name." He brushes a finger against Cole's cheek, and the baby turns his head toward him. "She didn't like it at first, but it grew on her. But as soon as Ava came out I knew no matter how many other children we had they would all be girls. I have no clue how I knew, but I did."

"I love the name." I watch Cole's face as it stretches into a yawn—his mouth open in a perfectly round circle, his eyes squeezed tightly shut. "It suits him."

David nods, a smile coming across his face. Cole's eyes drop closed, and his mouth starts moving, his lips suckling in his sleep.

"I miss her, Hannah. So much I can't breathe some days." Tears fall from David's eyes, dropping onto Cole's white-and-blue-striped hospital blanket. My breath catches, and I push the emotion threatening to spill out of me back down. I place my hand back on David's arm and squeeze, and he looks at me, tears streaking down his cheeks.

"I know," I say, wishing I could say something to make this easier for him, knowing there is nothing that can magically erase even a fraction of his pain. His loss is too great for any words to provide comfort. "I miss her, too. Desperately." I hastily wipe away my own tears. "I'm sorry I can't make this better for you."

"Don't be," he says, watching me. "She is…" He shakes his head, and his Adam's apple bobs a few times while he tries to get the words out. "She was your best friend."

"Yes, but she's your wife. And Ava and Josie's mother." I decided at the funeral, where everyone kept referring to Kate in the past tense, that I wouldn't let that happen—I wouldn't let her fade to only a memory, a two-dimensional picture on the wall, a person we all used to know. No, Kate would stay with us, relevant in our day-to-day lives—even if she wasn't physically here. "It doesn't matter what I... What matters is you and the girls. I hope you'll let us help you however we can."

"Hannah, you and Ben and Cole, you're family, okay? Kate would have been so mad about how I handled things," he says, laughing a little. It was not his usual laugh, however—easy and big—and the sound of it makes things hurt deep in my chest. "After she yelled at me for a few days, she would have given me the silent treatment, and I'm not sure which would have been worse." I laugh with him, knowing exactly what he means.

"I have a feeling I would have been on the receiving end of that silent treatment, as well," I say. "Besides, you did what you thought was best for her. You took care of her, David, the only way you could. Ben would have done the same for me."

"He told me that at the funeral," David replies. "But for what it's worth, I'm sorry."

"Well, apology not accepted," I reply, leaning over and kissing his cheek. "Even though Kate held the gold medal in stubbornness, I was certainly on the podium with her."

David nods and goes back to rocking Cole, who sleeps soundly—unaware of how the landscape has shifted so drastically around him since his birth. "So what now, Hannah? What do I do now?"

His voice is so lost, so void of the usual confidence I have come to associate with David, and I worry he may never get it back. I lean back in my chair, letting my head rest against its cushioned back, and turn to watch him, taking a moment to consider my answer.

"Now we figure out how to live without her."

"I don't know how to do that."

"Me neither," I reply. "But at least we don't have to do it alone, right?"

"Right," David says, his voice gruff. "Kate would be so

happy about Cole. All she wanted was for you to be a mother, to know how amazing it was to experience that. I'm glad she was able to give you that, Hannah."

I can't speak, now crying too hard to say anything. David shifts Cole deeper into the crook of his arm and clutches my hand. "Having Cole means you'll always have a piece of her with you. Just like I do with Ava and Josie. She gave us the greatest gift, our children."

He goes back to rocking, and soon my tears dry and my breathing becomes less ragged. But David doesn't let go of my hand through any of it, and I silently vow Cole will always know the woman who gave him life, and the people who loved her. After about ten minutes I gently tug my hand out of David's and reach into my purse, which rests beside my chair. I pull out an envelope, pink and tattered with age, and place it on my lap. Then I look over at David and say, "Remember how Kate and I met? The whole Darren and the swinging backpack incident?"

He nods. "Something about how you defended her honor and sent some delinquent kid to the hospital?"

"Something like that," I reply, chuckling. "I was saving this for Kate. To give her after…" My hands shake as I open the envelope—which I've kept in my purse since Cole was born, waiting for this moment—and hand the card inside to David. "I was going to give it back to her after Cole was born."

He looks at it for a long moment, taking it all in, before glancing at me with a smile. "She always kept her promises, didn't she?"

"That she did."

"Did you hear Darren had to get five stitches?" Kate asks me the next morning at school, while we stand at her locker. I had heard, from my quite furious mother who was forced to apologize profusely to Darren's mother when she called to give my mom a piece of her mind about me. My grandmother, however, winked after my mom's lecture

and pushed a piece of lemon cake toward me, whispering she thought that boy only got what was coming to him.

"Now every time he looks at that scar on his stupid head he'll think of you, and maybe he won't ever tell another girl she has a 'fat ass,'" Kate adds. She grins, and I can't help but grin back even though I've been grounded for the foreseeable future. "I made you something," she says, pulling an envelope out of her backpack.

"What is it?" I ask, turning it over in my hands. On the front of the soft pink envelope is written, "To Hannah," a big heart around the words.

"Just open it—you'll see," she says, shoving her backpack into her locker.

I slide my finger under the flap of the envelope and feel it release. Pulling out the card inside, a flurry of gold sparkles flutter into the air like snowflakes, and Kate giggles. "I may have gone overboard on the glitter," she says. The card is made of black construction paper, bordered with a thick band of sparkling gold. On the card in gold-inked bubble letters she has written, "Good for ONE giant awesome favor. Love, your BFF Kate."

"Whatever you want, whenever you want it. It's yours."

"Thank you, but you don't need to give me a favor, Kate," I say, tucking the card back into the envelope, the clingy glitter transferring to my jeans when I wipe my hands. "Darren's a jerk. You would have done the same for me." But I flush with happiness, grateful to have made a new friend who seems to like me as much as I like her.

"Keep it. You never know when you might need that," Kate replies, pointing to the envelope before I tuck it into my backpack.

We walk to class, laughing about the look on Darren's face after I smacked him with the backpack and making plans to have lunch together, no clue as to what the future holds for us, but happy that at least for this moment we have found each other.

★ ★ ★ ★ ★

ACKNOWLEDGMENTS

In many ways, this is the book I've been waiting to write. While a work of fiction—I have never lived in San Francisco, been a recipe developer or felt an earthquake rumble under my feet—hints of my personal story are scattered throughout the pages. And so, my first thank-you goes to my sister Jenna Free Davis (along with her husband, D'Arcy, and children, Emily and Gavin), who was our gestational surrogate and delivered into our arms a beautiful little girl we named Addison Mae. Without Jenna I would not be a mother. It's that simple; I'm that grateful.

While the procedures and emotional impact of infertility were familiar and unfortunately easy to write, I relied on a number of people to bring life to this book and to make it real.

Thanks to Google and the folks who post beautiful photos and descriptions of San Francisco so I could imagine it without living there, and especially to Catherine Nomura for sending me a travel-book-worthy email detailing not just the places and things, but the cultural feel of the city—and also for letting me know no one there calls it "San Fran." Closer to home, thanks to Starbucks and Chapters on Fairview Street for providing an away-from-home office, as well as plenty of hot coffee.

To Kristen Eppich—food stylist, writer and recipe developer extraordinaire—thank you for sharing what it's like to create magic with simple ingredients, and for answering mildly inappropriate questions like, "So, how much weight did you gain at your first job?"

To attorney Richard Vaughn, of the California-based International Fertility Law Group Inc., thank you for not only answering my (many) questions via phone and email, but also for reading sections of the book to ensure I wasn't screwing up the legalese. And thanks to Toronto lawyer and friend Sara Cohen for introducing me to Rich, and for indulging my surrogacy law questions over morning coffee. Thanks also to ICU physician Dr. Heather Whittingham, who graciously debated horrific medical scenarios and outcomes while our daughters attended art lessons, and to Dr. Kim Foster, who offered medical advice along with eagle-eyed feedback. Any and all errors in this book are mine and mine alone.

To my editor Michelle Meade, who seems to understand what I'm trying to do with my words even when I don't, thank you for always having your door open and for sitting on my shoulder as I write. We make the best team. And to Carolyn Forde, my agent and chief cheerleader, your faith in my books—current and future—does not go unnoticed. Thank you for the exclamation marks and reassurances—I knew I made the right choice way back when. To the teams at MIRA Books, Harlequin, HarperCollins and BookSparks, I literally could not call myself an author without your support and tireless work to turn these words of mine into real, on-the-shelf books. You certainly make me look good, and make it look easy.

To all the readers out there, thank you for buying, borrowing, reading and discussing our stories! Without you there is little reason to write. To my writer friends, beta readers, and the awesome book bloggers (especially Melissa Amster, Andrea Peskind Katz and Jennifer O'Regan), thank you for the support. To Rosey Kaes, Kim Foster, Becky Stanisic and Annabel Fitzsimmons—thank you for hashing out plot lines and reading my words, even when they were a giant mess. A special thanks to Tracey Garvis Graves, Lori Nelson Spielman, Taylor Jenkins Reid, Mary Kubica, Rachel Goodman, Amy E. Reichert, Colleen Oakley, Sona Charaipotra, Shelly King and the Tall Poppies for helping me navigate debut author land—I'd be lost without all of you.

To Tracy Chappell, a mother, writer and editor friend who died suddenly of a brain aneurysm at the too-young age of forty-one, right around the time I was revising this novel—thank you for reminding me that while this book is not my story, someone else may be living it. This story is better because of you.

To my parents, Bob and Judy, and their significant others, Brenda and Jürgen, along with my siblings—it's been easy to strive for what I want because you've always given me a soft place to land. I love you.

And finally, to Adam and Addison—I couldn't do any of this without you. I love you more than the moon and the stars combined.

THE CHOICES WE MAKE

KARMA BROWN

Reader's Guide

MIRA®

1. Hannah is desperate to become a mother, but she is extremely hesitant to consider adopting. Do her concerns seem valid to you? Why do you think surrogacy appeals to her as a better option?

2. Hannah and Ben have a number of difficult and tense conversations over the years as they've dealt with infertility. For a long time, they seem at odds when it comes to deciding on an alternative option, and it puts obvious strain on their relationship. What do you think of the way she and Ben handle these conversations?

3. While Kate is lucky enough to have two healthy daughters, she's also experienced difficult loss in her life. Discuss the role of her parents in this novel. How do you think the death of her mother affects the decisions she's making? What do you think about the way her father is attempting to reenter her life at this late stage?

4. When Kate first broaches the idea of being Hannah and Ben's surrogate, David is not only firmly opposed but furious at the suggestion. Discuss his reaction, and the way Kate handles it.

5. What do you think of the characters' decision to go through with a surrogate pregnancy? Have you or anyone you've known used a surrogate, and what was that experience like? If not, what do you imagine the most challenging part of the process would be?

6. Lyla, at first, seemed the perfect solution for Hannah to become a mother. How did you feel when Lyla backed out of the surrogacy because of racial discrimination?

7. After Kate's aneurysm and coma, Hannah and David struggle to find common ground. Did you think Hannah handled things appropriately by pushing back so strongly against David? Do you think Hannah did the right thing by pushing to continue the pregnancy after Kate's collapse?

8. Was David unreasonable when he kicked Hannah out of Kate's hospital room? Did Hannah and Ben have a moral obligation to support David's decision?

9. What do you think Kate would have done, if the situation were reversed? Put yourself in Hannah's shoes—what might you have done differently?

The Choices We Make is a very personal story for you. Can you explain where the idea for this story came from, and how it relates to your own experience?

I have always wanted to write a story about surrogacy, and in fact, one of my earlier "practice" (read: never to be published) books focused on a similar theme. The Choices We Make was inspired by my own story of becoming a mother (my sister was our surrogate after cancer left me unable to carry a pregnancy), as well as a news story about a pregnant woman who became comatose, and the heartbreaking battle that raged for months between the hospital and her family about whether or not to continue the pregnancy.

While you drew on your own emotional experience when writing this book, the details surrounding the surrogacy process and the complications are completely different. What kind of research went into creating this story?

My sister was our gestational carrier, meaning we provided the bun and she provided the oven. So my daughter is biologically ours, whereas in The Choices We Make, Kate is the biological mother as well as the surrogate mother. Despite not having personal experience with traditional surrogacy, much of the process is similar to gestational surrogacy (where the surrogate mother carries an embryo created by another couple)—especially the fertility procedures and emotional aspects. In terms of the medical and legal research, I was fortunate to work with knowledgeable and highly skilled fertility law attorneys and physicians, who all generously answered every question I asked (there were many).

Much of the novel is told in dual perspective, giving the reader a glimpse into the hearts of both Kate and Hannah as they embark on this incredible journey together. Can you talk about what it was like to write about these women and the bond they share?

In some ways this novel is a (very long) thank-you note and love letter to my sister Jenna, who carried our daughter for us. While most people assume our journey was simple—easy because of our close relationship—there were challenges along the way and moments when we both struggled. It's not easy to carry a baby for someone else, nor is it easy to be the one unable to experience pregnancy firsthand. So I wanted to capture both sides of that, to show it as the honest, challenging, heartwarming and miraculous experience it is.

Like *The Choices We Make*, your previous novel, *Come Away with Me*, is a heart-wrenching, emotional story about love and loss—exploring themes of grief, healing, motherhood and intimate relationships between lovers and friends. Can you discuss the significance of these themes in your writing?

I keep telling people I'm a very happy person who writes heartbreaking stories! But if I dig deeper, the truth is I write about things that scare me, make me weep and keep me up at night. I'm fascinated by how people rebound from tragedies, how they get on with the business of living even when the life they know crumbles around them. That's a kind of courage I'm incredibly drawn to, and I love exploring it through my writing.

What was your greatest challenge in writing *The Choices We Make*? What about your greatest pleasure?

The hardest part about writing this book was how emotional it was for me—while our situation was completely different, much of what happens to Kate and Hannah and their families came from my fears when we were doing our own surrogacy. The thought of something tragic happening to my sister—however remote—was for me almost a deal breaker. The greatest pleasure was the opportunity to tell a story that's been trying to burst out of me for a long time. I hope, as they turn the pages, readers feel the emotion that went into writing it.

Do you read other fiction while you're doing your own writing or do you find it distracting?

I'm always reading—whether I'm drafting my own story, or deep into revisions, or between projects. And I'm often reading more than one book at a time, something my husband thinks is one of my superpowers—the ability to keep track of three or four plotlines and sets of characters all at once. But I wouldn't be able to write a single word without reading. It provides great inspiration and motivation for my writing, and is, in my opinion, one of the greatest luxuries of life.

Can you describe your writing process? Do you outline first or dive right in? Do you have a routine? Do you let anyone read early drafts, or do you keep the story private until it's finished?

When I'm drafting a book I'm up early...5:00 a.m. every day, until it's done! I'm a little more relaxed through the rest of the book's life cycle, though I still tend to be an early riser. There's nothing better for my writer's brain than a presunrise dark sky, a giant mug of coffee and the stillness of the morning. It's taken me a few books to find the process that works best, but generally I start with a detailed synopsis of the book idea, then move to Scrivener (a workhorse of a writing tool I would be lost without) to outline the chapters, and only then do I start writing. But even though I outline 90 percent of the book before I write it, I leave wiggle room for surprises as I go. And the little secret I'm certain drives my editor crazy is that I never know how a book will end until I'm about halfway through writing it.

With two books under your belt now, what's on the horizon for you? Are you working on a new project?

I am always working on a new project! I'm one of those authors with too many ideas and not enough time to write them in... which is a great, if not frustrating, problem to have. Though I can't share specifics on what's coming next, I can say my stories will continue to be big, emotional novels featuring honest, relatable characters—and that you will likely always need a box of tissues nearby.